60p

Best Sea Stories

BEST SEA STORIES

EDITED

WITH AN INTRODUCTION

BY

OLIVER WARNER

FABER AND FABER

24 Russell Square

London

First published in mcmlxv
by Faber and Faber Limited
24 Russell Square London WC1
Printed in Great Britain by
Purnell & Sons Ltd, Paulton

TO
RICHARD GOFFIN

Contents

Introduction

Anyone who has peered down into the limpid recession of a tropical sea will have realised that there is never likely to be a sea story in the stricter sense, for ways of expression pertaining to the inner life of the sea have nothing to do with literature. Writers must confine themselves mainly to the surface, to ships and human seafarers. Their themes will touch upon the sea in relation to people, and the setting is not, by and large, a subject in itself, though it will impinge, through beauty, majesty, terror or threat, and it is always of consequence.

The best sea story is probably the *Odyssey,* and Homer's lead has been followed by a succession of writers who have either made the sea the background for much of their work, or have produced one or more sea stories which show mastery. To call any selection "best" is to invite dissent: what is claimed for the present choice is that it includes no author who has not shown that he understands something of the sea as a calling or adventure.

There is an embarrassment of riches such as makes necessary selection only from this side of the Atlantic, and from writers not earlier than Defoe. If the range were to be extended, passages from *Moby Dick* would cry aloud for extract, and there is at least a handful of American sea writers fit to stand beside Melville. Sometimes the chosen writers are masters of the novel, sometimes of the short story, occasionally of both. Whenever possible, a complete story has been included, though in the majority of cases it has been an excision from a longer work, to which appropriate reference is made in the acknowledgments.

For convenience, the items have been placed in the chronological order in which their authors were born, and it so happens that in general the arrangement fits the texture of the work. There is an omission much to be regretted: it is Erskine Childers, author of *The Riddle of the Sands,* a book so close-knit that it proved impossible to lift a chapter or so which might have done it justice. Another absentee is R. L. Stevenson, but here the reason is because, in the editor's view, the very best of its kind is the chapter in *A Footnote to History* which describes that Samoan hurricane of 1889 which had so striking an effect on maritime affairs in the Pacific. As the items are confined to imaginative prose, this had, by definition, to be ruled out: and indeed the collection will be judged not by what is missing, by what is in.

If anyone were to be asked who are the Founding Fathers of English fiction concerned with the sea, he would not be far wrong in naming Defoe, Smollett and Marryat, though a pedigree can be traced without much difficulty earlier than the eighteenth century.

Much of Defoe's life was mysterious, underground, unrecorded: it is in contrast to what he wrote for the public press, so abundant and diverse in subject, so frank in expression. And if there is one thing more certain than another it is that he knew ships and the sea at first hand, and could enter into the mariner's way of thinking with that natural and graphic clarity which characterises everything he wrote.

The classic desert-island story is *Robinson Crusoe.* The classic pirate story is *Captain Singleton,* though it is not a fraction as well known as a comparative late-comer, Stevenson's *Treasure Island.* It dates from 1720—the year after Crusoe's advent—and it is an account not merely of a Brother of the Coast in the style of Conrad's much later creation, old Peyrol in *The Rover,* but one who did well for himself and successfully got away with his plunder.

Much of the narrative in *Captain Singleton* relates to events ashore in Africa. Defoe's knowledge of the broad geography of that Continent, almost certainly derived from Portuguese sources, has surprised a succession of modern scholars, but there are a number of incidents afloat, and among them is a typical account of how a pirate set about his business on the high seas. It stands well on its own. It is also notable for the character of William the Quaker, a man as convincing as Defoe knew how to make him. Professor J. R. Sutherland once called Defoe a "fascinating primitive": the words are surely apt.

Smollett was not born when *Captain Singleton* appeared, yet by the year 1748, when he produced *Roderick Random,* he not only had had a taste of active service as a surgeon's mate in the West Indies and off the coast of Central America, but was busy turning himself into a novelist of the school of Le Sage and *Gil Blas*. There are many accounts in fiction of the wicked ways of the Press Gang. None are more convincing than that which belongs to Smollett's novel. Roderick Random himself is as unprincipled as Bob Singleton, and in the end, contrary to the rules of conventional morality, meets with an equally happy fate. Meanwhile, his adventures in the fleet which was sent against the Spanish overseas possessions during the War of the Austrian Succession would have given most readers a distaste for the life in the King's service afloat. We are introduced to the Press Gang: we also learn something of the sick-bay. The knowledge is not, alas, very edifying, but we are in the eighteenth century, and for all its sometimes elegant surface, it was a brutal time for the common man. Smollett returned to the Navy in *Peregrine Pickle,* where he drew that remarkable old sea-dog Commodore Hawser Trunnion, and where the best scenes are ashore.

The eighteenth century saw the birth of Frederick Marryat, the first writer of natural gifts and vigorous energy who not only served long enough in the Navy to attain the rank of post-captain and the Order of the Bath, but who—unlike Defoe and Smollett, to whom the sea is incidental—made his experience the basis of a series of tales in which the Navy of the greatest era of fighting sail is re-created.

Defoe and Smollett are deemed to be appropriate subjects of study by formal students of English Literature. Marryat has been side-tracked, a fate which at least has the result that he may be rediscovered and read for fun. In fact, there is no single writer who has had more influence, direct and through imitators, both on the sea-story written for grown-ups and on the kind designed for younger readers. Long before he set out to take the juvenile market by storm with *Masterman Ready,* Marryat had shown, through a series of novels of which *Peter Simple* is the most considerable, that he was in the high tradition of the picaresque.

No one has written better about Marryat than a successor, Conrad.

"His novels," said Conrad in his *Notes on Life and Letters,* "are not the outcome of his art, but of his character, like the deeds which make up his record of naval service. To the artist his work is interesting as a completely successful expression of an unartistic nature. It is absolutely amazing to us, as the disclosure of the spirit animating the stirring time when the nineteenth century was young. There is an air of fable about it. Its loss would be irreparable, like the curtailment of national story or the loss of an historical document."

Marryat's novels, whether the scene is land or sea, are riot and abundance, as Conrad suggests. It might have been expected that the severe discipline imposed by the short story form would have been too much for him, and in general that is so: but in a miscellany which he published in 1840 under the title of *Olla Podrida*—the name is that of a Spanish stew of meat and vegetables—he included one story which, though it has a measure of fantastic nonsense not often met with elsewhere, conveys the speed, spirit and zest which animate nearly everything he wrote. The story "S.W. and by W. ¾ W.", is forgotten, and if it serves the purpose of leading anyone to discover the diverse qualities to be remarked elsewhere in this author, together with the excellence of his prose, it will not have been reprinted in vain. It is not, however, an item representative of the rest of this selection, being tragi-comic, which most of the later authors are not: yet of

14

Marryat's fugitive pieces, many of which have disappeared without trace, it was perhaps worth salvaging, if only as showing so many of his attributes in a nut-shell.

Hardy is not usually regarded as a writer of the sea, and with reason, but he never wrote with more feeling than when engaged in themes relating to the era of Napoleon, and his pastoral, *The Trumpet Major,* is felicitous of its kind. The passage from this novel which describes his heroine's sight of the *Victory* as she made her way down Channel towards Spain and Trafalgar—seascape seen from ashore—seems to sum up all Hardy's feelings about that great vessel and her cargo of courage. This is the old Navy, rendered in a glimpse all the more vivid, perhaps, from Hardy's pride in his kinship with Nelson's flag-captain, the only officer of rank to be present at every one of his admiral's achievements in battle.

It is a natural transition from Hardy to Conrad, for they were contemporaries, and although they seem to belong to a distant and perhaps more colourful age of literature than our own, there are still a number living who knew them well and who recognised them for what they were in their lifetime.

While Conrad saw in Marryat something like a prince of maritime writers, there can be little doubt that Conrad was himself the greatest sea writer who ever honoured the English language by learning to use it. He was far more than a sea writer, indeed he once complained to his friend Richard Curle about being labelled as such, but *The Nigger of the Narcissus, Youth, Typhoon, Chance, Victory, The Rover* and many another story testify to the use Conrad made of an experience of twenty years. It would not be difficult to fill an entire anthology of fine passages drawn from his work, indeed this has been done. The pages herein from *Typhoon* should not be taken as representing Conrad's stature in the sea succession, but as a token of the work of his best period.

Conrad was a master of the long-short story as well as of the novel, but to have reprinted entire one of the best, such as *The*

Shadow Line, The Secret Sharer, Youth or *The End of the Tether,* presented serious difficulties and might in any case have disturbed the balance of the whole.

In considering Conrad and his predecessor, Marryat, it is worth remarking that they knew both sail and steam at first hand. Marryat, always forward-looking, insisted on the employment of one of the early steam vessels during the course of the Burma War of 1824, at a time when he was in charge of operations in the immediate theatre of conflict. Conrad's allegiance was to sail, but he had served in steam, and was never one to deceive himself about the realities of the age in which he lived.

Rudyard Kipling, an ardent admirer of Conrad's book of memories and reflections, *The Mirror of the Sea,* was a writer of enviable gifts, and of an unevenness which is often startling. He never wrote better of the seafarer than in his tribute to the fishermen of the Newfoundland Banks in *Captains Courageous,* and at one time he was liable to produce a story or two in which richly endowed characters were summoned from what might be termed the Fisher era of the Navy. "The Ship that Found Herself", a well-known example of Kipling-didactic, is from an early collection, *The Day's Work* (1898). It has distinct "period" flavour today, when the steamship, like the full-rigged ship before her, is becoming part of history. No writer can avoid an element of naïveté when he attempts to personalise technical matters. This may be forgiven (and even welcomed) if he is as expert as Kipling in putting his matter across.

Senior among those writers happily still living who knew deep-sea sail through direct experience is John Masefield. Perhaps his greatest quality, in verse and prose, has been that of compassion. No one has written in quite his terms of the sufferings of those who built his country's fortune upon the waters, and, in his younger days particularly, he had a gift of comedy which tempted the inclusion of the slight but pleasing story "The Devil and the Old Man" from *A Mainsail Haul.* It is juster to the author's standing to include a passage from a later work, *The Bird of*

Dawning, which gives play to the resources of his style and scope for his admiration of those clipper ships which were once the pride of the Port of London. In his novels the Poet Laureate provides the reader with that string of odd and even awkward incidents and touches which makes him say, as he does when he reads Defoe, "Yes; that's *exactly* how it happened. He must have been there himself." He has innocence, as well as peculiar narrative skill.

To those of an age euphemistically termed as being "of a certain maturity", a little book bound in blue cloth and published just before the opening of the First World War was, of its kind, a sea-mark. It must, indeed, have opened many younger eyes—not unpleasantly—to some of the realities of life in the most powerful fleet this country ever assembled. It was *Naval Occasions,* and the author, who used the pseudonym "Bartimeus", has long been known: it was Captain Sir Lewis Ritchie. The first sketch in the book set the tone for the whole, and if there is a certain nostalgia in recalling the brass-funnelled picket-boats of a vanished era, the men who did duty in them are worth evoking, while the midshipman with the face "of a very tired child" possibly survived to become a senior officer in World War II, when his Service endured the greatest trials in all its checkered history.

To represent the Royal and the Merchant Navies, to say nothing of the unabashed pirate, and to have left out the fishermen would have been unpardonable. Of their various recorders, few have shown more skill than Mr. Leo Walmsley, who in a series of stories has given a notable impression of the hazards and rivalries to which fishermen are subject. The writer's own career has been diverse, like Dr. Masefield's, but it is by his novels that he is likely to be remembered longest, and there is not a more characteristic example than *Three Fevers* in which he describes the adventures of a group of men and women making their living through a calling which is of its nature full of risk, which is invaluable to the rest of the community, and which is

INTRODUCTION

sometimes made additionally exciting by the oddest turns of
fortune.

Mr. C. S. Forester is a great master of verisimilitude. It is not
without significance that earlier in his career he produced a series
of historical biographies which were a starting point from which
to develop the even more exacting form of creative fiction.
Horatio Hornblower, exemplar of the successful naval officer of
the time of Nelson, convinces by his adventures as much as by
his personality, and Hornblower is but one of a series of character
studies which illuminate, for instance, episodes in the Peninsula,
aspects of the First World War on land and sea, and that
remarkable action in the Mediterranean, during the darker days
of World War II, when a handful of well-handled light cruisers
and destroyers successfully defied the power of enemy capital
ships. Mr. Forester's care for detail, which is consistent, is never
exercised at the cost of speed of narrative. He has allowed the inclusion of an incident in Hornblower's earlier life not yet to be
found in any collected work. Although it is a tragic piece, it illus-
trates some of Hornblower's best characteristics—his humanity,
his caution, above all perhaps, his paramount power of decision.

Mr. Richard Hughes has never been a prolific writer, a fact
which makes every new novel a cause for stir. There was a nine-
year interval between *A High Wind in Jamaica* and *In Hazard,*
and a far longer one between *In Hazard* and *A Fox in the Attic.*
In Hazard invited direct challenge with Conrad's *Typhoon,* and
it will stand the comparison. The extract included herein does
some justice to the work of the engineers upon whom, in the
last resort, the safety of a modern vessel depends, even though
they have no control whatever as to her direction, and feel, but
do not see, the consequence of orders from the bridge. It also
gives an idea of the strain of ordeal by violence. Incidents which
would appear extravagant on land seem natural enough at sea,
and indeed they are so.

In Hazard appeared shortly before the outbreak of World
War II. Mr. Nicholas Monsarrat's *The Cruel Sea* is a monument

to those who lost their lives in the Battle of the Atlantic, that long, protracted, agonised struggle upon the course of which victory so much depended. His hero, Commander Ericson, R.N.R., made foray into Arctic waters, and it is his successful hunting of a U-boat, while on the very edge of mental and physical exhaustion, which has been detached from the main narrative as forming an episode complete in itself. To some readers, *The Cruel Sea* was flawed by what seemed to be the deliberate insertion of spiced passages, but its persuasion is such that it has gained acceptance as a book which needed to be written if justice were to be done to those with whom the author served in highly critical years. Direct experience of events described is not always necessary to an author, but that it has notable advantages is proved overwhelmingly where the sea is concerned. Scarcely one of the writers included have been without experience of the behaviour of a ship or a boat under command. *The Cruel Sea* is actuality transmuted, and the events it describes seem a long way from the sun-lit episodes of Defoe.

The Cruel Sea is horrific, but so is modern war, and so, in a very different way, are passages in the stories of Mr. William Golding. His memorable novel, *Lord of the Flies,* ends with a glimpse of the Navy as the restorer of something like sanity to a world of disordered children. In a successor, *Pincher Martin,* the sea plays a much greater part. The work as a whole has been interpreted with varying degrees of ingenuity. Without traversing such fields of controversy as exist about its innermost core, its most *apparent* content is the graphic description of experiences on Rockall, that bleak stump which thrusts up far out into the Atlantic. Whether the narrative is allegorical or not in character, it has the conviction which the best allegory so often carries with it. The opening, which is quoted herein, is an impression of the chaos and horror which can follow disaster at sea: it is also, what many other items are not, highly "personalised".

Pincher Martin is a modern story with such a difference that it seems a not inappropriate work from which to close the selection, particularly as there is general agreement that Mr Golding is in the authentic line of succession of highly serious, accomplished writers.

Sound traditions do not readily atrophy, and the sea ingredient in English letters is so rich and diversified that it is likely to continue for as long as men and women find virtue and reward in matching their skill against wind, tide and current. These stories and episodes are, in fact, part of a continuing process, and there is no reason to believe that the future will be any less well endowed than the past.

DANIEL DEFOE

Captain Singleton

I shipped myself, in an evil hour to be sure, on a voyage to Cadiz, in a ship called the ——, and in the course of our voyage, being on the coast of Spain, was obliged to put into the Groyn, by a strong southwest wind.

Here I fell into company with some masters of mischief; and, among them, one, forwarder than the rest, began an intimate confidence with me, so that we called one another brothers, and communicated all our circumstances to one another. His name was Harris. This fellow came to me one morning, asking me if I would go on shore, and I agreed; so we got the captain's leave for the boat, and went together. When we were together, he asked me if I had a mind for an adventure that might make amends for all past misfortunes. I told him, yes, with all my heart; for I did not care where I went, having nothing to lose, and no one to leave behind me.

He then asked me if I would swear to be secret, and that, if I did not agree to what he proposed, I would nevertheless never betray him. I readily bound myself to that, upon the most solemn imprecations and curses that the devil and both of us could invent.

He told me, then, there was a brave fellow in the other ship, pointing to another English ship which rode in the harbour, who, in concert with some of the men, had resolved to mutiny the next morning, and run away with the ship; and that, if we could get strength enough among our ship's company, we might do the same. I liked the proposal very well, and he got eight of us to join with him, and he told us, that as soon as his friend had begun the work, and was master of the ship, we should be ready to do the like. This was his plot; and I, without the least hesitation, either at the villainy of the fact or the difficulty of performing it, came immediately into the wicked conspiracy, and so it went on among us; but we could not bring our part to perfection.

Accordingly, on the day appointed, his correspondent in the other ship, whose name was Wilmot, began the work, and, having seized the captain's mate and other officers, secured the ship, and gave the signal to us. We were but eleven in our ship, who were in the conspiracy, nor could we get any more that we could trust; so that, leaving the ship, we all took the boat, and went off to join the other.

Having thus left the ship I was in, we were entertained with a great deal of joy by Captain Wilmot and his new gang; and, being well prepared for all manner of roguery, bold, desperate (I mean myself), without the least checks of conscience for what I was entered upon, or for anything I might do, much less with any apprehension of what might be the consequence of it; I say, having thus embarked with this crew, which at last brought me to consort with the most famous pirates of the age, some of whom have ended their journals at the gallows, I think the giving an account of some of my other adventures may be an agreeable piece of story; and this I may venture to say beforehand, upon the word of a pirate, that I shall not be able to recollect the full, no, not by far, of the great variety which has formed one of the most reprobate schemes that ever man was capable to present to the world.

I that was, as I have hinted before, an original thief, and a pirate, even by inclination before, was now in my element, and never undertook anything in my life with more particular satisfaction.

Captain Wilmot (for so we are now to call him) being thus possessed of a ship, and in the manner as you have heard, it may be easily concluded he had nothing to do to stay in the port, or to wait either the attempts that might be made from the shore, or any change that might happen among his men. On the contrary, we weighed anchor the same tide, and stood out to sea, steering away for the Canaries. Our ship had twenty-two guns, but was able to carry thirty; and besides, as she was fitted out for a merchant-ship only, she was not furnished either with ammunition or small-arms sufficient for our design, or for the occasion we might have in case of a fight. So we put into Cadiz, that is to say, we came to an anchor in the bay; and the captain, and one whom we called young Captain Kidd, who was the gunner, landed, and some of the men who could best be trusted, among whom was my comrade Harris, who was made second mate, and myself, who was made a lieutenant. Some bales of English goods were proposed to be carried on shore with us for sale, but my comrade, who was a complete fellow at his business, proposed a better way for it; and having been in the town before, told us, in short, that he would buy what powder and bullet, small-arms, or anything else we wanted, on his own word, to be paid for when they came on board, in such English goods as we had there. This was much the best way, and accordingly he and the captain went on shore by themselves, and having made such a bargain as they found for their turn, came away again in two hours' time, and bringing only a butt of wine and five casks of brandy with them, we all went on board again.

The next morning two *barcos longos* came off to us, deeply laden, with five Spaniards on board them, for traffic. Our captain sold them good pennyworths, and they delivered us sixteen barrels of powder, twelve small rundlets of fine powder for our small-arms, sixty muskets, and twelve fuses for the officers; seventeen ton of cannon-ball, fifteen barrels of musket-bullets, with some swords and twenty good pair of pistols. Besides this, they brought thirteen butts of wine (for we, that were now all become gentlemen, scorned to drink the ship's beer), also sixteen puncheons of brandy, with twelve barrels of raisins and twenty chests of lemons; all which we paid for in English goods; and, over and

23

above, the captain received six hundred pieces of eight in money. They would have come again, but we would stay no longer.

From hence we sailed to the Canaries, and from thence onward to the West Indies, where we committed some depredation upon the Spaniards for provisions, and took some prizes, but none of any great value, while I remained with them, which was not long at that time; for, having taken a Spanish sloop on the coast of Carthagena, my friend made a motion to me, that we should desire Captain Wilmot to put us into the sloop, with a proportion of arms and ammunition, and let us try what we could do; she being much fitter for our business than the great ship, and a better sailer. This he consented to, and we appointed our rendezvous at Tobago, making an agreement, that whatever was taken by either of our ships should be shared among the ship's company of both; all which we very punctually observed, and joined our ships again, about fifteen months after, at the island of Tobago, as above.

We cruised near two years in those seas, chiefly upon the Spaniards; not that we made any difficulty of taking English ships, or Dutch, or French, if they came in our way; and particularly, Captain Wilmot attacked a New England ship bound from the Madeiras to Jamaica, and another bound from New York to Barbados, with provisions; which last was a very happy supply to us. But the reason why we meddled as little with English vessels as we could, was, first, because, if they were ships of any force, we were sure of more resistance from them; and, secondly, because we found the English ships had less booty when taken, for the Spaniards generally had money on board, and that was what we best knew what to do with. Captain Wilmot was, indeed, more particularly cruel when he took any English vessel, that they might not too soon have advice of him in England; and so the men-of-war had orders to look out for him. But this part I bury in silence for the present.

We increased our stock in these two years considerably, having taken 60,000 pieces of eight in one vessel, and 100,000 in another;

and being thus first grown rich, we resolved to be strong too, for we had taken a brigantine built at Virginia, an excellent sea-boat, and a good sailer, and able to carry twelve guns; and a large Spanish frigate-built ship, that sailed incomparably well also, and which afterwards, by the help of good carpenters, we fitted up to carry twenty-eight guns. And now we wanted more hands, so we put away for the Bay of Campeachy, not doubting we should ship as many men there as we pleased; and so we did.

Here we sold the sloop that I was in; and Captain Wilmot keeping his own ship, I took the command of the Spanish frigate as captain, and my comrade Harris as eldest lieutenant, and a bold enterprising fellow he was, as any the world afforded. One culverdine was put into the brigantine, so that we were now three stout ships, well manned, and victualled for twelve months; for we had taken two or three sloops from New England and New York, laden with flour, peas, and barrelled beef and pork, going for Jamaica and Barbados; and for more beef we went on shore on the island of Cuba, where we killed as many black cattle as we pleased, though we had very little salt to cure them.

Out of all the prizes we took here we took their powder and bullet, their small-arms and cutlasses; and as for their men, we always took the surgeon and the carpenter, as persons who were of particular use to us upon many occasions; nor were they always unwilling to go with us, though for their own security, in case of accidents, they might easily pretend they were carried away by force; of which I shall give a pleasant account in the course of my other expeditions.

We had one very merry fellow here, a Quaker, whose name was William Walters, whom we took out of a sloop bound from Pennsylvania to Barbados. He was a surgeon, and they called him doctor; but he was not employed in the sloop as a surgeon, but was going to Barbados to get a berth, as the sailors call it. However, he had all his surgeon's chests on board, and we made him go with us, and take all his implements with him. He was a comic fellow indeed, a man of very good solid sense, and an excellent surgeon; but, what was worth all, very good-humoured and pleasant in his conversation, and a bold, stout, brave fellow too, as any we had among us.

I found William, as I thought, not very averse to go along with us, and yet resolved to do it so that it might be apparent he was taken away by force, and to this purpose he comes to me. "Friend," says he, "thou sayest I must go with thee, and it is not in my power to resist thee if I would; but I desire thou wilt oblige the master of the sloop which I am on board to certify under his hand, that I was taken away by force and against my will." And this he said with so much satisfaction in his face, that I could not but understand him. "Ay, ay," says I, "whether it be against your will or no, I'll make him and all the men give you a certificate of it, or I'll take them all along with us, and keep them till they do." So I drew up a certificate myself, wherein I wrote that he was taken away by main force, as a prisoner, by a pirate ship; that they carried away his chest and instruments first, and then bound his hands behind him and forced him into their boat; and this was signed by the master and all his men.

Accordingly I fell a-swearing at him, and called to my men to tie his hands behind him, and so we put him into our boat and carried him away. When I had him on board, I called him to me. "Now, friend," says I, "I have brought you away by force, it is true, but I am not of the opinion I have brought you away so much against your will as they imagine. Come," says I, "you will be a useful man to us, and you shall have very good usage among us." So I unbound his hands, and first ordered all things that belonged to him to be restored to him, and our captain gave him a dram.

"Thou hast dealt friendly by me," says he, "and I will be plain with thee, whether I came willingly to thee or not. I shall make myself as useful to thee as I can, but thou knowest it is not my business to meddle when thou art to fight." "No, no," says the captain, "but you may meddle a little when we share the money." "Those things are useful to furnish a surgeon's chest," says William, and smiled, "but I shall be moderate."

In short, William was a most agreeable companion; but he had the better of us in this part, that if we were taken we were sure to be hanged, and he was sure to escape; and he knew it well enough. But, in short, he was a sprightly fellow, and fitter to be captain than any of us. I shall have often an occasion to speak of him in the rest of the story.

Our cruising so long in these seas began now to be so well known, that not in England only, but in France and Spain, accounts had been made public of our adventures, and many stories told how we murdered the people in cold blood, tying them back to back, and throwing them into the sea; one half of which, however, was not true, though more was done than is fit to speak of here.

The consequence of this, however, was, that several English men-of-war were sent to the West Indies, and were particularly instructed to cruise in the Bay of Mexico, and the Gulf of Florida, and among the Bahama islands, if possible, to attack us. We were not so ignorant of things as not to expect this, after so long a stay in that part of the world; but the first certain account we had of them was at Honduras, when a vessel coming in from Jamaica told us that two English men-of-war were coming directly from Jamaica thither in quest of us. We were indeed as it were embayed, and could not have made the least shift to have got off, if they had come directly to us; but, as it happened, somebody had informed them that we were in the Bay of Campeachy, and they went directly thither, by which we were not only free of them, but were so much to the windward of them, that they could not make any attempt upon us, though they had known we were there.

We took this advantage, and stood away for Carthagena, and from thence with great difficulty beat it up at a distance from under the shore for St. Martha, till we came to the Dutch island of Curaçao, and from thence to the island of Tobago, which, as before, was our rendezvous; which, being a deserted, uninhabited island, we at the same time made use of for a retreat. Here the captain of the brigantine died, and Captain Harris, at that time my lieutenant, took the command of the brigantine.

Here we came to a resolution to go away to the coast of Brazil, and from thence to the Cape of Good Hope, and so for the East Indies; but Captain Harris, as I have said, being now captain of the brigantine, alleged that his ship was too small for so long a voyage, but that, if Captain Wilmot would consent, he would take the hazard of another cruise, and he would follow us in the first ship he could take. So we appointed our rendezvous to be at Madagascar, which was done by my recommendation of the place, and the plenty of provisions to be had there.

Accordingly, he went away from us in an evil hour; for, instead of taking a ship to follow us, he was taken, as I heard afterwards, by an English man-of-war, and being laid in irons, died of mere grief and anger before he came to England. His lieutenant, I have heard, was afterwards executed in England for a pirate; and this was the end of the man who first brought me into this unhappy trade.

We parted from Tobago three days after, bending our course for the coast of Brazil, but had not been at sea above twenty-four hours, when we were separated by a terrible storm, which held three days, with very little abatement or intermission. In this juncture Captain Wilmot happened, unluckily, to be on board my ship, to his great mortification; for we not only lost sight of his ship, but never saw her more till we came to Madagascar, where she was cast away. In short, after having in this tempest lost our foretopmast, we were forced to put back to the isle of Tobago for shelter, and to repair our damage, which brought us all very near our destruction.

We were no sooner on shore here, and all very busy looking out for a piece of timber for a topmast, but we perceived standing in for the shore an English man-of-war of thirty-six guns. It was a great surprise to us indeed, because we were disabled so much;

but, to our great good fortune, we lay pretty snug and close among the high rocks, and the man-of-war did not see us, but stood off again upon his cruise. So we only observed which way she went, and at night, leaving our work, resolved to stand off to sea, steering the contrary way from that which we observed she went; and this, we found, had the desired success, for we saw him no more. We had gotten an old mizzen-topmast on board, which made us a jury fore-topmast for the present; and so we stood away for the isle of Trinidad, where, though there were Spaniards on shore, yet we landed some men with our boat, and cut a very good piece of fir to make us a new topmast, which we got fitted up effectually; and also we got some cattle here to eke out our provisions; and calling a council of war among ourselves, we resolved to quit those seas for the present, and steer away for the coast of Brazil.

The first thing we attempted here was only getting fresh water, but we learnt that there lay the Portuguese fleet at the bay of All Saints, bound for Lisbon, ready to sail, and only waited for a fair wind. This made us lie by, wishing to see them put to sea, and accordingly as they were with or without convoy, to attack or avoid them.

It sprung up a fresh gale in the evening at S.W. by W., which, being fair for the Portugal fleet, and the weather pleasant and agreeable, we heard the signal given to unmoor, and running in under the island of Si——, we hauled our mainsail and foresail up in the brails, lowered the topsails upon the cap, and clewed them up, that we might lie as snug as we could, expecting their coming out, and the next morning saw the whole fleet come out accordingly, but not all to our satisfaction, for they consisted of twenty-six sail, and most of them ships of force, as well as burthen, both merchantmen and men-of-war; so, seeing there was no meddling, we lay still where we were also, till the fleet was out of sight, and then stood off and on, in hopes of meeting with further purchace.

It was not long before we saw a sail, and immediately gave her chase; but she proved an excellent sailer, and, standing out to sea, we saw plainly she trusted to her heels—that is to say, to her sails. However, as we were a clean ship, we gained upon her, though slowly, and had we had a day before us, we should certainly have come up with her; but it grew dark apace, and in that case we knew we should lose sight of her.

Our merry Quaker, perceiving us to crowd still after her in the dark, wherein we could not see which way she went, came very dryly to me. "Friend Singleton," says he, "dost thee know what we are a-doing?" Says I, "Yes; why, we are chasing yon ship, are we not?" "And how dost thou know that?" says he, very gravely still. "Nay, that's true," says I again; "we cannot be sure." "Yes, friend," says he, "I think we may be sure that we are running away from her, not chasing her. I am afraid," adds he, "thou art turned Quaker, and hast resolved not to use the hand of power, or art a coward, and art flying from thy enemy."

"What do you mean?" says I (I think I swore at him). "What do you sneer at now? You have always one dry rub or another to give us."

"Nay," says he, "it is plain enough the ship stood off to sea due east, on purpose to lose us, and thou mayest be sure her business does not lie that way; for what should she do at the coast of Africa in this latitude, which should be as far south as Congo or Angola? But as soon as it is dark, that we would lose sight of her, she will tack and stand away west again for the Brazil coast and for the bay, where thou knowest she was going before; and are we not, then, running away from her? I am greatly in hopes, friend," says the dry, gibing creature, "thou wilt turn Quaker, for I see thou art not for fighting."

"Very well, William," says I; "then I shall make an excellent pirate." However, William was in the right, and I apprehended what he meant immediately; and Captain Wilmot, who lay very sick in his cabin, overhearing us, understood him as well as I, and called out to me that William was right, and it was our best way to change our course, and stand away for the bay, where it was ten to one but we should snap her in the morning.

Accordingly we went about-ship, got our larboard tacks on board, set the top-gallant sails, and crowded for the bay of All Saints, where we came to an anchor early in the morning, just out of gunshot of the forts; we furled our sails with rope-yarns, that we might haul home the sheets without going up to loose them, and, lowering our main and fore-yards, looked just as if we had lain there a good while.

In two hours afterwards we saw our game standing in for the bay with all the sail she could make, and she came innocently into our very mouths, for we lay still till we saw her almost within gunshot, when, our foremast gears being stretched fore and aft, we first ran up our yards, and then hauled home the top-sail sheets, the rope-yarns that furled them giving way of themselves; the sails were set in a few minutes; at the same time slipping our cable, we came upon her before she could get under way upon the other tack. They were so surprised that they made little or no resistance, but struck after the first broadside.

We were considering what to do with her, when William came to me. "Hark thee, friend," says he, "thou hast made a fine piece of work of it now, hast thou not, to borrow thy neighbour's ship here just at thy neighbour's door, and never ask him leave? Now, dost thou not think there are some men-of-war in the port? Thou hast given them the alarm sufficiently; thou wilt have them upon thy back before night, depend upon it, to ask thee wherefore thou didst so."

"Truly, William," said I, "for aught I know, that may be true; what, then, shall we do next?" Says he, "Thou hast but two things to do: either to go in and take all the rest, or else get thee gone before they come out and take thee; for I see they are hoisting a topmast to yon great ship, in order to put to sea immediately, and they won't be long before they come to talk with thee, and what wilt thou say to them when they ask thee why thou borrowedst their ship without leave?"

As William said, so it was. We could see by our glasses they were all in a hurry, manning and fitting some sloops they had there, and a large man-of-war, and it was plain they would soon be with us. But we were not at a loss what to do; we found the ship we had taken was laden with nothing considerable for our purpose, except some cocoa, some sugar, and twenty barrels of flour; the rest of her cargo was hides; so we took out all we thought fit for our turn, and, among the rest, all her ammunition, great shot, and small-arms, and turned her off. We also took a cable and three anchors she had, which were for our purpose, and some of her sails. She had enough left just to carry her into port, and that was all.

Having done this, we stood on upon the Brazil coast, southward, till we came to the mouth of the river Janeiro. But as we had two days the wind blowing hard at S.E. and S.S.E., we were obliged to come to an anchor under a little island, and wait for a wind. In this time the Portuguese had, it seems, given notice over land to the governor there, that a pirate was upon the coast; so that, when we came in view of the port, we saw two men-of-war riding just without the bar, whereof one, we found, was getting under sail with all possible speed, having slipped her cable on purpose to speak with us; the other was not so forward, but was preparing to follow. In less than an hour they stood both fair after us, with all the sail they could make.

Had not the night come on, William's words had been made good; they would certainly have asked us the question what we did there, for we found the foremost ship gained upon us, especially upon one tack, for we plied away from them to windward; but in the dark losing sight of them, we resolved to change our course and stand away directly for sea, not doubting that we should lose them in the night.

Whether the Portuguese commander guessed we would do so or no, I know not; but in the morning when the daylight appeared, instead of having lost him, we found him in chase of us about a league astern; only, to our great good fortune, we could see but one of the two. However, this one was a great ship, carried six-and-forty guns, and an admirable sailer, as appeared by her outsailing us; for our ship was an excellent sailer too, as I have said before.

When I found this, I easily saw there was no remedy, but we must engage; and as we knew we could expect no quarter from those scoundrels the Portuguese, a nation I had an original aversion to, I let Captain Wilmot know how it was. The captain, sick as he was, jumped up in the cabin, and would be led out upon the deck (for he was very weak) to see how it was. "Well," says he, "we'll fight them!"

Our men were all in good heart before, but to see the captain so brisk, who had lain ill of a calenture ten or eleven days, gave them double courage, and they went all hands to work to make a clear ship and be ready. William, the Quaker, comes to me with a kind of a smile. "Friend," says he, "what does yon ship follow us for?" "Why," says I, "to fight us, you may be sure." "Well," says he, "and will he come up with us, dost think?" "Yes," said I, "you see she will." "Why, then, friend," says the dry wretch, "why dost thou run from her still, when thou seest she will overtake thee? Will it be better for us to be overtaken farther off than here?" "Much as one for that," says I; "why, what would you have us do?" "Do!" says he; "let us not give the poor man more trouble than needs must; let us stay for him and hear what he has to say to us." "He will talk to us in powder and ball," said I. "Very well, then," says he, "if that be his country language, we must talk to him in the same, must we not? or else how shall he understand us?" "Very well, William," says I, "we understand you." And the captain, as ill as he was, called to me, "William's right again," says he; "as good here as a league farther." So he gives a word of command, "Haul up the main-sail; we'll shorten sail for him."

Accordingly we shortened sail, and as we expected her upon our lee-side, we being then upon our starboard tack, brought eighteen of our guns to the larboard side, resolving to give him a broadside that should warn him. It was about half-an-hour before he came up with us, all which time we luffed up, that we might keep the wind of him, by which he was obliged to run up under our lee, as we designed him; when we got him upon our quarter, we edged down, and received the fire of five or six of his guns. By this time you may be sure all our hands were at their quarters, so we clapped our helm hard a-weather, let go the lee-braces of the maintop sail, and laid it a-back, and so our ship fell athwart the Portuguese ship's hawse; then we immediately poured in our broadside, raking them fore and aft, and killed them a great many men.

The Portuguese, we could see, were in the utmost confusion; and not being aware of our design, their ship having fresh way, ran their bowsprit into the fore part of our main shrouds, as that they could not easily get clear of us, and so we lay locked after that manner. The enemy could not bring above five or six guns, besides their small-arms, to bear upon us, while we played our whole broadside upon him.

In the middle of the heat of this fight, as I was very busy upon the quarter-deck, the captain calls to me, for he never stirred from us, "What the devil is friend William a-doing yonder?" says the captain; "has he any business upon deck?" I stepped forward, and there was friend William, with two or three stout fellows, lashing the ship's bowsprit fast to our main-mast, for fear they should get away from us; and every now and then he pulled a bottle out of his pocket, and gave the men a dram to encourage them. The shot flew about his ears as thick as may be supposed in such an action, where the Portuguese, to give them their due, fought very briskly, believing at first they were sure of their game, and trusting to their superiority; but there was William, as composed, and in as perfect tranquillity as to danger, as if he had been over a bowl of punch, only very busy securing the matter, that a ship of forty-six guns should not run away from a ship of eight-and-twenty.

This work was too hot to hold long; our men behaved bravely:

our gunner, a gallant man, shouted below, pouring in his shot at such a rate, that the Portuguese began to slacken their fire; we had dismounted several of their guns by firing in at their forecastle, and raking them, as I said, fore and aft. Presently comes William up to me. "Friend," says he, very calmly, "what dost thou mean? Why dost thou not visit thy neighbour in the ship, the door being open for thee?" I understood him immediately, for our guns had so torn their hull, that we had beat two portholes into one, and the bulk-head of their steerage was split to pieces, so that they could not retire to their close quarters; so I gave the word immediately to board them. Our second lieutenant, with about thirty men, entered in an instant over the forecastle, followed by some more with the boatswain, and cutting in pieces about twenty-five men that they found upon the deck, and then throwing some grenadoes into the steerage, they entered there also; upon which the Portuguese cried quarter presently, and we mastered the ship, contrary indeed to our own expectation; for we would have compounded with them if they would have sheered off: but laying them athwart the hawse at first, and following our fire furiously, without giving them any time to get clear of us and work their ship; by this means, though they had six-and-forty guns, they were not able to fight above five or six, as I said above, for we beat them immediately from their guns in the forecastle, and killed them abundance of men between decks, so that when we entered they had hardly found men enough to fight us hand to hand upon their deck.

The surprise of joy to hear the Portuguese cry quarter, and see their ancient struck, was so great to our captain, who, as I have said, was reduced very weak with a high fever, that it gave him new life. Nature conquered the distemper, and the fever abated that very night; so that in two or three days he was sensibly better, his strength began to come, and he was able to give his orders effectually in everything that was material, and in about ten days was entirely well and about the ship.

In the meantime I took possession of the Portuguese man-of-war; and Captain Wilmot made me, or rather I made myself, captain of her for the present. About thirty of their seamen took service with us, some of which were French, some Genoese; and we set the rest on shore the next day on a little island on the coast of Brazil, except some wounded men, who were not in a condition to be removed, and whom we were bound to keep on board; but we had an occasion afterwards to dispose of them at the Cape, where, at their own request, we set them on shore.

TOBIAS SMOLLETT

Roderick Random

As for my own part, I saw no resource but the army or navy, between which I hesitated so long, that I found myself reduced to a starving condition. My spirit began to accommodate itself to my beggarly fate, and I became so mean as to go down towards Wapping, with an intention to inquire for an old schoolfellow, who, I understood, had got the command of a small coasting vessel, then in the river, and implore his assistance. But my destiny prevented this abject piece of behaviour; for, as I crossed Tower Wharf, a squat tawny fellow, with a hanger by his side, and a cudgel in his hand, came up to me, calling, "Yo, ho! brother, you must come along with me." As I did not like his appearance, instead of answering his salutation, I quickened my pace, in hope of ridding myself of his company; upon which he whistled aloud, and immediately another sailor appeared before me, who laid hold of me by the collar, and began to drag me along.

Not being of a humour to relish such treatment, I disengaged myself of the assailant, and with one blow of my cudgel, laid him motionless on the ground; and perceiving myself surrounded in a trice, by ten or a dozen more, exerted myself with such dexterity and success, that some of my opponents were fain to attack me with drawn cutlasses; and, after an obstinate engagement, in which I received a large wound on my head, and another on my left cheek, I was disarmed, taken prisoner, and carried on board a pressing tender, where, after being pinioned like a malefactor,

I was thrust down into the hold among a parcel of miserable wretches, the sight of whom well-nigh distracted me.

As the commanding officer had not humanity enough to order my wounds to be dressed, and I could not use my own hands, I desired one of my fellow-captives, who was unfettered, to take a handkerchief out of my pocket, and tie it round my head to stop the bleeding. He pulled out my handkerchief, 'tis true; but, instead of applying it to the use for which I designed it, went to the grating of the hatchway, and with astonishing composure, sold it before my face to a bum-boat woman then on board, for a quart of gin, with which he treated my companions, regardless of my circumstances and intreaties.

I complained bitterly of this robbery to the midshipman on deck, telling him at the same time, that unless my hurts were dressed, I should bleed to death. But compassion was a weakness of which no man could justly accuse this person, who, squirting a mouthful of dissolved tobacco upon me through the gratings, told me, "I was a mutinous dog, and that I might die and be d—d." Finding there was no other remedy, I appealed to patience, and laid up this usage in my memory, to be recalled at a fitter season.

In the meantime, loss of blood, vexation, and want of food, contributed, with the noisome stench of the place, to throw me into a swoon; out of which I was recovered by a tweak of the nose, administered by the tar who stood sentinel over us, who at the same time regaled me with a draught of flip, and comforted me with the hopes of being put on board the *Thunder* next day, where I should be freed of my handcuffs, and cured of my wounds by the doctor. I no sooner heard him name the *Thunder,* than I asked if he had belonged to that ship long? and he giving me to understand he had belonged to her five years, I inquired if he knew Lieutenant Bowling? "Know Lieutenant Bowling?" said he,—"odds my life! and that I do! and a good seaman he is, as ever stepp'd upon forecastle,—and a brave fellow as ever crack'd bisket;—none of your Guinea pigs,—nor your fresh-water, wishy-washy, fair-weather fowls. Many a taut gale of wind has honest Tom Bowling and I weathered together. Here's his health with all my heart, wherever he is, aloft or alow—in heaven or in hell—all's one for that—he needs not be ashamed to show himself."

I was so much affected with this eulogium, that I could not refrain from telling him that I was Lieutenant Bowling's kinsman; in consequence of which connexion he expressed an inclination to serve me, and, when he was relieved, brought some cold boiled beef in a platter, and biscuit, on which we supped plentifully, and afterwards drank another can of flip together. While we were thus engaged, he recounted a great many exploits of my uncle, who, I found, was very much beloved by the ship's company.

Having, by accident, in my pocket, my uncle's letter, written from Port Louis, I gave it to my benefactor, whose name was Jack Rattlin, for his perusal; but honest Jack told me frankly he could not read, and desired to know the contents; which I immediately communicated. When he heard that part of it in which he says he had writ to his landlord in Deal, he cried, "Body o' me; that was old Ben Block—he was dead before the letter came to hand. Ey, ey, had Ben been alive, Lieutenant Bowling would have had no occasion to skulk so long. Honest Ben was the first man that taught him to hand, reef, and steer.—Well, well, we must all die, that's certain,—we must all come to port sooner or later—at sea, or on shore; we must be fast moored one day; death's like the best bower anchor, as the saying is, it will bring us all up."

I could not but signify my approbation of the justness of Jack's reflections; and inquired into the occasion of the quarrel between Captain Oakum and my uncle; which he explained in this manner: "Captain Oakum to be sure is a good man enough,—besides he's my commander;—but what's that to me?—I do my duty, and value no man's anger or a rope's end.—Now the report goes, as how he's a lord or baron knight's brother, whereby, d'ye see me, he carries a straight arm, and keeps aloof from his officers, tho', may hap, they may be as good men in the main as he. Now we lying at anchor in Tuberoon Bay, Lieutenant Bowling had the middle watch, and as he always kept a good look out, he made, d'ye see, three lights in the offing, whereby he ran down to the great cabin for orders, and found the captain asleep; whereupon he waked him, which put him in a main high passion, and he swore woundily at the Lieutenant, and called him lousy Scotch son of a whore (for I being then sentinel in the steerage, heard all), and swab, and lubber, whereby the lieutenant returned the salute, and they jawed together, fore and aft, a good spell, till at last the captain turned out, and laying hold of a rattan, came athwart Mr. Bowling's quarter; whereby he told the captain, that, if he was not his commander, he would heave him overboard, and demanded satisfaction ashore; whereby, in the morning watch, the captain went ashore in the pinnace, and afterwards the lieutenant carried the cutter ashore; and so they, leaving their boats' crews on their oars, went away together; and so, d'ye see, in less than a quarter of an hour we heard firing, whereby we made for the place, and found the captain lying wounded on the beach, and so brought him on board to the doctor, who cured him in less than six weeks. But the lieutenant clapp'd on all the sail he could bear, and had got far enow ahead before we knew anything of the matter; so that we could never after get sight of him, for which we were not sorry, because the captain was mainly wroth and would certainly have done him a mischief;—for he afterwards caused him to be run on the ship's books, whereby he lost all his pay, and if he should be taken, would be tried as a deserter."

This account of the captain's behaviour gave me no advantageous idea of his character; and I could not help lamenting my own fate, that had subjected me to such a commander. However, making a virtue of necessity, I put a good face on the matter, and next day was, with the other pressed men, put on board of the *Thunder*, lying at the Nore. When we came alongside, the mate who guarded us thither ordered my handcuffs to be taken off, that I might get on board the easier. This circumstance being perceived by some of the company, who stood upon the gang-boards to see us enter, one of them called to Jack Rattlin, who was busied in doing this friendly office for me, "Hey, Jack, what Newgate galley have you boarded in the river as you came along? Have we not thieves enow among us already?" Another, observ-ing my wounds, which remained exposed to the air, told me that my seams were uncaulked, and that I must be new paved. A third, seeing my hair clotted together with blood, as it were, into distinct cords, took notice, that my bows were manned with the red ropes, instead of my side. A fourth asked me, if I could not keep my yards square without iron braces? And, in short, a thousand witticisms of the same nature were passed upon me before I could get up the ship's side. After we had been all entered upon the ship's books, I inquired of one of my shipmates where the surgeon was, that I might have my wounds dressed, and had actually got as far as the middle deck, (for our ship carried eighty guns,) in my way to the cock-pit, when I was met by the same midshipman who had used me so barbarously in the tender. He, seeing me free from my chains, asked, with an insolent air, who had released me? To this question I foolishly answered, with a countenance that too plainly declared the state of my thoughts, "Whoever did it, I am persuaded did not consult you in the affair." I had no sooner uttered these words, then he cried, "D—n you, you saucy son of a bitch, I'll teach you to talk so to your officer." So saying, he bestowed on me several severe stripes with a supple-jack he had in his hand; and, going to the commanding officer, made such a report of me, that I was immediately put in irons by the master-at-arms, and a sentinel placed over me. Honest Rattlin, as soon as he heard of my condition, came to me, and administered all the consolation he could, and then went to the surgeon in my behalf, who sent one of his mates to dress my wounds. This mate was no other than my old friend Thompson, with whom I became acquainted at the Navy Office.

If I knew him at first sight, it was not easy for him to recognise me, disfigured with blood and dirt, and altered by the misery I had undergone. Unknown as I was to him, he surveyed me with looks of compassion, and handled my sores with great tenderness. When he had applied what he thought proper, and was about to leave me, I asked him, if my misfortunes had disguised me so much that he could not recollect my face? Upon this address, he observed me with great earnestness for some time, and at length protested he could not recollect one feature of my countenance.

To keep him no longer in suspense, I told him my name; which when he heard, he embraced me with affection, and professed his sorrow in seeing me in such a disagreeable situation. I made him acquainted with my story; and when he heard how inhumanely I had been used in the tender, he left me abruptly, assuring me that I should see him again soon. I had scarce time to wonder at his sudden departure, when the master-at-arms came to the place of my confinement, and bade me follow him to the quarter-deck, where I was examined by the first lieutenant, who commanded the ship in the absence of the captain, touching the treatment I had received in the tender from my friend the midshipman, who was present to confront me. I recounted the particulars of his behaviour to me, not only in the tender, but since my being on board the ship, part of which being proved by the evidence of Jack Rattlin and others, who had no great devotion for my oppressor, I was discharged from confinement, to make way for him, who was delivered to the master-at-arms to take his turn in the bilboes. And this was not the only satisfaction I enjoyed; for I was, at the request of the surgeon, exempted from all other duty than that of assisting his mates in making and administering medicines to the sick. This good office I owed to the friendship of Mr. Thompson, who had represented me in such a favourable light to the surgeon, that he demanded me of the lieutenant to supply the place of his third mate, who was lately dead. When I had obtained this favour, my friend

Thompson carried me down to the cock-pit, which is the place allotted for the habitation of the surgeon's mates; and when he had shown me their berth, as he called it, I was filled with astonishment and horror.

We descended by divers ladders to a space as dark as a dungeon, which I understood was immersed several feet under water, being immediately above the hold. I had no sooner approached this dismal gulf, than my nose was saluted with an intolerable stench of putrefied cheese and rancid butter, that issued from an apartment at the foot of the ladder, resembling a chandler's shop, where, by the faint glimmering of a candle, I could perceive a man with a pale meagre countenance, sitting behind a kind of desk, having spectacles on his nose, and a pen in his hand. This, I learned of Mr. Thompson, was the ship's steward, who sat there to distribute provisions to the several messes, and to mark what each received. He therefore presented my name to him, and desired I might be entered in his mess; then, taking a light in his hand, conducted me to the place of his residence, which was a square of about six feet, surrounded with the medicine chest, that of the first mate, his own, and a board, by way of table, fastened to the after powder-room; it was also enclosed with canvas, nailed round to the beams of the ship, to screen us from the cold, as well as from the view of the midshipman and quarter-masters, who lodged within the cable-tiers on each side of us.

In this gloomy mansion he entertained me with some cold salt pork, which he brought from a sort of locker, fixed above the table; and, calling for the boy of the mess, sent for a can of beer, of which he made excellent flip to crown the banquet. By this time I began to recover my spirits, which had been exceedingly depressed by the appearance of everything about me, and could no longer refrain from asking particulars of Mr. Thomson's fortune, since I had seen him in London. He told me, that, being disappointed in his expectations of borrowing money to gratify the rapacious secretary at the Navy Office, he found himself utterly unable to subsist any longer in town, and had actually offered his service in quality of mate to the surgeon of a merchant's ship bound to Guinea, on the slaving trade; when one morning, a young fellow, of whom he had some acquaintance, came to his lodgings, and informed him, that he had seen a warrant made out in his name at the Navy Office, for surgeon's second mate of a third rate. This unexpected piece of good news he could scarcely believe to be true, more especially as he had been found qualified at Surgeon's Hall for third mate only; but, that he might not be wanting to himself, he went thither to be assured, and actually found it so. Whereupon, demanding his warrant, it was delivered to him, and the oaths administered immediately. That very afternoon he went to Gravesend in the tilt-boat, from whence he took a place in the tide-coach for Rochester; next morning, got on board the *Thunder,* for which he was appointed, then lying in the harbour of Chatham; and the same day was mustered by the clerk of the cheque. And well it was for him that such expedition was used; for, in less than twelve hours after his arrival, another William Thomson came on board, affirming that he was the person for whom the warrant was expedited, and that the other was an impostor.

My friend was grievously alarmed at this accident—the more so, as his namesake had very much the advantage over him both in assurance and dress. However, to acquit himself of the suspicion of imposture, he produced several letters, written from Scotland to him in that name, and recollecting that his indentures were in a box on board, he brought them up, and convinced all present that he had not assumed a name which did not belong to him. His competitor, enraged that they should hesitate in doing him justice, (for, to be sure, the warrant had been designed for him,) behaved with so much indecent heat, that the commanding officer, who was the same gentleman I had seen, and the surgeon, were offended at his presumption, and, making a point of it with their friends in town, in less than a week got the first confirmed in his station. "I have been on board," said he, "ever since, and, as this way of life is become familiar to me, have no cause to complain of my situation. The surgeon is a good-natured indolent man; the first mate, who is now on shore on duty, is, indeed, a little proud and choleric, as all Welshmen are, but, in the main, a friendly honest fellow. The lieutenants I have no concern with; and as for the captain, he is too much of a gentleman to know a surgeon's mate, even by sight."

FREDERICK MARRYAT

S.W. and by W. ¾ W.

Jack Littlebrain was, physically considered, as fine grown, and moreover as handsome a boy as ever was seen, but it must be acknowledged that he was not very clever. Nature is, in most instances, very impartial; she has given plumage to the peacock, but, as everyone knows, not the slightest ear for music. Throughout the feathered race it is almost invariably the same; the homeliest clad are the finest songsters. Among animals the elephant is certainly the most intelligent, but, at the same time, he cannot be considered as a beauty. Acting upon this well-ascertained principle, nature imagined that she had done quite enough for Jack when she endowed him with such personal perfection; and did not consider it was at all necessary that he should be very clever; indeed, it must be admitted not only that he was not very clever, but (as the truth must be told) remarkably dull and stupid. However, the Littlebrains have been for a long while a well-known, numerous, and influential family, so that, if it were possible that Jack could have been taught anything, the means were forthcoming: he was sent to every school in the country; but it was in vain; at every following vacation, he was handed over from the one pedagogue to the other, of those whose names were renowned for the Busbian system of teaching by stimulating both ends: he was horsed every day and still remained an ass, and at the end of six months, if he did not run away before that period was over, he was invariably sent back to his parents as incorrigible and unteachable. What was to be done with him?

46

The Littlebrains had always got on in the world, somehow or another, by their interest and connections; but here was one who might be said to have no brains at all. After many *pros* and *cons,* and after a variety of consulting letters had passed between the various members of his family, it was decided, that as his maternal uncle, Sir Theophilus Blazers, G.C.B., was at that time second in command in the Mediterranean, he should be sent to sea under his command; the Admiral, having in reply to a letter on the subject, answered that it was hard indeed if he did not lick him into some shape or another; and that, at all events, he'd warrant that Jack should be able to box the compass before he had been three months nibbling the ship's biscuit; further, that it was very easy to get over the examination necessary to qualify him for lieutenant, as a turkey and a dozen of brown stout sent in the boat with him on the passing day, as a present to each of the passing captains, would pass him, even if he were as incompetent as a camel (or, as they say at sea, a cable,) to pass through the eye of a needle; that having once passed, he would soon have him in command of a fine frigate, with a good nursing first lieutenant; and that if he did not behave himself properly, he would make his signal to come on board of the flag-ship, take him into the cabin, and give him a sound horsewhipping, as other admirals have been known to inflict on their sons under similar circumstances. The reader must be aware that, from the tenour of Sir Theophilus's letter, the circumstances which we are narrating must have occurred some fifty years ago.

When Jack was informed that he was to be a midshipman, he looked up in the most innocent way in the world (and innocent he was, sure enough), turned on his heels, and whistled as he went for want of thought. For the last three months he had been at home, and his chief employment was kissing and romping with the maids, who declared him to be the handsomest Littlebrain that the country had ever produced. Our hero viewed the preparations made for his departure with perfect indifference, and wished everybody good-bye with the utmost composure. He was a happy, good-tempered fellow who never calculated, because he could not; never decided, for he had not wit enough to choose; never foresaw, although he could look straight before him; and never remembered, because he had no memory. The line, "If ignorance is bliss, 'tis folly to be wise," was certainly made especially for Jack: nevertheless he was not totally deficient: he knew what was good to eat or drink, for his taste was perfect, his eyes were very sharp, and he could discover in a moment if a peach was ripe on the wall; his hearing was quick, for he was the first in the school to detect the footsteps of his pedagogue; and he could smell anything savoury nearly a mile off, if the wind lay the right way. Moreover, he knew that if he put his fingers in the fire that he would burn himself; that knives cut severely; that birch tickled, and several other little axioms of this sort which are generally ascertained by children at an early age, but which Jack's capacity had not received until a much later date. Such as he was, our hero went to sea; his stock in his sea-chest being very abundant, while his stock of ideas was proportionally small.

We will pass over all the trans-shipments of Jack until he was eventually shipped on board of the *Mendacious,* then lying at Malta with the flag of Sir Theophilus Blazers at the fore—a splendid ship, carrying 120 guns, and nearly 120 midshipmen of different calibres. (I pass over captain, lieutenant, and ship's company, having made mention of her most valuable qualifications.) Jack was received with a hearty welcome by his uncle, for he came in pudding-time, and was invited to dinner; and the Admiral made the important discovery, that if his nephew was a fool in other points, he was certainly no fool at his knife and fork. In a short time his messmates found out that he was no fool at his fists, and his knock-down arguments ended much disputation. Indeed, as the French would say, Jack was perfection in the *physique,* although so very deficient in the *morale.*

But if Pandora's box proved a plague to the whole world, Jack had his individual portion of it, when he was summoned to *box* the compass by his worthy uncle Sir Theophilus Blazers; who in the course of six months discovered that he could not make his nephew box it in the three, which he had warranted in his letter; every day our hero's ears were boxed, but the compass never. It required all the cardinal virtues to teach him the cardinal points during the forenoon, and he made a point of forgetting them before the sun went down. Whenever they attempted it (and various were the teachers employed to drive the compass into Jack's head) his head drove round the compass; and try all he could, Jack never could compass it. It appeared, as some people are said only to have one idea, as if Jack could only have one *point* in his head at a time, and to that point he would stand like a well-broken pointer. With him the wind never changed until the next day. His uncle pronounced him to be a fool, but that did not hurt his nephew's feelings; he had been told so too often already.

I have said that Jack had a great respect for good eating and drinking, and, moreover, was blessed with a good appetite: every person has his peculiar fancies, and if there was anything which more titillated the palate and olfactory nerves of our hero, it was a roast goose with sage and onions. Now it so happened, that having been about seven months on board of the *Mendacious,* Jack had one day received a summons to dine with the Admiral, for the steward had ordered a roast goose for dinner, and knew not only that Jack was partial to it, but also that Jack was the Admiral's nephew, which always goes for something on board of a flag-ship. Just before they were sitting down to table, the Admiral wishing to know how the wind was, and having been not a little vexed with the slow progress of his nephew's nautical acquirements, said, "Now, Mr. Littlebrain, go up, and bring me down word how the wind is; and mark me, as, when you are sent, nine times out of ten you make a mistake, I shall now bet you five guineas against your dinner, that you make a mistake this time: so now be off and we will soon ascertain whether you lose your dinner or I lose my money. Sit down, gentlemen, we will not wait for Mr. Littlebrain."

Jack did not much admire this bet on the part of his uncle, but still less did he like the want of good manners in not waiting for him. He had just time to see the covers removed, to scent a whiff of the goose, and was off.

"The Admiral wants to know how the wind is, sir," said Jack to the officer of the watch.

The officer of the watch went to the binnacle, and setting the wind as nearly as he could, replied, "Tell Sir Theophilus that it is S.W. and by W. ¾ W."

"That's one of those confounded long points that I never can remember," cried Jack, in despair.

"Then you'll 'get goose,' as the saying is," observed one of the midshipmen.

"No; I'm afraid that I sha'n't get any," replied Jack, despondingly. "What did he say, S.W. and by N. ¾ E.?"

"Not exactly," replied his messmate, who was a good-natured lad, and laughed heartily at Jack's version. "S.W. and by W. ¾ W."

"I never can remember it," cried Jack. "I'm to have five guineas if I do, and no dinner if I don't; and if I stay here much longer, I shall get no dinner at all events, for they are all terribly peckish, and there will be none left."

"Well, if you'll give me one of the guineas, I'll show you how to manage it," said the midshipman.

"I'll give you two, if you'll only be quick and the goose a'n't all gone," replied Jack.

The midshipman wrote down the point from which the wind blew, at full length, upon a bit of paper, and pinned it to the rim of Jack's hat. "Now," said he, "when you go into the cabin, you can hold your hat so as to read it, without their perceiving you."

"Well, so I can; I never should have thought of that," said Jack.

"You hav'n't wit enough," replied the midshipman.

"Well, I see no wit in the compass," replied Jack.

"Nevertheless, it's full of point," replied the midshipman; "now be quick."

Our hero's eyes served him well, if his memory was treacherous; and as he entered the cabin door he bowed over his hat very politely, and said as he read it off, "S.W. and by W. ¾ W.," and then he added, without reading at all, "if you please, Sir Theophilus."

"Steward," said the Admiral, "tell the officer of the watch to step down."

"How's the wind, Mr. Growler?"

"S.W. and by W. ¾ W.," replied the officer.

"Then, Mr. Littlebrain, you have won your five guineas, and now you may sit down and enjoy your dinner."

Our hero was not slow in obeying the order, and ventured, upon the strength of his success, to send his plate twice for goose. Having eaten their dinner, drunk their wine, and taken their coffee, the officers, at the same time, took the hint which invariably accompanies the latter beverage, made their bows and retreated. As Jack was following his seniors out of the cabin, the Admiral put the sum which he had staked into his hands, observing, that "it was an ill wind that blew nobody good".

So thought Jack, who, having faithfully paid the midshipman the two guineas for his assistance, was now on the poop keeping his watch, as midshipmen usually do; that is, stretched out on the signal lockers, and composing himself to sleep after the most approved fashion, answering the winks of the stars by blinks of his eyes, until at last he shut them to keep them warm. But, before he had quite composed himself, he thought of the goose and the five guineas. The wind was from the same quarter, blowing soft and mild; Jack lay in a sort of reverie, as it fanned his cheek, for the weather was close and sultry.

"Well," muttered Jack to himself, "I do love that point of the compass, at all events, and I think that I never shall forget S.W. and by W. ¾ W. No I never—never liked one before, though——"

"Is that true?" whispered a gentle voice in his ear; "do you love 'S.W. and by W. ¾ W.,' and will you, as you say, never forget her?"

"Why, what's that?" said Jack, opening his eyes, and turning half round on his side.

"It's me—'S.W. and by W. ¾ W.,' that you say you love."

Littlebrain raised himself and looked round;—there was no one on the poop except himself and two or three of the afterguard, who were lying down between the guns. "Why, who was it that spoke?" said Jack, much astonished.

"It was the wind you love, and who has long loved you," replied the same voice; "do you wish to see me?"

"See you,—see the wind?—I've been already sent on that message by the midshipman," thought Jack.

"Do you love me as you say, and as I love you?" continued the voice.

"Well, I like you better than any other point of the compass, and I'm sure I never thought I should like one of them," replied Jack.

"That will not do for me; will you love only me?"

"I'm not likely to love the others," replied Jack, shutting his eyes again; "I *hate* them all."

"And love me?"

"Well, I do love you, that's a fact," replied Jack, as he thought of the goose and the five guineas.

"Then look round, and you shall see me," said the soft voice.

Jack, who hardly knew whether he was asleep or awake, did at this summons once more take the trouble to open his eyes, and beheld a fairy female figure, pellucid as water, yet apparently possessing substance; her features were beautifully soft and mild, and her outline trembled and shifted as it were, waving gently to and fro. She smiled sweetly, hung over him, played with his chestnut curls, softly touched his lips with her own, passed her trembling fingers over his cheeks, and her warm breath appeared as if it melted into his. Then she grew more bold,—embraced his person, searched into his neck and collar, as if curious to examine him.

Jack felt a pleasure and a gratification which he could not well comprehend: once more the charmer's lips trembled upon his own, now remaining for a moment, now withdrawing, again returning to kiss and kiss again, and once more did the soft voice put the question—

"Do you love me?"

"Better than goose," replied Jack.

"I don't know who goose may be," replied the fairy form, as she tossed about Jack's waving locks; "you must love only me, promise me that before I am relieved."

"What, have you got the first watch, as well as me?" replied Jack.

"I am on duty just now, but I shall not be so long. We southerly winds are never kept long in one place; some of my sisters will probably be sent here soon."

"I don't understand what you talk about," replied Jack. "Suppose you tell me who you are, and what you are, and I'll do all I can to keep awake; I don't know how it is, but I've felt more inclined to go to sleep since you have been fanning me about, than I did before."

"Then I will remain by your side while you listen to me. I am, as I told you, a wind——"

"That's puzzling," said Jack, interrupting her.

"My name is 'S.W. and by W. ¾ W.'"

"Yes, and a very long name it is. If you wish me to remember you, you should have had a shorter one."

This ruffled the wind a little, and she blew rather sharp into the corner of Jack's eye,—however, she proceeded—

"You are a sailor, and of course you know all the winds on the compass by name."

"I wish I did; but I don't," replied Littlebrain. "I can recollect you, and not one other."

Again the wind trembled with delight on his lips, and she proceeded:— "You know that there are thirty-two points on the

53

compass, and these points are divided into quarters; so that there are, in fact, 128 different winds."

"There are more than I could ever remember; I know that," said Jack.

"Well, we are in all 128. All the winds which have northerly in them, are coarse and ugly; all the southern winds are pretty."

"You don't say so?" replied our hero.

"We are summoned to blow, as required, but the hardest duty generally falls to the northerly winds, as it should do, for they are the strongest; although we southerly winds can blow hard enough when we choose. Our characters are somewhat different. The most unhappy in disposition, and I may say, the most malevolent, are the north and easterly winds; the N.W. winds are powerful, but not unkind; the S.E. winds vary, but, at all events, we of the S.W. are considered the mildest and most beneficent. Do you understand me?"

"Not altogether. You're going right round the compass, and I never could make it out, that's a fact. I hear what you say, but I cannot promise to recollect it; I can only recollect S.W. and by W. ¾ W."

"I care only for your recollecting me; if you do that, you may forget all the rest. Now you see we South Wests are summer winds, and are seldom required but in this season; I have often blown over your ship these last three months, and I always have lingered near you, for I loved you."

"Thank you—now go on, for seven bells have struck some time, and I shall be going to turn in. Is your watch out?"

"No, I shall blow for some hours longer. Why will you leave me—why won't you stay on deck with me?"

"What, stay on deck after my watch is out! No, if I do, blow me! We midshipmen never do that—but I say, why can't you come down with me, and turn in my hammock; it's close to the hatchway, and you can easily do it."

"Well, I will, upon one promise. You say that you love me. Now I'm very jealous, for we winds are always supplanting one another. Promise me that you will never mention any other wind in the compass but me, for if you do, they may come to you, and if I hear of it I'll blow the masts out of your ship, that I will."

"You don't say so?" replied Jack, surveying her fragile trembling form.

"Yes, I will, and on a lee shore too; so that the ship shall go to pieces on the rocks, and the Admiral and every soul on board her be drowned."

"No, you wouldn't, would you?" said our hero, astonished.

"Not if you promise me. Then I'll come to you and pour down the windsails, and dry your washed clothes as they hang on the rigging, and just ripple the waves as you glide along, and hang upon the lips of my dear love, and press him in my arms. Promise me, then, on no account ever to recollect or mention any other wind but me."

"Well, I think I may promise that," replied Jack, "for I'm very clever at forgetting; and then you'll come to my hammock, wo'n't you, and sleep with me? you'll be a nice cool bedfellow these warm nights."

"I can't sleep on my watch as midshipmen do; but I'll watch you while you sleep, and I'll fan your cheeks, and keep you cool and comfortable, till I'm relieved."

"And when you go, when will you come again?"

"That I cannot tell—when I'm summoned; and I shall wait with impatience, that you may be sure of."

"There's eight bells," said Jack, starting up; "I must go down and call the officer of the middle watch; but I'll soon turn in, for my relief is not so big as myself, and I can thrash him."

Littlebrain was as good as his word; he cut down his relief, and then thrashed him for venturing to expostulate. The consequence was, that in ten minutes he was in his hammock, and "S.W. and by W. ¾ W." came gently down the hatchway, and rested in his arms. Jack soon fell fast asleep, and when he was wakened up the next morning by the quarter-master, his bedfellow was no longer there. A mate inquiring how the wind was,

was answered by the quarter-master that they had a fresh breeze from the N.N.W., by which Jack understood that his sweetheart was no longer on duty.

Our hero had passed such a happy night with his soft and kind companion, that he could think of nothing else; he longed for her to come again, and, to the surprise of everybody, was now perpetually making inquiries as to the wind which blew. He thought of her continually; and in fact was as much in love with "S.W. and by W. ¾ W." as he possibly could be. She came again—once more did he enjoy her delightful company; again she slept with him in his hammock, and then, after a short stay, she was relieved by another.

We do not intend to accuse the wind of inconstancy, as that was not her fault; nor of treachery, for she loved dearly; nor of violence, for she was all softness and mildness; but we do say, that "S.W. and by W. ¾ W." was the occasion of Jack being very often in a scrape, for our hero kept his word; he forgot all other winds, and, with him, there was no other except his dear "S.W. and by W. ¾ W." It must be admitted of Jack, that, at all events, he showed great perseverance, for he stuck to his point.

Our hero would argue with his messmates, for it is not those who are most capable of arguing who are most fond of it; and, like all arguers not very brilliant, he would flounder and diverge away right and left, just as the flaws of ideas came into his head.

"What nonsense it is your talking that way," would his opponent say. "Why don't you come to the point?"

"And so I do," cried Jack.

"Well then, what is your point?"

"S.W. and by W. ¾ W.," replied our hero.

Who could reply to this? But in every instance, and through every difficulty, our hero kept his promise, until his uncle Sir Theophilus was very undecided, whether he should send him home to be locked up in a Lunatic Asylum, or bring him on in the service to the rank of post-captain. Upon mature consideration, however, as a man in Bedlam is a very useless member of society, and a tee-total non-productive, whereas a captain in the navy is a responsible agent, the Admiral came to the conclusion, that Littlebrain must follow up his destiny.

At last, Jack was set down as the greatest fool in the ship, and was pointed out as such. The ladies observed, that such might possibly be the case, but at all events he was the handsomest young man in the Mediterranean fleet. We believe that both parties were correct in their assertions.

Time flies—even a midshipman's time, which does not fly quite so fast as his money—and the time came for Mr. Littlebrain's examination. Sir Theophilus, who now commanded the whole fleet, was almost in despair. How was it possible that a man could navigate a ship, with only one quarter point of the compass in his head?

Sir Theophilus scratched his wig; and the disposition of the Mediterranean fleet, so important to his country, was altered according to the dispositions of the captains who commanded the ships. In those days, there were martinets in the service; officers who never overlooked an offence, or permitted the least deviation from strict duty; who were generally hated, but at the same time were most valuable to the service. As for his nephew passing his examination before any of those of the first, or second, or even of the third degree, the Admiral knew that it was impossible. The consequence was, that one was sent away on a mission to Genoa, about nothing; another to watch for vessels never expected, off Sardinia; two more to cruise after a French frigate which had never been built: and thus, by degrees, did the Admiral arrange, so as to obtain a set of officers sufficiently pliant to allow his nephew to creep under the gate which barred his promotion, and which he never could have vaulted over. So the signal was made —our hero went on board—his uncle had not forgotten the propriety of a little *douceur* on the occasion; and, as the turkeys were all gone, three couple of geese were sent in the same boat, as a present to each of the three passing captains. Littlebrain's heart failed him as he pulled to the ship; even the geese hissed at him, as much as to say, "If you were not such a stupid ass, we might have been left alive in our coops." There was a great deal of truth in that remark, if they did say so.

Nothing could have been made more easy for Littlebrain than his examination. The questions had all been arranged beforehand; and some kind friend had given him all the answers written down. The passing captains apparently suffered from the heat of the weather, and each had his hands on his brow, looking down on the table at the time that Littlebrain gave his answers, so that of course they did not observe that he was reading them off. As soon as Littlebrain had given his answer, and had had sufficient time to drop his paper under the table, the captains felt better and looked up again.

There were but eight questions for our hero to answer. Seven had been satisfactorily got through; then came the eighth, a very simple one:— "What is your course and distance from Ushant to the Start?" This question having been duly put, the captains were again in deep meditation, shrouding their eyes with the palms of their hands.

Littlebrain had his answer—he looked at the paper. What could be more simple than to reply?—and the captains would have all risen up, shaken him by the hand, complimented him upon the talent he had displayed, sent their compliments to the commander-in-chief, and their thanks for the geese. Jack was just answering, "North——"

"Recollect your promise!" cried a soft voice, which Jack well recollected.

Jack stammered—the captains were mute—and waited patiently.

"I must say it," muttered Jack.

"You shan't," replied the little Wind.

"Indeed I must," said Jack, "or I shall be turned back."

The captains, surprised at this delay and the muttering of Jack, looked up, and one of them gently inquired if Mr. Littlebrain had not dropped his handkerchief or something under the table? and then they again fixed their eyes upon the green cloth.

"If you dare, I'll never see you again," cried "S.W. and by W. ¾ W.,"—"never come to your hammock,—but I'll blow the ship on shore, every soul shall be lost, Admiral and all; recollect your promise!"

"Then I shall never pass," replied Jack.

"Do you think that any other point in the compass shall pass you except me?—never! I'm too jealous for that; come now, dearest," and the Wind again deliciously trembled upon the lips of our hero, who could no longer resist.

"S.W. and by W. ¾ W.," exclaimed Jack firmly.

"You have made a slight mistake, Mr. Littlebrain," said one of the captains. "*Look* again—I meant to say, *think* again."

"S.W. and by W. ¾ W.," again repeated Jack.

"Dearest! how I love you!" whispered the soft wind.

"Why, Mr. Littlebrain," said one of the captains, for Jack had actually laid the paper down on the table, "what's in the wind now?"

"She's obstinate," replied Jack.

"You appear to be so, at all events," replied the captain. "Pray try once more."

"I have it!" thought Jack, who tore off the last answer from his paper. "I gained five guineas by that plan once before." He then handed the bit of paper to the passing captain: "I believe that's right, sir," said our hero.

"Yes, that is right; but could you not have said it instead of writing it, Mr. Littlebrain?"

Jack made no reply; his little sweetheart pouted a little, but said nothing; it was an evasion which she did not like. A few seconds of consultation then took place, as a matter of form. Each captain asked of the other if he was perfectly satisfied as to Mr. Littlebrain's capabilities, and the reply was in the affirmative; and they were perfectly satisfied, that he was either a fool or a madman. However, as we have had both in the service by way of precedent, Jack was added to the list, and the next day was appointed lieutenant.

Our hero did his duty as lieutenant of the forecastle; and as all the duty of that officer is, when hailed from the quarter-deck, to answer *"Ay, ay, sir,"* he got on without making many mistakes. And now he was very happy; no one dared to call him a fool except his uncle; he had his own cabin, and many was the time that his dear little "S.W. and by W. ¾ W." would come in by the scuttle, and nestle by his side.

"You won't see so much of me soon, dearest," said she, one morning, gravely.

"Why not, my soft one?" replied Jack.

"Don't you recollect that the winter months are coming on?"

"So they are," replied Jack. "Well, I shall long for you back."

And Jack did long, and long very much, for he loved his dear wind, and the fine weather which accompanied her. Winter came on, and heavy gales and rain, and thunder and lightning; nothing but double-reefed topsails, and wearing in succession; and our hero walked the forecastle, and thought of his favourite wind. The N.E. winds came down furiously, and the weather was bitter cold. The officers shook the rain and spray off their garments when their watch was over, and called for grog.

"Steward, a glass of grog," cried one, "and let it be strong."

"The same for me," said Jack; "only I'll mix it myself."

Jack poured out the rum till the tumbler was half full.

"Why, Littlebrain," said his messmate, "that is a dose, that's what we call a regular *Nor-wester*."

"Is it?" replied Jack. "Well then, Nor-westers suit me exactly, and I shall stick to them like cobbler's wax."

And during the whole of the winter months our hero showed a great predilection for Nor-westers.

It was in the latter end of February that there was a heavy gale; it had blown furiously from the northward for three days, and then it paused and panted as if out of breath—no wonder; and then the wind shifted, and shifted again, with squalls and heavy rain, until it blew from every quarter of the compass.

Our hero's watch was over, and he came down and called for a "Nor-wester" as usual.

"How is the wind, now?" asked the first lieutenant to the master, who came down dripping wet.

"S.S.W., but drawing fast to the Westward," said old Spun-yarn.

And so it was; and it veered round until "S.W. and by W. ¾ W.", with an angry gust, came down the sky-light, and blowing strongly into our hero's ear, cried—

"Oh! you false one!!"

"False!" exclaimed Jack. "What! you here, and so angry too?—what's the matter?"

"What's the matter—do you think I don't know? What have you been doing ever since I was away, comforting yourself during my absence with *Nor-westers?*"

"Why, you an't jealous of a Nor-wester, are you?" replied Littlebrain. "I confess, I'm rather partial to them."

"What!—this to my face!—I'll never come again—without you promise me that you will have nothing to do with them, and never call for one again. Be quick—I cannot stay more than two minutes, for it is hard work now, and we relieve quick—say the word."

"Well, then," replied Littlebrain, "you've no objection to *half-and-half?*"

"None in the world; that's quite another thing, and has nothing to do with the wind."

"It has, though," thought Jack, "for it gets a man in the wind; but I wo'n't tell her so; and," continued he, "you don't mind a raw nip, do you?"

"No—I care for nothing except a Nor-wester."

"I'll never call for one again," replied Jack; "it is but making my grog a little stronger; in future it shall be half-and-half."

"That's a dear!—now I'm off, don't forget me;" and away went the wind in a great hurry.

It was about three months after this short visit, the fleet being off Corsica, that our hero was walking the deck, thinking that he soon should see the object of his affections, when a privateer brig was discovered at anchor a few miles from Bastia. The signal was made for the boats of the fleet to cut her out, and the Admiral, wishing that his nephew should distinguish himself somehow, gave him the command of one of the finest boats. Now Jack was as brave as brave could be; he did not know what danger was; he hadn't wit enough to perceive it, and there was no doubt but he would distinguish himself. The boats went on the service. Jack was the very first on board, cheering his men as he darted into the closed ranks of his opponents. Whether it was that he did not think that his head was worth defending, or that he was too busy in breaking the heads of others to look after his own; this is certain, that a tomahawk descended upon it with such force as to bury itself in his skull (and his was a thick skull, too). The privateer's men were overpowered by numbers, and then our hero was discovered, under a pile of bodies, still breathing heavily. He was hoisted on board, and taken into his uncle's cabin: the surgeon shook his head when he had examined that of our hero.

"It must have been a most tremendous blow," said he to the Admiral, "to have penetrated——"

"It must have been, indeed," replied the Admiral, as the tears rolled down his cheeks; for he loved his nephew.

The surgeon having done all that his art would enable him, left the cabin to attend to others who were hurt; the Admiral also went on the quarter-deck, walking to and fro for an hour in a melancholy mood. He returned to the cabin, and bent over his nephew; Jack opened his eyes.

"My dear fellow," said the Admiral, "how's your head now?"

"S.W. and by W. ¾ W.," faintly exclaimed our hero, constant in death, as he turned a little on one side and expired.

It was three days afterwards, as the fleet were on a wind, making for Malta, that the bell of the ship tolled, and a body, sewed up in a hammock and covered with the Union Jack, was

carried to the gangway by the Admiral's bargemen. It had been
a dull cloudy day, with little wind; the hands were turned up,
the officers and men stood uncovered; the Admiral in advance
with his arms folded, as the chaplain read the funeral service over
the body of our hero,—and as the service proceeded, the sails
flapped, for the wind had shifted a little; a motion was made,
by the hand of the officer of the watch, to the man at the helm
to let the ship go off the wind, that the service might not be disturbed, and a mizzling soft rain descended. The wind had shifted
to our hero's much loved *point,* his fond mistress had come to
mourn over the loss of her dearest, and the rain that descended
were the tears which she shed at the death of her handsome but
not over-gifted lover.

THOMAS HARDY

A Speck On The Sea

From the moment of Bob's return to the bosom of the deep Anne had had no existence on land; people might have looked at her human body and said she had flitted thence. The sea and all that belonged to the sea was her daily thought and her nightly dream. She had the whole two-and-thirty winds under her eye, each passing gale that ushered in returning autumn being mentally registered; and she acquired a precise knowledge of the direction in which Portsmouth, Brest, Ferrol, Cadiz, and other such likely places lay. Instead of saying her own familiar prayers at night she substituted, with some confusion of thought, the Forms of Prayer to be used at sea. John at once noticed her lorn, abstracted looks, pitied her,—how much he pitied her!— and asked when they were alone if there was anything he could do.

"There are two things," she said, with almost childish eagerness in her tired eyes.

"They shall be done."

"The first is to find out if Captain Hardy has gone back to his ship; and the other is—O if you will do it, John!—to get me newspapers whenever possible."

After this duologue John was absent for a space of three hours, and they thought he had gone back to barracks. He entered, however, at the end of that time, took off his forage-cap, and wiped his forehead.

"You look tired, John," said his father.

"O no." He went through the house till he had found Anne Garland.

"I have only done one of those things," he said to her.

"What, already? I didn't hope for or mean to-day."

"Captain Hardy is gone from Pos'ham. He left some days ago. We shall soon hear that the fleet has sailed."

"You have been all the way to Pos'ham on purpose? How good of you!"

"Well, I was anxious to know myself when Bob is likely to leave. I expect now that we shall soon hear from him."

Two days later he came again. He brought a newspaper, and what was better, a letter for Anne, franked by the first lieutenant of the *Victory*.

"Then he's aboard her," said Anne, as she eagerly took the letter.

It was short, but as much as she could expect in the circumstances, and informed them that the captain had been as good as his word, and had gratified Bob's earnest wish to serve under him. The ship, with Admiral Lord Nelson on board, and accompanied by the frigate *Euryalus,* was to sail in two days for Plymouth, where they would be joined by others, and thence proceed to the coast of Spain.

Anne lay awake that night thinking of the *Victory,* and of those who floated in her. To the best of Anne's calculation that ship of war would, during the next twenty-four hours, pass within a few miles of where she herself then lay. Next to seeing Bob, the thing that would give her more pleasure than any other in the world was to see the vessel that contained him—his floating city, his sole dependence in battle and storm—upon whose safety from winds and enemies hung all her hope.

The morrow was market-day at the seaport, and in this she saw her opportunity. A carrier went from Overcombe at six o'clock thither, and having to do a little shopping for herself she gave it as a reason for her intended day's absence, and took a place in the van. When she reached the town it was still early morning, but the borough was already in the zenith of its daily bustle and show. The King was always out-of-doors by six o'clock, and such cock-crow hours at Gloucester Lodge produced an equally forward stir among the population. She alighted and passed down the esplanade, as fully thronged by persons of fashion at this time of mist and level sunlight as a watering-place in the present day is at four in the afternoon. Dashing bucks and beaux in cocked hats, black feathers, ruffles, and frills, stared at her as she hurried along; the beach was swarming with bathing women, wearing waistbands that bore the national refrain, "God save the King," in gilt letters; the shops were all open, and Sergeant Stanner, with his sword-stuck bank-notes and heroic gaze, was beating up at two guineas and a crown, the crown to drink his Majesty's health.

She soon finished her shopping, and then, crossing over into the old town, pursued her way along the coast-road to Portland. At the end of an hour she had been rowed across the Fleet (which then lacked the convenience of a bridge), and reached the base of Portland Hill. The steep incline before her was dotted with houses, showing the pleasant peculiarity of one man's doorstep being behind his neighbour's chimney, and slabs of stone as the common material for walls, roof, floor, pigsty, stable-manger, door-scraper, and garden-stile. Anne gained the summit, and followed along the central track over the huge lump of freestone which forms the peninsula, the wide sea prospect extending as she went on. Weary with her journey, she approached the extreme southerly peak of rock, and gazed from the cliff at Portland Bill, or Beal, as it was in those days more correctly called.

The wild, herbless, weather-worn promontory was quite a solitude, and, saving the one old lighthouse about fifty yards up the slope, scarce a mark was visible to show that humanity had ever been near the spot. Anne found herself a seat on a stone, and swept with her eyes the tremulous expanse of water around her that seemed to utter a ceaseless unintelligible incantation. Out of the three hundred and sixty degrees of her complete horizon two hundred and fifty were covered by waves, the *coup d'œil* including the area of troubled waters known as the Race, where two seas met to effect the destruction of such vessels as could not be mastered by one. She counted the craft within her view: there were five; no, there were only four; no, there were seven, some of the specks having resolved themselves into two. They were all small coasters, and kept well within sight of land.

Anne sank into a reverie. Then she heard a slight noise on her left hand, and turning beheld an old sailor, who had approached with a glass. He was levelling it over the sea in a direction to the south-east, and somewhat removed from that in which her own eyes had been wandering. Anne moved a few steps thitherward, so as to unclose to her view a deeper sweep on that side, and by this discovered a ship of far larger size than any which had yet dotted the main before her. Its sails were for the most part new and clean, and in comparison with its rapid progress before the wind the small brigs and ketches seemed standing still. Upon this striking object the old man's glass was bent.

"What do you see, sailor?" she asked.

"Almost nothing," he answered. "My sight is so gone lately that things, one and all, be but a November mist to me. And yet I fain would see to-day. I am looking for the *Victory*."

"Why?" she said quickly.

"I have a son aboard her. He's one of the three from these parts. There's the captain, there's my son Ned, and there's young Loveday of Overcombe—he that lately joined."

"Shall I look for you?" said Anne, after a pause.

"Certainly, mis'ess, if so be you please."

Anne took the glass, and he supported it by his arm. "It is a large ship," she said, "with three masts, three rows of guns along the side, and all her sails set."

"I guessed as much."

"There is a little flag in front—over her bowsprit."

"The jack."

"And there's a large one flying at her stern."

"The ensign."

"And a white one on her fore-topmast."

"That's the admiral's flag, the flag of my Lord Nelson. What is her figure-head, my dear?"

"A coat-of-arms, supported on this side by a sailor."

Her companion nodded with satisfaction. "On the other side of that figure-head is a marine."

"She is twisting round in a curious way, and her sails sink in like old cheeks, and she shivers like a leaf upon a tree."

"She is in stays, for the larboard tack. I can see what she's been doing. She's been re'ching close in to avoid the flood tide, as the wind is to the sou'west, and she's bound down; but as soon as the ebb made, d'ye see, they made sail to the west'ard. Captain Hardy may be depended upon for that; he knows every current about here, being a native."

"And now I can see the other side; it is a soldier where a sailor was before. You are *sure* it is the *Victory*?"

"I am sure."

After this a frigate came into view—the *Euryalus*—sailing in the same direction. Anne sat down, and her eyes never left the ships. "Tell me more about the *Victory*," she said.

"She is the best sailer in the service, and she carries a hundred guns. The heaviest be on the lower deck, the next size on the middle deck, the next on the main and upper decks. My son Ned's place is on the lower deck, because he's short, and they put the short men below."

Bob, though not tall, was not likely to be specially selected for shortness. She pictured him on the upper deck, in his snow-white trousers and jacket of navy blue, looking perhaps towards the very point of land where she then was.

The great silent ship, with her population of blue-jackets, marines, officers, captain, and the admiral who was not to return alive, passed like a phantom the meridian of the Bill. Sometimes her aspect was that of a large white bat, sometimes that of a grey one. In the course of time the watching girl saw that the ship had passed her nearest point; the breadth of her sails diminished by foreshortening, till she assumed the form of an egg on end. After this something seemed to twinkle, and Anne, who had previously withdrawn from the old sailor, went back to him, and looked again through the glass. The twinkling was the light falling upon the cabin windows of the ship's stern. She explained it to the old man.

"Then we see now what the enemy have seen but once. That was in seventy-nine, when she sighted the French and Spanish fleet of Scilly, and she retreated because she feared a landing. Well, 'tis a brave ship and she carries brave men!"

Anne's tender bosom heaved, but she said nothing, and again became absorbed in contemplation.

The *Victory* was fast dropping away. She was on the horizon, and soon appeared hull down. That seemed to be like the beginning of a greater end than her present vanishing. Anne Garland could not stay by the sailor any longer, and went about a stone's-throw off, where she was hidden by the inequality of the cliff from his view. The vessel was now exactly end on, and stood out in the direction of the Start, her width having contracted to the proportion of a feather. She sat down again, and mechanically took out some biscuits that she had brought, foreseeing that her waiting might be long. But she could not eat one of them; eating seemed to jar with the mental tenseness of the moment; and her undeviating gaze continued to follow the lessened ship with the fidelity of a balanced needle to a magnetic stone, all else in her being motionless.

The courses of the *Victory* were absorbed into the main, then her topsails went, and then her top-gallants. She was now no more than a dead fly's wing on a sheet of spider's web; and even this fragment diminished. Ann could hardly bear to see the end, and yet she resolved not to flinch. The admiral's flag sank behind the watery line, and in a minute the very truck of the last topmast stole away. The *Victory* was gone.

JOSEPH CONRAD

Typhoon

The Nan-Shan, *Captain MacWhirr in command, is facing the worst of the storm. She carries Chinese coolies, each with his separate store of dollars. In the confusion and fury, dollars and coolies have become almost inextricably mixed up. Rout and Beale are engine-room officers; Jukes is chief mate.*

He waited. Before his eyes the engines turned with slow labour, that in the moment of going off into a mad fling would stop dead at Mr. Rout's shout, "Look out, Beale!" They paused in an intelligent immobility, stilled in mid-stroke, a heavy crank arrested on the cant, as if conscious of danger and the passage of time. Then, with a "Now, then," from the chief, and the sound of a breath expelled through clenched teeth, they would accomplish the interrupted revolution and begin another.

There was the prudent sagacity of wisdom and the deliberation of enormous strength in their movements. This was their work—this patient coaxing of a distracted ship over the fury of the waves and into the very eye of the wind. At times Mr. Rout's chin would sink on his breast, and he watched them with knitted eyebrows as if lost in thought.

The voice that kept the hurricane out of Jukes' ear began, "Take the hands with you . . ." and left off unexpectedly.

"What could I do with them, sir?"

A harsh, abrupt, imperious clang exploded suddenly. The three pairs of eyes flew up to the telegraph dial to see the hand jump from FULL to STOP, as if snatched by a devil. And then these three men in the engine-room had the intimate sensation of a check upon the ship, of a strange shrinking, as if she had gathered herself for a desperate leap.

"Stop her!" bellowed Mr. Rout.

Nobody—not even Captain MacWhirr, who alone on deck had caught sight of a white line of foam coming on at such a height that he couldn't believe his eyes—nobody was to know the steepness of that sea and the awful depth of the hollow the hurricane had scooped out behind the running wall of water.

It raced to meet the ship, and, with a pause, as of girding the loins, the *Nan-Shan* lifted her bows and leaped. The flames in all the lamps sank, darkening the engine-room. One went out. With a tearing crash and a swirling, raving tumult, tons of water fell upon the deck, as though the ship had darted under the foot of a cataract.

Down there they looked at each other, stunned.

"Swept from end to end, by God!" bawled Jukes.

She dipped into the hollow straight down, as if going over the edge of the wind. The engine-room toppled forward menacingly, like the inside of a tower nodding in an earthquake. An awful racket, of iron things falling, came from the stokehold. She hung on this appalling slant long enough for Beale to drop on his hands and knees and begin to crawl as if he meant to fly on all fours out of the engine-room, and for Mr. Rout to turn his head slowly, rigid, cavernous, with the lower jaw dropping. Jukes had shut his eyes, and his face in a moment became hopelessly blank and gentle, like the face of a blind man.

At last she rose slowly, staggering, as if she had to lift a mountain with her bows.

Mr. Rout shut his mouth; Jukes blinked; and little Beale stood up hastily.

"Another one like this, and that's the last of her," cried the chief.

He and Jukes looked at each other, and the same thought came into their heads. The captain! Everything must have been swept away. Steering-gear gone—ship like a log. All over directly.

"Rush!" ejaculated Mr. Rout thickly, glaring with enlarged doubtful eyes at Jukes, who answered him by an irresolute glance.

The clang of the telegraph gong soothed them instantly. The black hand dropped in a flash from STOP to FULL.

"Now then, Beale!" cried Mr. Rout.

The steam hissed low. The piston-rods slid in and out. Jukes put his ear to the tube. The voice was ready for him. It said, "Pick up all the money. Bear a hand now. I'll want you up here." And that was all.

"Sir?" called up Jukes. There was no answer.

He staggered away like a defeated man from the field of battle. He had got, in some way or other, a cut above his left eyebrow —a cut to the bone. He was not aware of it in the least: quantities of the China Sea, large enough to break his neck for him, had gone over his head, had cleaned, washed, and salted that wound. It did not bleed, but only gaped red; and this gash over the eye, his dishevelled hair, the disorder of his clothes, gave him the aspect of a man worsted in a fight with fists.

"Got to pick up the dollars," he appealed to Mr. Rout, smiling pitifully at random.

"What's that?" asked Mr. Rout wildly. "Pick up . . . ? I don't care . . ." Then, quivering in every muscle, but with an exaggeration of paternal tone, "Go away now, for God's sake. You deck people 'll drive me silly. There's that second mate been going for the old man. Don't you know? You fellows are going wrong for want of something to do. . . ."

At these words Jukes discovered in himself the beginnings of anger. Want of something to do—indeed. . . . Full of hot scorn against the chief, he turned to go the way he had come. In the stokehold the plump donkeyman toiled with his shovel mutely, as if his tongue had been cut out; but the second was carrying on like a noisy, undaunted maniac, who had preserved his skill in the art of stoking under a marine boiler.

"Hallo, you wandering officer! Hey! Can't you get some of your slush-slingers to wind up a few of them ashes? I am getting choked with them here. Curse it! Hallo! Hey! Remember the articles: *Sailors and firemen to assist each other.* Hey! D'ye hear?"

Jukes was climbing out frantically and the other, lifting up his face after him, howled, "Can't you speak? What are you poking about here for? What's your game, anyhow?"

A frenzy possessed Jukes. By the time he was back amongst the men in the darkness of the alleyway, he felt ready to wring all their necks at the slightest sign of hanging back. The very thought of it exasperated him. *He* couldn't hang back. They shouldn't.

The impetuosity with which he came amongst them carried them along. They had already been excited and startled at all his comings and goings—by the fierceness and rapidity of his movements; and more felt than seen in his rushes, he appeared formidable—busied with matters of life and death that brooked no delay. At his first word he heard them drop into the bunker one after another obediently, with heavy thumps.

They were not clear as to what would have to be done. "What is it? What is it?" they were asking each other. The boatswain tried to explain; the sounds of a great scuffle surprised them: and the mighty shocks, reverberating awfully in the black bunker, kept them in mind of their danger. When the boatswain threw open the door it seemed that an eddy of the hurricane, stealing through the iron sides of the ship, had set all these bodies whirling like dust. There came to them a confused uproar, a tempestuous tumult, a fierce mutter, gusts of screams dying away, and the tramping of feet mingling with the blows of the sea.

For a moment they glared amazed, blocking the doorway. Jukes pushed through them brutally. He said nothing, and simply

73

darted in. Another lot of coolies on the ladder, struggling suicidally to break through the battened hatch to a swamped deck, fell off as before, and he disappeared under them like a man overtaken by a landslide. The boatswain yelled excitedly. "Come along. Get the mate out. He'll be trampled to death. Come on."

They charged in, stamping on breasts, on fingers, on faces, catching their feet in heaps of clothing, kicking broken wood; but before they could get hold of him, Jukes emerged waist deep in a multitude of clawing hands. In an instant he had been lost to view, all the buttons of his jacket had gone, its back had got split up to the collar, his waistcoat had been torn open. The central struggling mass of Chinamen went over to the roll, dark, indistinct, helpless, with a wild gleam of many eyes in the dim light of the lamps.

"Leave me alone—damn you. I am all right," screeched Jukes. "Drive them forward. Watch your chance when she pitches. Forward with 'em. Drive them against the bulkhead. Jam 'em up."

The rush of the sailors into the seething 'tween-deck was like a splash of cold water into a boiling cauldron. The commotion sank for a moment.

The bulk of the Chinamen were locked into such a compact scrimmage that, linking their arms and aided by an appalling dive of the ship, the seamen sent it forward in one great shove, like a solid block. Behind their backs small clusters and loose bodies tumbled from side to side.

The boatswain performed prodigious feats of strength. With his long arms open, and each great paw clutching at a stanchion, he stopped the rush of seven entwined Chinamen rolling like a boulder. His joints cracked; he said, "Ha!" and they flew apart. But the carpenter showed the greater intelligence. Without saying a word to anybody he went back into the alleyway, to fetch several coils of cargo gear he had seen there—chain and rope. With these life-lines were rigged.

There was really no resistance. The struggle, however it began, had turned into a scramble of blind panic. If the coolies had started up after their scattered dollars they were by that time fighting only for their footing. They took each other by the throat merely to save themselves from being hurled about. Whoever got a hold anywhere would kick at the others who caught at his legs and hung on, till a roll sent them flying together across the deck.

The coming of the white devils was a terror. Had they come to kill? The individuals torn out of the ruck became very limp in the seamen's hands: some, dragged aside by the heels, were passive, like dead bodies, with open, fixed eyes. Here and there a coolie would fall on his knees as if begging for mercy; several, whom the excess of fear made unruly, were hit with hard fists between the eyes, and cowered; while those who were hurt submitted to rough handling, blinking rapidly without a plaint. Faces streamed with blood; there were raw places on the shaven heads, scratches, bruises, torn wounds, gashes. The broken porcelain out of the chests was mostly responsible for the latter. Here and there a Chinaman, wild-eyed, with his tail unplaited, nursed a bleeding sole.

They had been ranged closely, after having been shaken into submission, cuffed a little to allay excitement, addressed in gruff words of encouragement that sounded like promises of evil. They sat on the deck in ghastly, drooping rows, and at the end the carpenter, with two hands to help him, moved busily from place to place, setting taut and hitching the life-lines. The boatswain, with one leg and one arm embracing a stanchion, struggled with a lamp pressed to his breast, trying to get a light, and growling all the time like an industrious gorilla. The figures of seamen stooped repeatedly, with the movements of gleaners, and everything was being flung into the bunker: clothing, smashed wood, broken china, and the dollars too, gathered up in men's jackets. Now and then a sailor would stagger towards the doorway with his arms full of rubbish; and dolorous, slanting eyes followed his movements.

75

With every roll of the ship the long rows of sitting Celestials would sway forward brokenly, and her headlong dives knocked together the line of shaven polls from end to end. When the wash of water rolling on the deck died away for a moment, it seemed to Jukes, yet quivering from his exertions, that in his mad struggle down there he had overcome the wind somehow: that a silence had fallen upon the ship, a silence in which the sea struck thunderously at her sides.

Everything had been cleared out of the 'tween-deck—all the wreckage, as the men said. They stood erect and tottering above the level of heads and drooping shoulders. Here and there a coolie sobbed for his breath. Where the high light fell, Jukes could see the salient ribs of one, the yellow, wistful face of another; bowed necks; or would meet a dull stare directed at his face. He was amazed that there had been no corpses; but the lot of them seemed at their last gasp, and they appeared to him more pitiful than if they had been all dead.

Suddenly one of the coolies began to speak. The light came and went on his lean, straining face: he threw his head up like a baying hound. From the bunker came the sounds of knocking and the tinkle of some dollars rolling loose; he stretched out his arm, his mouth yawned black, and the incomprehensible guttural sounds, that did not seem to belong to a human language, penetrated Jukes with a strange emotion as if a brute had tried to be eloquent.

Two more started mouthing what seemed to Jukes fierce denunciations; the others stirred with grunts and growls. Jukes ordered the hands out of the 'tween-decks hurriedly. He left last himself, backing through the door, while the grunts rose to a loud murmur and hands were extended after him as after a malefactor. The boatswain shot the bolt, and remarked uneasily, "Seems as if the wind has dropped, sir."

The seamen were glad to get back into the alleyway. Secretly each of them thought that at the last moment he could rush out on deck—and that was a comfort. There is something horribly repugnant in the idea of being drowned under a deck. Now they had done with the Chinamen, they again became conscious of the ship's position.

Jukes on coming out of the alleyway found himself up to the neck in the noisy water. He gained the bridge, and discovered he could detect obscure shapes as if his sight had become preternaturally acute. He saw faint outlines. They recalled not the familiar aspect of the *Nan-Shan,* but something remembered— an old dismantled steamer he had seen years ago rotting on a mudbank. She recalled that wreck.

There was no wind, not a breath, except the faint currents created by the lurches of the ship. The smoke tossed out of the funnel was settling down upon her deck. He breathed it as he passed forward. He felt the deliberate throb of the engines, and heard small sounds that seemed to have survived the great uproar: the knocking of broken fittings, the rapid tumbling of some piece of wreckage on the bridge. He perceived dimly the squat shape of his captain holding on to a twisted bridge-rail, motionless and swaying as if rooted to the planks. The unexpected stillness of the air oppressed Jukes.

"We have done it, sir," he gasped.

"Thought you would," said Captain MacWhirr.

"Did you?" murmured Jukes to himself.

"Wind fell all at once," went on the captain.

Jukes burst out, "If you think it was an easy job——"

But the captain, clinging to the rail, paid no attention. "According to the books the worst is not over yet."

"If most of them hadn't been half dead with seasickness and fright, not one of us would have come out of that 'tween-deck alive," said Jukes.

"Had to do what's fair by them," mumbled MacWhirr stolidly. "You don't find everything in books."

"Why, I believe they would have risen on us if I hadn't ordered the hands out of that pretty quick," continued Jukes with warmth.

After the whisper of their shouts, their ordinary tones, so distinct, rang out very loud to their ears in the amazing stillness of the air. It seemed to them they were talking in a dark and echoing vault.

Through a jagged aperture in the dome of clouds the light of a few stars fell upon the black sea, rising and falling confusedly. Sometimes the head of a watery cone would topple on board and mingle with the rolling flurry of foam on the swamped deck; and the *Nan-Shan* wallowed heavily at the bottom of a circular cistern of clouds. This ring of dense vapours, gyrating madly round the calm of the centre, encompassed the ship like a motionless and unbroken wall of an aspect inconceivably sinister. Within, the sea, as if agitated by an internal commotion, leaped in peaked mounds that jostled each other, slapping heavily against her sides; and a low moaning sound, the infinite plaint of the storm's fury, came from beyond the limits of the menacing calm. Captain MacWhirr remained silent, and Jukes' ready ear caught suddenly the faint, long-drawn roar of some immense wave rushing unseen under that thick blackness, which made the appalling boundary of his vision.

"Of course," he started resentfully, "they thought we had caught at the chance to plunder them. Of course! You said— pick up the money. Easier said than done. They couldn't tell what was in our heads. We came in, smash—right into the middle of them. Had to do it by a rush."

"As long as it's done . . ." mumbled the captain, without attempting to look at Jukes. "Had to do what's fair."

"We shall find yet there's the devil to pay when this is over," said Jukes, feeling very sore. "Let them only recover a bit, and you'll see. They will fly at our throats, sir. Don't forget, sir, she isn't a British ship now. These brutes know it well, too. The damn'd Siamese flag."

"We are on board, all the same," remarked Captain MacWhirr.

"The trouble's not over yet," insisted Jukes prophetically, reeling and catching on. "She's a wreck," he added faintly.

"The trouble's not over yet," assented Captain MacWhirr, half aloud . . . "Look out for her a minute."

"Are you going off the deck, sir?" asked Jukes hurriedly, as if the storm were sure to pounce upon him as soon as he had been left alone with the ship.

He watched her, battered and solitary, labouring heavily in a wild scene of mountainous black waters lit by the gleams of distant worlds. She moved slowly, breathing into the still core of the hurricane the excess of her strength in a white cloud of steam —and the deep-toned vibration of the escape was like the defiant trumpeting of a living creature of the sea impatient for the renewal of the contest. It ceased suddenly. The still air moaned. Above Jukes' head a few stars shone into the pit of black vapours. The inky edge of the cloud-disc frowned upon the ship under the patch of glittering sky. The stars too seemed to look at her intently, as if for the last time, and the cluster of their splendour sat like a diadem on a lowering brow.

Captain MacWhirr had gone into the chart-room. There was no light there; but he could feel the disorder of that place where he used to live tidily. His armchair was upset. The books had tumbled out on the floor; he scrunched a piece of glass under his boot. He groped for the matches and found a box on a shelf with a deep ledge. He struck one, and puckering the corners of his eyes, held out the little flame towards the barometer whose glittering top of glass and metal nodded at him continuously.

It stood very low—incredibly low, so low that Captain MacWhirr grunted. The match went out, and hurriedly he extracted another, with thick, stiff fingers.

Again a little flame flared up before the nodding glass and metal of the top. His eyes looked at it, narrowed with attention, as if expecting an imperceptible sign. With his grave face he resembled a booted and misshapen pagan burning incense before the oracle of a Joss. There was no mistake. It was the lowest reading he had ever seen in his life.

Captain MacWhirr emitted a low whistle. He forgot himself

till the flame diminished to a blue spark, burnt his fingers and vanished. Perhaps something had gone wrong with the thing!

There was an aneroid glass screwed above the couch. He turned that way, struck another match, and discovered the white face of the other instrument looking at him from the bulkhead, meaningly, not to be gainsaid, as though the wisdom of men were made unerring by the indifference of matter. There was no room for doubt now. Captain MacWhirr pshawed at it, and threw the match down.

The worst was to come, then—and if the books were right this worst would be very bad. The experience of the last six hours had enlarged his conception of what heavy weather could be like. "It'll be terrific," he pronounced mentally. He had not consciously looked at anything by the light of the matches except at the barometer; and yet somehow he had seen that his water-bottle and the two tumblers had been flung out of their stand. It seemed to give a more intimate knowledge of the tossing the ship had gone through. "I wouldn't have believed it," he thought. And his table had been cleared too; his rulers, his pencils, the inkstand—all the things that had their safe appointed places—they were gone, as if a mischievous hand had plucked them out one by one and flung them on the wet floor. The hurricane had broken in upon the orderly arrangements of his privacy. This had never happened before, and the feeling of dismay reached the very seat of his composure. And the worst was to come yet! He was glad the trouble in the 'tween-deck had been discovered in time. If the ship had to go after all, then, at least, she wouldn't be going to the bottom with a lot of people in her fighting tooth and claw. That would have been odious. And in that feeling there was a humane intention and a vague sense of the fitness of things.

These instantaneous thoughts were yet in their essence heavy and slow, partaking of the nature of the man. He extended his hand to put back the matchbox in its corner of the shelf. There were always matches there—by his order. The steward had his instructions impressed upon him long before. "A box . . . just there, see? Not so very full . . . where I can put my hand on it, steward. Might want a light in a hurry. Can't tell on board ship *what* you might want in a hurry. Mind, now."

And of course on his side he would be careful to put it back in its place scrupulously. He did so now, but before he removed his hand it occurred to him that perhaps he would never have occasion to use that box any more. The vividness of the thought checked him, and for an infinitesimal fraction of a second his fingers closed again on the small object as though it had been the symbol of all those little habits that chain us to the weary round of life. He released it at last, and letting himself fall on the settee, listened for the first sounds of returning wind.

Not yet. He heard only the wash of water, the heavy splashes, the dull shocks of the confused seas boarding his ship from all sides. She would never have a chance to clear her decks.

But the quietude of the air was startlingly tense and unsafe, like a slender hair holding a sword suspended over his head. By this awful pause the storm penetrated the defences of the man and unsealed his lips. He spoke out in the solitude and the pitch darkness of the cabin, as if addressing another being awakened within his breast.

"I shouldn't like to lose her," he said half aloud.

He sat unseen, apart from the sea, from his ship, isolated, as if withdrawn from the very current of his own existence, where such freaks as talking to himself surely had no place. His palms reposed on his knees, he bowed his short neck and puffed heavily, surrendering to a strange sensation of weariness he was not enlightened enough to recognise for the fatigue of mental stress.

From where he sat he could reach the door of a wash-stand locker. There should have been a towel there. There was. Good. . . . He took it out, wiped his face, and afterwards went on rubbing his wet head. He towelled himself with energy in the dark, and then remained motionless with the towel on his knees. A moment passed, of a stillness so profound that no one could have guessed there was a man sitting in that cabin. Then a murmur arose.

"She may come out of it yet."

When Captain MacWhirr came out on deck, which he did brusquely, as though he had suddenly become conscious of having stayed away too long, the calm had lasted already more than fifteen minutes—long enough to make itself intolerable even to his imagination. Jukes, motionless on the forepart of the bridge, began to speak at once. His voice, blank and forced as though he were talking through hard-set teeth, seemed to flow away on all sides into the darkness, deepening again upon the sea.

"I had the wheel relieved. Hackett began to sing out that he was done. He's lying in there alongside the steering-gear with a face like death. At first I couldn't get anybody to crawl out and relieve the poor devil. That boss'en's worse than no good, I always said. Thought I would have had to go myself and haul out one of them by the neck."

"Ah, well," muttered the captain. He stood watchful by Jukes' side.

"The second mate's in there too, holding his head. Is he hurt, sir?"

"No—crazy," said Captain MacWhirr, curtly.

"Looks as if he had a tumble, though."

"I had to give him a push," explained the captain.

Jukes gave an impatient sigh.

"It will come very sudden," said Captain MacWhirr, "and from over there, I fancy. God only knows, though. These books are only good to muddle your head and make you jumpy. It will be bad, and there's an end. If we only can steam her round in time to meet it . . . ."

A minute passed. Some of the stars winked rapidly and vanished.

"You left them pretty safe?" began the captain abruptly, as though the silence were unbearable.

"Are you thinking of the coolies, sir? I rigged life-lines all ways across that 'tween deck."

"Did you? Good idea, Mr. Jukes."

"I didn't . . . think you cared to . . . know," said Jukes—the lurching of the ship cut his speech as though somebody had been jerking him around while he talked—"how I got on with . . . that infernal job. We did it. And it may not matter in the end."

"Had to do what's fair, for all—they are only Chinamen. Give them the same chance with ourselves—hang it all. She isn't lost yet. Bad enough to be shut up below in a gale——"

"That's what I thought when you gave me the job, sir," interjected Jukes moodily.

"—without being battered to pieces," pursued Captain Mac-Whirr with rising vehemence. "Couldn't let that go on in my ship, if I knew she hadn't five minutes to live. Couldn't bear it, Mr. Jukes."

A hollow echoing noise, like that of a shout rolling in a rocky chasm, approached the ship and went away again. The last star, blurred, enlarged, as if returning to the fiery mist of its beginning, struggled with the colossal depth of blackness hanging over the ship—and went out.

"Now for it!" muttered Captain MacWhirr. "Mr. Jukes."

"Here, sir."

The two men were growing indistinct to each other.

"We must trust her to go through it and come out on the other side. That's plain and straight. There's no room for Captain Wilson's storm-strategy here."

"No, sir."

"She will be smothered and swept again for hours," mumbled the captain. "There's not much left by this time above deck for the sea to take away—unless you or me."

"Both, sir," whispered Jukes breathlessly.

"You are always meeting trouble half way, Jukes," Captain MacWhirr remonstrated quaintly. "Though it's a fact that the second mate is no good. D'ye hear, Mr. Jukes? You would be left alone if . . ."

Captain MacWhirr interrupted himself, and Jukes, glancing on all sides, remained silent.

"Don't you be put out by anything," the captain continued, mumbling rather fast. "Keep her facing it. They may say what they like, but the heaviest seas run with the wind. Facing it —always facing it—that's the way to get through. You are a young sailor. Face it. That's enough for any man. Keep a cool head."

"Yes, sir," said Jukes, with a flutter of the heart.

In the next few seconds the captain spoke to the engine-room and got an answer.

For some reason Jukes experienced an access of confidence, a sensation that came from outside like a warm breath, and made him feel equal to any demand. The distant muttering of the darkness stole into his ears. He noted it unmoved, out of that sudden belief in himself, as a man safe in a shirt of mail would watch a point.

The ship laboured without intermission amongst the black hills of water, paying with this hard tumbling the price of her life. She rumbled in her depths, shaking a white plummet of steam into the night, and Jukes' thought skimmed like a bird through the engine-room, where Mr. Rout—good man—was ready. When the rumbling ceased it seemed to him that there was a pause of every sound, a dead pause in which Captain Mac-Whirr's voice rang out startlingly.

"What's that? A puff of wind?"—it spoke much louder than Jukes had ever heard it before—"On the bow. That's right. She may come out of it yet."

The mutter of the winds drew near apace. In the forefront could be distinguished a drowsy waking plaint passing on, and far off the growth of a multiple clamour, marching and expanding. There was the throb as of many drums in it, a vicious rushing note, and like the chant of a tramping multitude.

Jukes could no longer see his captain distinctly. The darkness was absolutely piling itself upon the ship. At most he made out movements, a hint of elbows spread out, of a head thrown up.

Captain MacWhirr was trying to do up the top button of his oilskin coat with unwonted haste. The hurricane, with its power to madden the seas, to sink ships, to uproot trees, to overturn strong walls and dash the very birds of the air to the ground, had found this taciturn man in its path, and, doing its utmost, had managed to wring out a few words. Before the renewed wrath of winds swooped on his ship, Captain MacWhirr was moved to declare, in a tone of vexation, as it were, "I wouldn't like to lose her."

He was spared that annoyance.

RUDYARD KIPLING

The Ship that Found Herself

We now, held in captivity,
　Spring to our labour nor grieve!
See now, how it is blesseder,
　Brothers, to give than receive!
Keep trust, wherefore ye were made
　Paying the duty ye owe;
For a clean thrust and the sheer of the blade
　Shall carry us where we should go?
Song of the Engines.

It was her first voyage, and though she was but a cargo-steamer of twelve hundred tons, she was the very best of her kind, the outcome of forty years of experiments and improvements in framework and machinery; and her designers and owner thought as much of her as though she had been the *Lucania*. Any one can make a floating hotel that will pay expenses, if he puts enough money into the saloon, and charges for private baths, suites of rooms, and such like; but in these days of competition and low freights every square inch of a cargo-boat must be built for cheapness, great hold-capacity, and a certain steady speed. This boat was, perhaps, two hundred and forty feet long and thirty-two feet wide, with arrangements that enabled her to carry cattle on her main and sheep on her upper deck if she wanted to; but her great glory was the amount of cargo that she could store away in her holds. Her owners—they were a very well known Scotch firm—came round with her from the north, where she had been launched and christened and fitted, to Liverpool, where she was to take cargo for New York; and the owner's daughter, Miss Frazier, went to and fro on the clean decks, admiring the new paint and the brass work, and the patent winches, and particularly the strong, straight bow, over which she had cracked a bottle of champagne when she named the steamer the *Dimbula*. It was a beautiful September afternoon, and the boat in all her new-ness—she was painted lead-colour with a red funnel—looked very fine indeed. Her house-flag was flying, and her whistle from time to time acknowledged the salutes of friendly boats, who saw that she was new to the High and Narrow Seas and wished to make her welcome.

"And now," said Miss Frazier delightedly, to the captain, "she's a real ship, isn't she? It seems only the other day father gave the order for her, and now—and now—isn't she a beauty!" The girl was proud of the firm, and talked as though she were the controlling partner.

"Oh, she's no so bad," the skipper replied cautiously. "But I'm sayin' that it takes more than christenin' to mak' a ship. In the nature o' things, Miss Frazier, if ye follow me, she's just irons and rivets and plates put into the form of a ship. She has to find herself yet."

"I thought father said she was exceptionally well found."

"So she is," said the skipper, with a laugh. "But it's this way wi' ships, Miss Frazier. She's all here, but the parrts of her have not learned to work together yet. They've had no chance."

"The engines are working beautifully. I can hear them."

"Yes, indeed. But there's more than engines to a ship. Every inch of her, ye'll understand, has to be livened up and made to work wi' its neighbour—sweetenin' her, we call it, technically."

"And how will you do it?" the girl asked.

"We can no more than drive and steer her, and so forth; but if we have rough weather this trip—it's likely—she'll learn the rest by heart! For a ship, ye'll obsairve, Miss Frazier, is in no sense a reegid body closed at both ends. She's a highly complex structure o' various an' conflictin' strains, wi' tissues that must give an' tak' accordin' to her personal modulus of elasteecity." Mr. Buchanan, the chief engineer, was coming towards them. "I'm sayin' to Miss Frazier, here, that our little *Dimbula* has to be sweetened yet, and nothin' but a gale will do it. How's all wi' your engines, Buck?"

"Well enough—true by plumb an' rule, o' course; but there's no spontaneeity yet." He turned to the girl. "Take my word, Miss Frazier, and maybe ye'll comprehend later; even after a pretty girl's christened a ship it does not follow that there's such a thing as a ship under the men that work her."

"I was sayin' the very same, Mr. Buchanan," the skipper interrupted.

"That's more metaphysical than I can follow," said Miss Frazier, laughing.

"Why so? Ye're good Scotch, an'—I knew your mother's father, he was fra' Dumfries—ye've a vested right in metapheesics, Miss Frazier, just as ye have in the *Dimbula*," the engineer said.

"Eh, well, we must go down to the deep watters, an' earn Miss Frazier her deevidends. Will you not come to my cabin for tea?" said the skipper. "We'll be in dock the night, and when you're goin' back to Glasgie ye can think of us loadin' her down an' drivin' her forth—all for your sake."

In the next few days they stowed some two thousand tons' dead weight into the *Dimbula,* and took her out from Liverpool. As soon as she met the lift of the open water, she naturally began to talk. If you lay your ear to the side of the cabin the next time you are in a steamer, you will hear hundreds of little voices in every direction, thrilling and buzzing, and whispering and popping, and gurgling and sobbing and squeaking exactly like a telephone in a thunder-storm. Wooden ships shriek and growl and grunt, but iron vessels throb and quiver through all their hundreds of ribs and thousands of rivets. The *Dimbula* was very strongly built, and every piece of her had a letter or number, or both, to describe it; and every piece had been hammered, or forged, or rolled, or punched by man, and had lived in the roar and rattle of the ship-yard for months. Therefore, every piece had its own separate voice in exact proportion to the amount of trouble spent upon it. Cast-iron, as a rule, says very little; but mild steel plates and wrought-iron, and ribs and beams that have been much bent and welded and riveted, talk continuously. Their conversation, of course, is not half as wise as our human talk, because they are all, though they do not know it, bound down one to the other in a black darkness, where they cannot tell what is happening near them, nor what will overtake them next.

As soon as she had cleared the Irish coast a sullen, grey-headed old wave of the Atlantic climbed leisurely over her straight bows, and sat down on her steam-capstan used for hauling up the anchor. Now the capstan and the engine that drove it had been newly painted red and green; besides which, nobody likes being ducked.

"Don't you do that again," the capstan sputtered through the teeth of his cogs. "Hi! Where's the fellow gone?"

The wave had slouched overside with a plop and a chuckle; but "Plenty more where he came from," said a brother-wave, and went through and over the capstan, who was bolted firmly to an iron plate on the iron deck-beams below.

"Can't you keep still up there?" said the deck-beams. "What's the matter with you? One minute you weigh twice as much as you ought to, and the next you don't!"

"It isn't my fault," said the capstan. "There's a green brute outside that comes and hits me on the head."

"Tell that to the shipwrights. You've been in position for months and you've never wriggled like this before. If you aren't careful you'll strain *us*."

"Talking of strain," said a low, rasping, unpleasant voice, "are any of you fellows—you deck-beams, we mean—aware that those exceedingly ugly knees of yours happen to be riveted into our structure—*ours*?"

"Who might you be?" the deck-beams inquired.

"Oh, nobody in particular," was the answer. "We're only the port and starboard upper-deck stringers; and if you persist in heaving and hiking like this, we shall be reluctantly compelled to take steps."

Now the stringers of the ship are long iron girders, so to speak, that run lengthways from stern to bow. They keep the iron frames (what are called ribs in a wooden ship) in place, and also help to hold the ends of the deck-beams, which go from side to side of the ship. Stringers always consider themselves most important, because they are so long.

"You will take steps—will you?" This was a long echoing rumble. It came from the frames—scores and scores of them, each one about eighteen inches distant from the next, and each riveted to the stringers in four places. "We think you will have a certain amount of trouble in *that*"; and thousands and thousands of the little rivets that held everything together whispered: "You will. You will! Stop quivering and be quiet. Hold on, brethren! Hold on! Hot Punches! What's that?"

Rivets have no teeth, so they cannot chatter with fright; but they did their best as a fluttering jar swept along the ship from stern to bow, and she shook like a rat in a terrier's mouth.

An unusually severe pitch, for the sea was rising, had lifted the big throbbing screw nearly to the surface, and it was spinning round in a kind of soda-water—half sea and half air—going much faster than was proper, because there was no deep water for it to work in. As it sank again, the engines—and they were triple expansion, three cylinders in a row—snorted through all their three pistons. "Was that a joke, you fellow outside? It's an uncommonly poor one. How are we to do our work if you fly off the handle that way?"

"I didn't fly off the handle," said the screw, twirling huskily at the end of the screw-shaft. "If I had, you'd have been scrap-iron by this time. The sea dropped away from under me, and I had nothing to catch on to. That's all."

"That's all, d'you call it?" said the thrust-block, whose business it is to take the push of the screw; for if a screw had nothing to hold it back it would crawl right into the engine-room. (It is the holding back of the screwing action that gives the drive to a ship.) "I know I do my work deep down and out of sight, but I warn you I expect justice. All I ask for is bare justice. Why can't you push steadily and evenly, instead of whizzing like a whirligig, and making me hot under all my collars." The thrust-block had six collars, each faced with brass, and he did not wish to get them heated.

All the bearings that supported the fifty feet of screw-shaft as it ran to the stern whispered: "Justice—give us justice."

"I can only give you what I can get," the screw answered. "Look out! It's coming again!"

He rose with a roar as the *Dimbula* plunged, and "whack—flack—whack—whack" went the engines, furiously, for they had little to check them.

"I'm the noblest outcome of human ingenuity—Mr. Buchanan says so," squealed the high-pressure cylinder. "This is simply ridiculous!" The piston went up savagely, and choked, for half the steam behind it was mixed with dirty water. "Help! Oiler! Fitter! Stoker! Help! I'm choking," it gasped. "Never in the history of maritime invention has such a calamity overtaken one so young and strong. And if I go, who's to drive the ship?"

"Hush! oh, hush!" whispered the Steam, who, of course, had been to sea many times before. He used to spend his leisure ashore in a cloud, or a gutter, or a flower-pot, or a thunder-storm, or anywhere else where water was needed. "That's only a little priming, a little carrying-over, as they call it. It'll happen all night, on and off. I don't say it's nice, but it's the best we can do under the circumstances."

"What difference can circumstances make? I'm here to do my work—on clean, dry steam. Blow circumstances!" the cylinder roared.

"The circumstances will attend to the blowing. I've worked

on the North Atlantic run a good many times—it's going to be rough before morning."

"It isn't distressingly calm now," said the extra-strong frames —they were called web-frames—in the engine-room. "There's an upward thrust that we don't understand, and there's a twist that is very bad for our brackets and diamond-plates, and there's a sort of west-north-westerly pull that follows the twist, which seriously annoys us. We mention this because we happened to cost a good deal of money, and we feel sure that the owner would not approve of our being treated in this frivolous way."

"I'm afraid the matter is out of the owner's hands for the present," said the Steam, slipping into the condenser. "You're left to your own devices till the weather betters."

"I wouldn't mind the weather," said a flat bass voice below; "it's this confounded cargo that's breaking my heart. I'm the garboard-strake, and I'm twice as thick as most of the others, and I ought to know something."

The garboard-strake is the lowest plate in the bottom of a ship, and the *Dimbula's* garboard-strake was nearly three-quarters of an inch mild steel.

"The sea pushes me up in a way I should never have expected," the strake grunted, "and the cargo pushes me down, and, between the two, I don't know what I'm supposed to do."

"When in doubt, hold on," rumbled the Steam, making head in the boilers.

"Yes; but there's only dark, and cold, and hurry, down here; and how do I know whether the other plates are doing their duty? Those bulwark-plates up above, I've heard, ain't more than five-sixteenths of an inch thick—scandalous, I call it."

"I agree with you," said a huge web-frame by the main cargo-hatch. He was deeper and thicker than all the others, and curved half-way across the ship in the shape of half an arch, to support the deck where deck-beams would have been in the way of cargo coming up and down. "I work entirely unsupported, and I observe that I am the sole strength of this vessel, so far as my vision extends. The responsibility, I assure you, is enormous. I believe the money-value of the cargo is over one hundred and fifty thousand pounds. Think of that!"

"And every pound of it is dependent on my personal exertions." Here spoke a sea-valve that communicated directly with the water outside, and was seated not very far from the garboard-strake. "I rejoice to think that I am a Prince-Hyde Valve, with best Pará rubber facings. Five patents cover me—I mention this without pride—five separate and several patents, each one finer than the other. At present I am screwed fast. Should I open, you would immediately be swamped. This is incontrovertible!"

Patent things always use the longest words they can. It is a trick that they pick up from their inventors.

"That's news," said a big centrifugal bilge-pump. "I had an idea that you were employed to clean decks and things with. At least, I've used you for that more than once. I forget the precise number, in thousands, of gallons which I am guaranteed to throw per hour; but I assure you, my complaining friends, that there is not the least danger. I alone am capable of clearing any water that may find its way here. By my Biggest Deliveries, we pitched then!"

The sea was getting up in a workmanlike style. It was a dead westerly gale, blown from under a ragged opening of green sky, narrowed on all sides by fat, grey clouds; and the wind bit like pincers as it fretted the spray into lacework on the flanks of the waves.

"I tell you what it is," the foremast telephoned down its wire-stays. "I'm up here, and I can take a dispassionate view of things. There's an organised conspiracy against us. I'm sure of it, because every single one of these waves is heading directly for our bows. The whole sea is concerned in it and so's the wind. It's awful!"

"What's awful?" said a wave, drowning the capstan for the hundredth time.

"This organised conspiracy on your part," the capstan gurgled, taking his cue from the mast.

"Organised bubbles and spindrift! There has been a depression in the Gulf of Mexico. Excuse me!" He leaped overside; but his friends took up the tale one after another.

"Which has advanced——" That wave hove green water over the funnel.

"As far as Cape Hatteras——" He drenched the bridge.

"And is now going out to sea—to sea—to sea!" The third went free in three surges, making a clean sweep of a boat, which turned bottom up and sank in the darkening troughs alongside, while the broken falls whipped the davits.

"That's all there is to it," seethed the white water roaring through the scuppers. "There's no animus in our proceedings. We're only meteorological corollaries."

"Is it going to get any worse?" said the bow-anchor chained down to the deck, where he could only breathe once in five minutes.

"Not knowing, can't say. Wind may blow a bit by midnight. Thanks awfully. Good-bye."

The wave that spoke so politely had travelled some distance aft, and found itself all mixed up on the deck amidships, which was a well-deck sunk between high bulwarks. One of the bulwark plates, which was hung on hinges to open outward, had swung out, and passed the bulk of water back to the sea again with a clean smack.

"Evidently that's what I'm made for," said the plate, closing again with a sputter of pride. "Oh no, you don't, my friend!"

The top of a wave was trying to get in from the outside, but as the plate did not open in that direction, the defeated water spurted back.

"Not bad for five-sixteenths of an inch," said the bulwark-plate. "My work, I see, is laid down for the night"; and it began opening and shutting with the motion of the ship as it was designed to do.

"We are not what you might call idle," groaned all the frames together, as the *Dimbula* climbed a big wave, lay on her side at the top, and shot into the next hollow, twisting in the descent. A huge swell pushed up exactly under her middle, and her bow and stern hung free with nothing to support them. Then one joking wave caught her up at the bow, and another at the stern, while the rest of the water slunk away from under her just to see how she would like it; so she was held up at her two ends only, and the weight of the cargo and the machinery fell on the groaning iron keels and bilge-stringers.

"Ease off! Ease off, there!" roared the garboard-strake. "I want one-eighth of an inch fair play! D'you hear me, you rivets!"

"Ease off! Ease off!" cried the bilge-stringers. "Don't hold us so tight to the frames!"

"Ease off!" grunted the deck-beams, as the *Dimbula* rolled fearfully. "You've cramped our knees into the stringers, and we can't move. Ease off, you flat-headed little nuisances."

Then two converging seas hit the bows, one on each side, and fell away in torrents of streaming thunder.

"Ease off!" shouted the forward collision-bulkhead. "I want to crumple up, but I'm stiffened in every direction. Ease off, you dirty little forge-filings. Let me breathe!"

All the hundreds of plates that are riveted to the frames, and make the outside skin of every steamer, echoed the call, for each plate wanted to shift and creep a little, and each plate, according to its position, complained against the rivets.

"We can't help it! *We* can't help it!" they murmured in reply. "We're put here to hold you, and we're going to do it; you never pull us twice in the same direction. If you'd say what you were going to do next, we'd try to meet your views."

"As far as I could feel," said the upper-deck planking, and that was four inches thick, "every single iron near me was pushing or pulling in opposite directions. Now, what's the sense of that? My friends, let us all pull together."

"Pull any way you please," roared the funnel, "so long as you don't try your experiments on *me*. I need seven wire ropes, all pulling in different directions, to hold me steady. Isn't that so?"

"We believe you, my boy!" whistled the funnel-stays through their clenched teeth, as they twanged in the wind from the top of the funnel to the deck.

"Nonsense! We must all pull together," the decks repeated. "Pull lengthways."

"Very good," said the stringers; "then stop pushing sideways when you get wet. Be content to run gracefully fore and aft, and curve in at the ends as we do."

"No—no curves at the end! A very slight workmanlike curve from side to side, with a good grip at each knee, and little pieces welded on," said the deck-beams.

"Fiddle!" cried the iron pillars of the deep, dark hold. "Who ever heard of curves? Stand up straight; be a perfectly round column, and carry tons of good solid weight—like that! There!" A big sea smashed on the deck above, and the pillars stiffened themselves to the load.

"Straight up and down is not bad," said the frames, who ran that way in the sides of the ship, "but you must also expand yourselves sideways. Expansion is the law of life, children. Open out! Open out!"

"Come back!" said the deck-beams savagely, as the upward heave of the sea made the frames try to open. "Come back to your bearings, you slack-jawed irons!"

"Rigidity! Rigidity! Rigidity!" thumped the engines. "Absolute, unvarying rigidity—rigidity!"

"You see!" whined the rivets in chorus. "No two of you will ever pull alike, and—and you blame it all on us. We only know how to go through a plate and bite down on both sides so that it can't, and mustn't, and shan't move."

"I've got one-fraction of an inch play, at any rate," said the garboard-strake, triumphantly. So he had, and all the bottom of the ship felt the easier for it.

"Then we're no good," sobbed the bottom rivets. "We were ordered—we were ordered—never to give; and we've given, and the sea will come in, and we'll all go to the bottom together!

First we're blamed for everything unpleasant, and now we haven't the consolation of having done our work."

"Don't say I told you," whispered the Steam consolingly; "but, between you and me and the last cloud I came from, it was bound to happen sooner or later. You *had* to give a fraction, and you've given without knowing it. Now, hold on, as before."

"What's the use?" a few hundred rivets chattered. "We've given—we've given; and the sooner we confess that we can't keep the ship together, and go off our little heads, the easier it will be. No rivet forged can stand this strain."

"No one rivet was ever meant to. Share it among you," the Steam answered.

"The others can have my share. I'm going to pull out," said a rivet in one of the forward plates.

"If you go, others will follow," hissed the Steam. "There's nothing so contagious in a boat as rivets going. Why, I knew a little chap like you—he was an eighth of an inch fatter, though —on a steamer—to be sure, she was only nine hundred tons, now I come to think of it—in exactly the same place as you are. He pulled out in a bit of a bobble of a sea, not half as bad as this, and he started all his friends on the same butt-strap, and the plates opened like a furnace door, and I had to climb into the nearest fog-bank, while the boat went down."

"Now that's peculiarly disgraceful," said the rivet. "Fatter than me, was he, and in a steamer half our tonnage? Reedy little peg! I blush for the family, sir." He settled himself more firmly than ever in his place, and the Steam chuckled.

"You see," he went on, quite gravely, "a rivet, and especially a rivet in your position, is really the one indispensable part of the ship."

The Steam did not say that he had whispered the very same thing to every single piece of iron aboard. There is no sense in telling too much truth.

And all that while the little *Dimbula* pitched and chopped, and swung and slewed, and lay down as though she were going

G

to die, and got up as though she had been stung, and threw her nose round and round in circles half a dozen times as she dipped; for the gale was at its worst. It was inky black, in spite of the tearing white froth on the waves, and, to top everything, the rain began to fall in sheets, so that you could not see your hand before your face. This did not make much difference to the ironwork below, but it troubled the foremast a good deal.

"Now it's finished," he said dismally. "The conspiracy is too strong for us. There is nothing left but to——"

"*Hurraar! Brrrraaah! Brrrrrrp!*" roared the Steam through the fog-horn, till the decks quivered. "Don't be frightened, below. It's only me, just thowing out a few words, in case anyone happens to be rolling round to-night."

"You don't mean to say there's any one except *us* on the sea in such weather?" said the funnel in a husky snuffle.

"Scores of 'em," said the Steam, clearing its throat; "*Rrrrraaa! Brraaaaa! Prrrrp!* It's a trifle windy up here; and, Great Boilers! how it rains!"

"We're drowning," said the scuppers. They had been doing nothing else all night, but this steady thrash of rain above them seemed to be the end of the world.

"That's all right. We'll be easier in an hour or two. First the wind and then the rain: Soon you may make sail again! *Grrraaaaaah! Drrrraaaa! Drrrp!* I have a notion that the sea is going down already. If it does you'll learn something about rolling. We've only pitched till now. By the way, aren't you chaps in the hold a little easier than you were?"

There was just as much groaning and straining as ever, but it was not so loud or squeaky in tone; and when the ship quivered she did not jar stiffly, like a poker hit on the floor, but gave with a supple little waggle, like a perfectly balanced golf-club.

"We have made a most amazing discovery," said the stringers, one after another. "A discovery that entirely changes the situation. We have found, for the first time in the history of ship-building, that the inward pull of the deck-beams and the outward thrust

98

of the frames lock us, as it were, more closely in our places, and enable us to endure a strain which is entirely without parallel in the records of marine architecture."

The Steam turned a laugh quickly into a roar up the fog-horn. "What massive intellects you great stringers have," he said softly, when he had finished.

"We also," began the deck-beams, "are discoverers and geniuses. We are of opinion that the support of the hold-pillars materially helps us. We find that we lock up on them when we are subjected to a heavy and singular weight of sea above."

Here the *Dimbula* shot down a hollow, lying almost on her side—righting at the bottom with a wrench and a spasm.

"In these cases—are you aware of this, Steam?—the plating at the bows, and particularly at the stern—we would also mention the floors beneath us—help *us* to resist any tendency to spring." The frames spoke, in the solemn, awed voice which people use when they have just come across something entirely new for the very first time.

"I'm only a poor puffy little flutterer," said the Steam, "but I have to stand a good deal of pressure in my business. It's all tremendously interesting. Tell us some more. You fellows are so strong."

"Watch us and you'll see," said the bow-plates, proudly. "Ready, behind there! Here's the Father and Mother of Waves coming! Sit tight, rivets all!" A great sluicing comber thundered by, but through the scuffle and confusion the Steam could hear the low, quick cries of the ironwork as the various strains took them—cries like these: "Easy, now—easy! *Now* push for all your strength! Hold out! Give a fraction! Hold up! Pull in! Shove crossways! Mind the strain at the ends! Grip, now! Bite tight! Let the water get away from under—and there she goes!"

The wave raced off into the darkness, shouting, "Not bad, that, if it's your first run!" and the drenched and ducked ship throbbed to the beat of the engines inside her. All three cylinders were white with the salt spray that had come down through the engine-room hatch; there was white fur on the canvas-bound steam-pipes, and even the bright-work deep below was speckled and soiled; but the cylinders had learned to make the most of steam that was half water, and were pounding along cheerfully.

"How's the noblest outcome of human ingenuity hitting it?" said the Steam, as he whirled through the engine-room.

"Nothing for nothing in this world of woe," the cylinders answered, as though they had been working for centuries, "and precious little for seventy-five pounds' head. We've made two knots this last hour and a quarter! Rather humiliating for eight hundred horse-power, isn't it?"

"Well, it's better than drifting astern, at any rate. You seem rather less—how shall I put it?—stiff in the back than you were."

"If you'd been hammered as we've been this night, you wouldn't be stiff—iff—iff, either. Theoreti—retti—retti—cally, of course, rigidity is the thing. Purrr—purr—practically, there has to be a little give and take. We found that out by working on our sides for five minutes at a stretch—chch—chh. How's the weather?"

"Sea's going down fast," said the Steam.

"Good business," said the high-pressure cylinder. "Whack her up, boys. They've given us five pounds more steam"; and he began humming the first bars of "Said the young Obadiah to the old Obadiah", which, as you may have noticed, is a pet tune among engines not built for high speed. Racing-liners with twin-screws sing "The Turkish Patrol" and the overture to the "Bronze Horse", and "Madame Angot", till something goes wrong, and then they render Gounod's "Funeral March of a Marionette", with variations.

"You'll learn a song of your own some fine day," said the Steam, as he flew up the fog-horn for one last bellow.

Next day the sky cleared and the sea dropped a little, and the *Dimbula* began to roll from side to side till every inch of iron in her was sick and giddy. But luckily they did not all feel ill at the same time: otherwise she would have opened out like a wet paper box.

The Steam whistled warnings as he went about his business: it is in this short, quick roll and tumble that follows a heavy sea that most of the accidents happen, for then everything thinks that the worst is over and goes off guard. So he orated and chattered till the beams and frames and floors and stringers and things had learned how to lock down and lock up on one another, and endure this new kind of strain.

They found ample time to practise, for they were sixteen days at sea, and it was foul weather till within a hundred miles of New York. The *Dimbula* picked up her pilot, and came in covered with salt and red rust. Her funnel was dirty grey from top to bottom; two boats had been carried away; three copper ventilators looked like hats after a fight with the police; the bridge had a dimple in the middle of it; the house that covered the steam steering-gear was split as with hatchets; there was a bill for small repairs in the engine-room almost as long as the screw-shaft; the forward cargo-hatch fell into bucket-staves when they raised the iron cross-bars; and the steam-capstan had been badly wrenched on its bed. Altogether, as the skipper said, it was "a pretty general average".

"But she's soupled," he said to Mr. Buchanan. "For all her dead weight she rode like a yacht. Ye mind that last blow off the Banks? I am proud of her, Buck."

"It's vera good," said the chief engineer, looking along the dishevelled decks. "Now, a man judgin' superfeecially would say we were a wreck, but we know otherwise—by experience."

Naturally everything in the *Dimbula* fairly stiffened with pride, and the foremast and the forward collision-bulkhead, who are pushing creatures, begged the Steam to warn the Port of New York of their arrival. "Tell those big boats all about us," they said. "They seem to take us quite as a matter of course."

It was a glorious, clear, dead calm morning, and in single file, with less than half a mile between each, their bands playing and their tug-boats shouting and waving handkerchiefs, were the *Majestic*, the *Paris*, the *Touraine*, the *Servia*, the *Kaiser Wilhelm II.*, and the *Werkendam*, all statelily going out to sea. As the *Dimbula* shifted her helm to give the great boats clear way, the Steam (who knows far too much to mind making an exhibition of himself now and then) shouted:

"Oyez! Oyez! Oyez! Princes, Dukes, and Barons of the High Seas! Know ye by these presents, we are the *Dimbula,* fifteen days nine hours from Liverpool, having crossed the Atlantic with three thousand ton of cargo for the first time in our career! We have not foundered. We are here. 'Eer! 'Eer! We are not disabled. But we have had a time wholly unparalleled in the annals of ship-building! Our decks were swept! We pitched; we rolled! We thought we were going to die! *Hi! Hi!* But we didn't. We wish to give notice that we have come to New York all the way across the Atlantic, through the worst weather in the world; and we are the *Dimbula*! We are—arr—ha—ha—ha-r-r-r!"

The beautiful line of boats swept by as steadily as the procession of the Seasons. The *Dimbula* heard the *Majestic* say, "Hmph!" and the *Paris* grunted, "How!" and the *Touraine* said, "Oui!" with a little coquettish flicker of steam; and the *Servia* said, "Haw!" and the *Kaiser* and the *Werkendam* said, "Hoch!" Dutch-fashion—and that was absolutely all.

"I did my best," said the Steam, gravely, "but I don't think they were much impressed with us, somehow. Do you?"

"It's simply disgusting," said the bow-plates. "They might have seen what we've been through. There isn't a ship on the sea that has suffered as we have—is there, now?"

"Well, I wouldn't go so far as that," said the Steam, "because I've worked on some of those boats, and sent them through weather quite as bad as the fortnight that we've had, in six days; and some of them are a little over ten thousand tons, I believe. Now I've seen the *Majestic,* for instance, ducked from her bows to her funnel; and I've helped the *Arizona,* I think she was, to back off an iceberg she met with one dark night; and I had to run out of the *Paris's* engine-room, one day, because there was thirty foot of water in it. Of course, I don't deny——" The Steam shut off suddenly, as a tug-boat, loaded with a political club and a brass band, that had been to see a New York Senator off to Europe, crossed their bows, going to Hoboken. There was a long silence that reached, without a break, from the cut-water to the propeller-blades of the *Dimbula*.

Then a new, big voice said slowly and thickly, as though the owner had just waked up: "It's my conviction that I have made a fool of myself."

The Steam knew what had happened at once; for when a ship finds herself all the talking of the separate pieces ceases and melts into one voice, which is the soul of the ship.

"Who are you?" he said, with a laugh.

"I am the *Dimbula,* of course. I've never been anything else except that—and a fool!"

The tug-boat, which was doing its very best to be run down, got away just in time, its band playing clashily and brassily a popular but impolite air:

> *In the days of old Rameses—are you on?*
> *In the days of old Rameses—are you on?*
> *In the days of old Rameses,*
> *That story had paresis,*
> *Are you on—are you on—are you on?*

"Well, I'm glad you've found yourself," said the Steam. "To tell the truth I was a little tired of talking to all those ribs and stringers. Here's Quarantine. After that we'll go to our wharf and clean up a little, and—next month we'll do it all over again."

JOHN MASEFIELD

Bird Of Dawning

All night long she drove before the thrust of the wester, in a
succession of staggering and surging leaps that sent the crests of
the waves flying white before her. At midnight she was running
twelve, at two, thirteen, and at the changing of the watch fourteen knots. Though she had ever steered easily, she was now
more than one man's task: the lee wheel was manned, and kept
busy.

At five in the morning Cruiser turned out after an hour of
uneasy sleep in his hammock to find the ship roaring on up
Channel in the breaking darkness, a high grey Channel sea
running under a wild heaven, and the teeth of the waves gleaming out from the grey. He lurched to the mate, who was forward,
putting an extra tackle on the fore-tack. When the tack was
home, he asked:

"Have you picked up any light, Mister?"

"No, sir, all blind as you see."

"Well, we must be there or thereabouts."

"Yes, sir. It's been a good slant."

"Get a hand aloft when it lightens a bit; he may be able to
see the land."

"Very good, Captain Trewsbury." The mate hesitated for a
moment, then said:

"If you please, sir, we're doing more than fourteen, and we
haven't had a sight for four days. We're well into the Channel:

and thick as it is we may be on top of anything before we
see it."

"No: keep her going," Cruiser said. "Our luck's in. We'll
not throw it away."

"Very good, Captain Trewsbury."

The ship was running on, with the same desperate haste, an
hour later when Trewsbury returned. It was now in the wildness
of an angry morning, with a low, hurrying heaven and leaping
sea, that showed green under the grey, and rose and slipped away
with a roar. The ship was careering with an aching straining
crying from every inch of her, aloft and below. Her shrouds
strained and whined and sang, the wind boomed in her sail, the
sheet blocks beat, the chain of their pendants whacked the masts.
All the mighty weight of ship and cargo heaved itself aloft, and
surged and descended and swayed, smashing the seas white,
boring into and up and out of the hills and the hollows of the
water, and singing as she did it, and making all hands, as they
toiled, to sing.

"Run, you bright bird," Trewsbury said, "that's what you
were born to."

There was no chance of a sight with that low heaven: the man
aloft could see nothing: all hands were on deck getting the
anchors over. There came a sudden cry from them of "Steamer,
dead ahead."

She must have seen them on the instant, and ported on the
instant, enough to clear. Cruiser saw her as it were climbing
slowly and perilously to port for twenty seconds: then as
he leaped for the signal flags to ask, "Where are we?" she
was surging past close alongside, a little grey coastal tramp,
with a high bridge over her central structure, butting hard
into it with a stay foresail dark with wet to steady her, and her
muzzle white to the eyes. As she had just fired, a stream of
black smoke blew away and down from her, with sudden sparks
in it, as Cruiser thought. Cruiser saw two figures in yellow
oilskins staring at them from behind the dodger. He knew

well with what admiration and delight those sailors stared. Then the little coaster's stern hove up in a smother, as her head dipped to it, and she was past and away, with one man behind the dodger waving a hand. The reek of her smoke struck Cruiser's nostrils; then she was gone from them, her name unknown.

The mate was at Cruiser's side.

"That shows you how we're in the fairway, sir," he said. "We may be on top of something at any minute. We've only a minute to clear anything, in this."

"I know it."

"Yes, sir."

"Did you ever know of a China clipper throwing away a fair wind in soundings?"

"No, sir."

"Did you ever hear of a China clipper being sunk in the Channel when running?"

"No, Captain Trewsbury, and I don't want to be the first."

"Well, I do want to be the first, Mister, and I mean to be it, the first to London Docks, if you understand. And to get there, I have to use whatever chance throws in my way. It's going to break, presently."

There came a hail from the main cross-trees, where the look-out had a speaking trumpet. "Ship on starboard bow." They turned to look at her, and Cruiser who was ready now ran up the signal flags of, "What is my position?"

As the flags blew out clear the ship hove up alongside. She was a big full-rigged ship, painted black, and very loftily rigged with skysail yards on all three masts. She was now under her fore and main lower topsails and fore topmast staysail, beating her way down Channel. She was streaming with glittering water. At each 'scend the sea ran white along her rail, which bowed to it and lipped it in. Then, out of the pause, the bowed fabric seemed to dive forward, though with difficulty. Cruiser saw the watch gathered on the poop, all staring: even the man at the wheel was staring. The ship beat past them on a lurching leap, her main-deck full and spouting, no one answering the signal, not even acknowledging it.

"There's discourtesy," the mate said. "She wouldn't even dip her colours."

"She never saw our signal," Cruiser said. "She's an outward-bounder, with everything on top and nothing to hand. Besides she was watching us."

"We must be well worth the watching, sir," the mate said, moving away. To himself, as he moved, he added, "and I hope all who meet us will watch out for us."

It grew lighter in the sky, but no lighter to landward, they were running in a blind and moving seascape not a thousand yards across, all cloud and water, both mad. The ship strode into it, and streaked her way across it, smashing on to the greyness a track of paleness and a greenness of many million bubbles, over which the petrels scuttered.

Where they were Cruiser did not know, and did not much care. The exultation that was so movingly in the ship was in himself. They were getting up Channel with a marvellous slant, and who could tell that they were not leading the fleet. It would clear up presently, and they would see where they were, or pass something that would tell them.

"Forward there," he called. "Up there two of you, and get a good burton on the foreyard. Lively now, I'm going to give her a stunsail."

"Burton on the foreyard: ay, ay, sir."

He turned to the helmsmen. Coates, who had the weather spokes, was enjoying it; he loved to see a ship driven; but Bauer at the lee wheel was scared.

"How is she, Coates?" he asked.

"She's begun to be a bit kittenish," Coates said, "but nothing to hurt, sir."

"You're keeping a good course. You can steer, Coates."

"Yes, sir. And she can kick, I tell you."

"Keep your eyes forward, Bauer," Cruiser said. "There's nothing for you to look at behind you."

There was, though. There was a toppling, toppling running array of heaping water ever slipping over at the top.

"If you let her broach to, Bauer," he said, "you'll be the first man drowned and the last man God will forgive and that's what you'll get by it."

Bauer smiled a sickly smile, and licked his dry lips and said: "Yes, sir."

"All ready the burton, forward?"

"All ready, sir."

"Bowse it well taut." He went forward to see to the setting of the sail.

As the courses of the *Bird of Dawning* were very deep as well as square, the lower studding sail was a great sail, needing much care in the setting, in such a wind as was blowing. The boom was run forward and guyed. All hands mustered to the job. They well knew that if it were not done smartly, the sail would go. A wild sea spread from under their feet into the hurrying cloud; but those there felt, from the push of the rain that came down upon them, that the greyness was about to go. The rain that had streamed from all things relented suddenly and died into a pattering.

"Let her go," Cruiser called. The tackles skirled as the men went away with them; he paid out the tripping line as they ran. The boom dipped under as it went and the great sail darkened with the wet half up it. As the stops came adrift, the sail lifted and strove to flog itself clear, but the checks of the gear came on to it and stayed it. One instant before it had been a bulge of canvas, flapping at folds where the wind could catch it, now it was a straining curve of sail, held by check and countercheck, leaning like a wing to the ship over all that hurry of leaping sea. She put down her foot, and the foot of the sail stooped into it, as a gull stoops upon the wing. She rose, with the water dripping from the scoop, and again plunged and arose shaking.

"That's got her where she lives," Clutterbucke said. "That's made her lift her feet."

"Just as well she's got that burton on her yard-arm."

The effect on the ship was instantaneous. She had been leaping, now she seemed to lift from sea to sea, and to tread down their crests into subjection.

"I think she'll stand a topmast stunsail," Cruiser said to himself.

He went aft to watch the steering, which was grown the livelier for the sail. From the poop, he had a new impression of the power of her drive: she was swooping and swerving, like a thing alive; in fact, she was a thing alive: she had ceased to be wood and iron, laden with cases: she was something of the spirit of the wind, and of the kindled wit of man, that laughed as she flew.

Suddenly, as he stood by the wheel, watching her head, and letting his eyes run aloft to the curves of the leaches under strain, the greyness in the heaven parted as though the sheets had given, with the effect of a sail suddenly let go and clued up. The cloud tattered itself loose to windward and rived itself apart, and blue sky showed and spread. Instantly, a blueness and a brightness came upon the water. To leeward before them the storm passed away like a scroll. There, to port, far away, was the Chesil Beach, with the Needles beyond it, and the far and faint line of England stretching astern to the Start. The sun appeared and beauty came with him, so that all the tumbling and heaping brightness rejoiced.

One of the first things revealed was a fine clipper ship two miles ahead, lying almost the same course. On the starboard quarter, perhaps two miles away, another lofty ship came racing up Channel, and far astern a third showed. This third was perhaps not one of the China fleet.

"We've turned into the straight," Cruiser said. "There seem to be three left in it."

"Yes, sir," Fairford said, "unless the race is already won."

"We'll learn soon enough if it's already won," Cruiser said. "Get a tackle on the yard-arm there," he called. "All hands set studding sails." The mate and the men marvelled, but they leaped to the order. They were now as keen as Cruiser to bring their ship home. Not a man thought that perhaps the race had been already won by someone; to them the race was now beginning.

Cruiser was on the fo'c's'le head with the telescope trying to make out the ship ahead. Under the tapering clouds of sail he could see a dark green hull, with an old-fashioned transom look about her stern. She could be no other than the *Caer Ocvran*. She had been running with prudence, not knowing where she was; now that the sky had cleared she was making sail.

"All ready, the foretopmast stunsail, sir," Mr. Fairford reported, adding under his breath, "If you think she'll stand them, sir."

"No time for prudence now," Cruiser said, "hoist away there —lively now."

One at a time the mighty wings of studding sail swayed aloft and shook themselves out of their bundles with a roaring into service. Cruiser saw the topsail yard lift and the booms buckle as the strain came upon them; but the gear held. A whiteness boiled along the *Bird's* side and flew in a sheet over the waist as she felt the new power given to her. Cruiser watched for a minute, standing well forward, eyeing the straining booms. "They'll hold," he thought, "as long as the wind keeps steady and the helmsmen behave." He crossed the fo'c's'le and eyed the ship ahead. She had set her lower studding sail, and no doubt was setting more as fast as the men could move, but the *Bird of Dawning* seemed sailing two feet to her one.

He watched for half a moment; Fairford and others were at his side, staring.

"Ah, she's holding us," Fairford said suddenly. "Yes, she's holding us. There go her topmast studding sails: beautifully done too. She's got forty hands at stations. It's something to have a full crew."

"We've got twelve," Cruiser said. "Twelve good men upset the Roman Empire. Get the topgallant stunsails on her."

The men ran to it: he slipped aft with the telescope, partly to con the ship, partly to see what the ship astern might be. He steadied the glass against a mizen shroud and stared at the ship astern. She was on the starboard quarter, and plainly much nearer than she had been. She was not more than a mile and a half away. Not much of her showed except a tower of leaning sail, winged out with studding sails, a jib-boom poising and bowing, and a roll of white water under her bows. He broke off from his staring to rate Bauer at the lee wheel. "Never mind what's astern of you," he called. "Watch your steering or you'll have the masts out of her and we'll skin you alive."

He looked again at the ship astern. Someone forward had said that she was the *Min and Win.* He was satisfied that she was not the *Min and Win,* but a much bigger and newer ship, the *Fu-Kien,* commanded by a reckless dare-devil known as Bloody Bill China. "Well, what Bill can carry we can drag," he said, so he leaped down into the waist, to the job of getting more sail on to a ship that already had plenty.

"Doctor, there," he called to Perrot, "and you, Chedglow, get breakfast along on deck. Chedglow, get tongues and sardines and what you like out of the stores: the best there is. Hands must breakfast as they can, on deck, three at a time." He watched the setting of the new sail and its effect upon the ship. She was holding her own now, perhaps gaining a very little on the *Caer Ocvran,* and hardly losing to the *Fu-Kien.*

"She's gaining on us, though," Cruiser muttered. He could see now plainly, her anchors over the bows dripping brightness whenever she rose from the sea. "Well, I'll try what the skysail will do. Up there, one of you, and loose the skysail."

They loosed and hoisted it, and had the sight of the pole bending like a whip of whalebone to the strain. Bill replied by loosing his main skysail, which blew away in the setting. They raced on now, hardly changing position. All hands in all three ships had all that they could do: getting a pull there, a pull there, a better set on this and a better trim to the other. Even Stratton, sullen as he was, seemed interested in the race, even Efans forgot his rights in the thought of how much better Captain Duntisbourne would have handled her. They raced in the laughing morning, while the coast slipped by them, all the landmarks long looked for.

With blown-down streamers of smoke, a squadron of ironclads moved across the sea in front of them, going in line ahead from Spithead under steam with no canvas set. They were in a beam sea, making heavy weather of it, they laboured exceedingly, streaming like the half tide rock, yet keeping station. The sailors commented on their order aloft, the yards squared to a T, the bunts triced up with jiggers into perfect cones and secured with black gaskets a foot across. Two of them were barque-rigged, with double topsail yards. Cruiser dipped his colours to them, and then with rapid hoists of flags asked if the China race had already been won. There were no code hoists for this question: he had to spell it and was not sure of being understood. One of the ships hoisted the negative pennant, or so he thought, but he could not be sure, as the flag was blowing away from him, and even if it were the pennant he thought that it might be some private naval signal, or even a refusal to answer.

Cruiser had had prepared for two days on the poop a contrivance for sending letters and telegrams ashore in case of luck or need. He had lashed to a ship's life-buoy in upright positions two blue and white boat-flags, which the *Bird of Dawning's* boats had borne in the Foochow Regatta. He had then bent to the buoy a long line of small stuff ready to lower it over the side. To this buoy he now lashed with great care two bottles of brandy, frapped with bagwrinkle, and a canvas packet sewn up in oilskin, which contained a sovereign, presumably the only coin on board, that had been found in Captain Miserden's trouser pocket, and an urgent appeal to the finder to send two telegrams there plainly written out, ready to be sent.

Soon after the ironclads had passed, a big smack, under a reefed mainsail and jib, hove up, all gleaming, ahead. She was crossing their bows, making for some point on the Hampshire coast. It was what Cruiser had most longed for, during that morning. He signalled to her with a red weft that he wished to speak, and luckily the fisherman understood, and hove up into the wind with a shaking sail to let the *Bird of Dawning* pass.

As the great ship surged by, Cruiser in the mizen rigging shouted to the smack through his speaking trumpet asking them to send off the telegrams. He pointed to the buoy, which the mate smartly lowered to the sea and paid out upon. They saw the buoy lift high on the sea, with its flags blowing clear, and in an instant it was tossed away upon the following surge to the smack's bows. A man leaned over with a boat-hook, fished for it, caught it and hove it inboard, then bent over it as the sail filled. Cruiser saw the bottle pass from hand to hand while the skipper looked at the writing. The skipper presently waved vigorously to show that he understood.

"I only hope that he does understand," Cruiser thought. "And that nobody else has worked the same traverse." One telegram was to the London and Dover Tug Company to have two tugs for the *Bird of Dawning* off the South Foreland, the other was to his brother, now a young lawyer in London, to meet the ship in the Downs and advise about the claims for salvage.

"Mike is the only lawyer I know," Cruiser thought. "And I've been abroad for a year: if he should have died, I shall be up a gum-tree."

As he had expected, the change of the lifting of the gale brought with it a lessening of the wind and a shifting of it to two points to the north-west. All three ships now had set every sail that they could carry, to the royal studding sails and trust-to-gods. Cruiser had guyed out a boom below the jibboom and had set a spritsail: Bloody Bill China had bonnets on his courses and contrivances that he called puff-balls in the roaches of his topsails. What the *Caer Ocvran* was doing they could not clearly see: she was almost dead ahead of them. The three ships were drawing nearer to each other, the *Caer Ocvran* coming back, the *Fu-Kien* coming on. If the race had not been already won by some ship in ahead of them, it was the finest finish seen since the China prize was raced for.

An outward-bound ship came ratching past with the sprays like clouds of smoke at her bows. Her mate and various boys were on her fo'c's'le at work: they all knocked off to see those racers, no such sight had been seen in the Channel as those three driven clippers making the utmost of the day. Cruiser signalled to her an urgent signal, and asked, spelling the hoists, "Has any China ship arrived yet?" He could see the ship's captain with a couple of boys busy at the signal halliards, acknowledging each hoist. The answer, when they made it, was the affirmative pennant without any ship's number to show the winning ship.

"So we're beaten to it, then, sir," Fairford said. "I wonder if the *Natuna* got it."

Cruiser stared after the now receding ship, now being spoken to by Bloody Bill, to whom she gave nothing but her own number, the *Inkerman* of London, and a dipped ensign.

"I don't believe she understood," Cruiser said, "and I'm not going to take that as gospel. We'll race these two ships at least."

Still, something of the zest was gone from the contest when he thought that after all another ship might have docked even a couple of days before, and now lay discharging, with a gilt cock at her masthead. Then as the day drew on, the tide slackened and the wind dropped and shifted still more to the north: it gave them a beam sea and much anxiety for their gear, which held, but only just held.

At one that afternoon, as they passed Beachy all three ships began to feel the turn of the tide, the flying kites had to come in lest they should pitch the spars away. Then in little short spells of twenty minutes the wind would lull and the kites would be set again; and in this kind of sailing Bloody Bill China had an advantage: as Cruiser could see, he had the boys aloft in the tops all the time ready to race up to loose the light sails or take them in. He was creeping up a little and a little, and was now only about a mile astern, having gained certainly a mile and a half in five hours. In another five hours the *Fu-Kien* would be half a mile ahead, having the pick of the tugs at the South Foreland.

The *Caer Ocvran* was at a slight disadvantage, being not quite so happy in fresh or clearing weather as in light airs. However, her captain was fighting for every inch she lost. Cruiser with his small crew had only the miracle of the ship in his favour. He felt more and more keenly every instant that the ship was the best ship in the race. In other voyages she may not have been so: in this race all had conspired together, her builder and some happy combination in her trim, to make her supreme, but now she was short of hands, unable to do her best.

A darkness gathered into the heaven astern of them as the secondary moved up. The hours of the afternoon dragged by as the ships strained up Channel, all drawing nearer, all watched by thousands ashore, who now guessed that those three moving beauties were the clippers of the China fleet.

Just off the Fairlight a little steamer, going with coals for Fowey, edged close in to the *Bird of Dawning,* so as to have a good look at her. Cruiser hailed her through the trumpet.

"Ahoy, there, the *Chaffinch,* what China ship won the Race?"

"No ship," the *Chaffinch's* skipper shouted back. "You are the Race. Go in and win."

"Thank you," Cruiser shouted. "Is that straight?"

"Yes. Get to it. Knock the bastards silly."

This was greeted with a cheer from all hands: they had a chance still.

There came a sudden hurrying, greyness astern: it sent before it a hissing noise which put Cruiser's heart into his boots. He shouted out, "Let go your royal halliards. Stand by topgallant braces," and had let fly the main royal halliards as a rain squall swept over them and blotted out ships, sea and land in a deluge that filled the scupper. Out of the deluge there came wind in a gust that tore the flying royals into tatters. Something more than royals went, the topgallant stunsails went at tack and halliards, blew out in the rain like dirty flags, flogged once, twice and away, with whips of their gear lashing round anything they touched. The masts bent, the yards curved at the arms under the pull of the sheets, and the ship leaped forward as though suddenly lashed.

The men ran to the gear: nothing more was lost: the split sails were cleared and new ones bent but not set. The rain made a darkness about them for twenty minutes, during which Cruiser had two men on the fo'c's'le looking out.

As the squall cleared off, the sun drawing to the west shone out and made a rainbow upon its darkness. Under the arch of colours they saw the *Caer Ocvran* not two hundred yards from them on the starboard bow. She seemed to be stuck there in tossing waters that whitened about her in a great bubble.

Through the glass Cruiser could plainly see her captain, pacing his weather poop, glancing quickly aloft and at the *Bird of Dawning*. "Ah, yes, sir," Fairford said, as he watched, "you can glance and you can curse the helmsman, but the *Bird of Dawning's* got you beat to the wide."

"That's Captain Winstone," Cruiser said. "He was mate of the *Bidassoa* when I was in her. Look at that now: did you ever see a ship so wet?"

"She's famous for it, sir; the *Caer*. A fine ship, too."

Presently they were abreast of her, and forging ahead upon her, so that they could see her in her glory. She had a straight sheer and a transom stern, having been built upon the lines of the famous French frigate, *L'Aigle*. In a light air no ship of her time could touch her, and she could run with the swiftest. She had a name through the seven seas for being wet: her decks now were running bright: for she was a caution in a head sea. They were watching and tending her now, getting some of her after-sail off her to keep her from burying her bow. Cruiser dipped his colours to her as he passed, but would not hail his old captain. As he drew clear, he saw her famous figurehead of Queen Gwenivere bowing down into the smother, then rising and pausing, then plunging down till the fo'c's'le-rail was lipping green.

"Look at that," Cruiser said. "Did you ever see a ship pitch like that?"

As he spoke, she took a deeper 'scent than usual, and rose with a snapped stunsail boom lifting on a loose wing.

The *Fu-Kien* drew clear of the *Caer Ocvran* on her lee-side: she was now a quarter of a mile away and gaining perhaps twenty yards a minute. Dungeness lay ahead, distant perhaps eight miles, and somewhere about Dungeness there would be pilots and perhaps tugs. There or thereabouts the race would be decided, another hour would see it out. Cruiser's men had been hard at it all day, and were showing signs of wear. They drank strong tea, syrupy with sugar laced with brandy, as they got their hawsers ready forward and eyed the distant winning post.

All the issue from the gate of the Channel were about them: all the ships of a tide or two before from London and Antwerp, all the fishermen of Kent and Sussex. Every seaman who came past had no eyes for anything but those two superb clippers disputing for pride of place.

When the squall had passed by both had set every rag that could be brought to draw: they were now straining under clouds of canvas with a strong beam wind, and a head tide. Tarlton, who had been in the *Fu-Kien,* was not encouraging. "Just the wind she likes most," he said, "she's a glutton for it. And she laps up a head sea like a rum milk-punch." All the marvellous evening shone out mile after mile as they raced: the French coast plain as far as Calais, England white to windward, with occasional windows flashing like jewels, and a darkness of passing storm beyond. Occasional violent gusts kept men in both ships at the upper halliards; and still the *Fu-Kien* gained.

Cruiser was watching her now; she was not more than a hundred yards astern and to leeward, her decks full of men, and spare sails, all made up for bending, on each hatch, and the ship herself a picture of perfection, all bright for port, the paint-work and tarring finished; the hull black, with a white sheer-straik to set off her sheer, the yards black, man-of-war fashion, but with white yard-arms, and her masts all scraped clean with glass, of shining yellow pine. All her brass was bright, and the scroll below her bowsprit had been freshly gilt. She was driving on easily with great laughing leaps. Cruiser could see, in the bearing of the men in her, their certainty that they were winning. Both ships were hauling their wind now to turn the bend. Both could see now, coming out from Dungeness, the pilot cutter, standing towards them, not two miles away, and beyond, making for them what seemed to be tugs, but might be small coasters.

"Too bad, sir," old Fairford said. "We'd have done it if we'd had a bit more luck."

Cruiser was feeling broken-hearted at being passed on the post, but he could not take this view of it. "No, no," he said. "We've had such luck as no sailors ever had before. Think of what has come to us." All the same, he had to move away. When he was on the lee-poop staring at the *Fu-Kien*, old Fairford could not see how bitterly he felt.

As they hauled their wind, the *Fu-Kien* forged ahead upon them, standing close in upon them, intending to weather upon them and drive across their bows. Bloody Bill China was there on his poop, an unmistakable big figure with a hard tall grey hat jammed sideways on his head and a long pistol in his right hand. "That's Bloody Bill, sir," Tarlton said to Mr. Fairford. "Bloody Bill China, sir, the Captain. You'll see him send a bottle of brandy out to the yard-arm in a moment."

Sure enough a lad with a line went up the mizen-rigging and out to the crojick yard with it, rove it through a jewel block at the yard-arm, and brought it down on deck. A bottle of brandy was hauled out to the yard-arm upon it and dangled there. "That's Bloody Bill's way, sir," Tarlton said. "If ever he weathers on a ship he shoots a bottle of brandy at the yard-arm and then splits another on all hands."

Twenty faces stared at the *Bird of Dawning* from the *Fu-Kien's* side. Those men of the sea, negroes, Malays and Europeans, grinned and cheered as their ship slid past.

Bloody Bill China, who was certainly half drunk, shouted something to his steward, who was standing near the break of the poop beside a grog-kid. The steward put a corkscrew into the cork of a bottle which he held. Bloody Bill strode to the ship's rail, and yelled at Cruiser, whom he took to be Captain Miserden, "Give my love to the Prophet Habakkuk."

Voices from the *Fu-Kien's* waist, eager for the promised grog, and full of joy in their victory, shouted "Habakkuk, Yah Yah, Habakkuk", and instantly the *Fu-Kien's* mainmast was ahead of the *Bird of Dawning's* mizzen, and at once the *Fu-Kien's* crew manned the rail and cheered, and beat the fire signal on both her bells. Bloody Bill China brandished his pistol above his head, brought it down, and fired it as he fell: the bottle at the yard-arm was shattered—the brandy spilled. Instantly the steward drew his cork and Blood Bill China shouted, "Grog-oh! The *Fu-Kien* wins the China Race."

She tore past the *Bird of Dawning*. She cleared her by a cable, then by three hundred yards. "Look out, sir," Tarlton cried to Cruiser. "He'll cross your bows as sure as God made Sunday."

And instantly Bloody Bill China did; he luffed up out of bravado, so as to get to windward of the *Bird of Dawning*.

He was going to cross her bows, just to show her. As he luffed, one of the violent gusts beat down upon both ships. Cruiser saw it coming and let go in time, but it caught the *Fu-Kien* fairly, and whipped her topgallant masts clean off in succession as one might count one, two, three. The great weight of gear swung to and from on each mast, the fore-upper topsail halliards parted and the yard coming down brought the lower topsail with it, bending the truss and cockbilling the yard. The helmsman let her go off, she fell off, thumping and thrashing while gear came flying down from the ruin. With a crash, the wreck of the fore-topgallant mast, with its three yards, and stunsail booms and weight of sail and half a mile of rigging, collapsed about the forehatch.

It all had happened in a moment. Cruiser had been warned and had just time to heave the helm up. The *Bird of Dawning* always steered like a bird: she answered to a touch; she answered to it now, but the *Fu-Kien* was right athwart her hawse not three hundred yards away, falling off and coming down on her, with all the wreck of her mainmast visibly shaking the whole mast. One active daredevil soul was already racing with axe to the splintered mast-head, to hack through the shrouds.

Cruiser saw her come round on her heel, straight at the *Bird of Dawning*. For about half a minute it seemed certain that the two would go into each other and sink each other. The mizen royal yard slid out of its bands and smote the *Fu-Kien's* deck end-on like a harpoon. The terrified helmsman hove the helm hard down; the ship, having still way on her, swung back into the wind; with a running, ripping, walloping crash, her main topgallant wreck came down into her waist, going through the bunt of the mainsail as it went.

The *Bird of Dawning* went past her and missed her by thirty yards. As they passed, Bloody Bill China leaped on to the top of the wheel-box, hurled his hard hat at Cruiser, and while it was still in the air, settling to the sea, put three bullets through it with his pistol: he then hurled his pistol after it and leaped down cursing on to the main-deck to clear the wreck.

Cruiser left him to clear it; there, ranging down upon him, was the pilot cutter. In another minute that graceful boat rounded to with her pilot, who caught the tackle flung, and in an instant was swung high and brought upon the *Bird of Dawning's* deck.

The Pilot was a short man of enormous breadth, with a gentle manner. He seemed puzzled at the smallness of the crew and at the unusual untidiness of the deck, the planks not scrubbed nor oiled, the paint not freshened. He came up the weather ladder to Cruiser and shook him by the hand.

"I'm proud to welcome you, Captain," he said. "You're the first China clipper to take a pilot this year."

About five minutes later two tugs bore down upon them. Cruiser hoped as they drew near that they would be those telegraphed for by him. They were, however, two pirates, anxious to make the most of the situation. "Take you in, and dock you, for £100 a tug, Captain," their spokesman said.

"Are you the London and Dover Tug Company?"

"No, Captain; the South Foreland Tug Company. What about it?"

"Nothing doing."

"Now Captain," the tugman cried. "You give us your line. £100 a tug is nothing to you if you win the prize. And with us you can't fail to win the prize. What's £100 a tug to honour and glory?"

"I'll give you £50 a tug," Cruiser said.

"Is that your last word?"

"Yes."

"Adew, my bucko," the tugman cried. Both tugs sheered off, in what Cruiser took to be the familiar gesture of a tugman driving a bargain. In this he was wrong, both tugs bore down on the *Fu-Kien* in such obvious distress astern. They had no doubt hoped that they might get a little salvage there. He saw them hang round the stern of the *Fu-Kien* while they drove their bargain and though Bill China was an ill man to bargain with, they drove it, for he saw them take the position ahead to take the *Fu-Kien's* lines. But there was some little delay in their getting the lines, because the *Fu-Kien's* forward deck was a jumble of wreck not yet cleared. Old Fairford shook his head. "Ah, Captain Trewsbury," he said, "if you'll excuse my saying it, sir, 'Agree with thy adversary quickly' is wisdom when you're dealing with tugs. Now we're past the bend of land this wind will fall and be tricky: we'll be as like as not becalmed before we're in the Downs: and there aren't too many tugs, sir. It'd be hard to see the *Fu-Kien* go past with those two fellows. Besides, sir, if the wind should fall light, as it will, we shall have the *Caer Ocvran* on us again. They say her captain can get way on her by blowing a flute on the poop."

"I daresay I was an ass," Cruiser said, "but we'll soon know."

There came a shout from forward on the starboard side. Efans came running aft.

"What's the matter? Cruiser asked.

"The *Serica,* sir. She's been on the French side, look you, and is standing ofer ahead of us."

"What of it?" Cruiser asked. "She can't sail against the wind." He had watched that ship to leeward for some time, wondering if she could be one of the fleet. He had not thought her to be the *Serica.* If she were the *Serica,* then she, too, would be in the running, and might get a tug before him and beat them all. He had looked at her through the telescope, and thought that she was liker the *Min and Win*; but a ship ahead of them by any name would be as ugly. "Well, I suppose I was an ass," he concluded to himself, as the evening closed in and the sun dipped into the clouds above England.

As old Fairford had foretold from the depth of his knowledge, the wind fell light and was tricky. Sheltered there in the Channel under the lee of the land, with the tide still ebbing, there was a little lop on the water, which was of a dark grey now under the cliffs, and stretching green, with pinkish mottlings from the clouds to distant France. Dover Pier and Castle and cliffs rose up: and there bearing down on him were two tugs, with tall scarlet smoke-stacks banded at the top with black. "There are the London and Dover tugs," he said.

"Them's them," old Fairford said. "The *Morning* and *Evening Star.*" He sheered away to utter his real comment unheard: "And them two the *Fu-Kien's* got will eat the pair of them for breakfast."

As the *Evening Star* swung round, and came almost alongside, Cruiser saw his brother, the lawyer, standing on the bridge with the tug-captain.

"Hallo, Mike," he hailed. "How goes it?"

"Hallo, Cyril."

"You got my telegram?"

"Yes. I've settled with these tugs. I've settled everything."

"Give us your line, Captain," the tugman cried. The lines were tossed down: in a few minutes the hawsers were passed and the tow to London River had begun.

Soon after they had started towing and before it had become too dark to see, the ship that men had thought to be the *Serica* showed clearly that she could not be the China clipper, but some unknown lofty ship bound for Dunkirk. Cruiser was able to judge the speed of the *Fu-Kien* under tow as less than his. He had a start of at least a couple of miles of her, and hoped to be able to maintain it.

In the last of the light he saw the *Caer Ocvran* come gliding up on a breath and signalling for steam. There was no tug for her. Presently the wind ceased, so that even the *Caer Ocvran* lay still in the calm.

The September night closed in upon them as they drew into the Downs. Deal lights twinkled to port; on ahead, on the starboard bow, the Gull Stream light gleamed out and vanished and again gleamed. Presently, as they finished with the sails and came from aloft in the dark, a big moon rose on the one hand, while on the other came the Kentish lights, Ramsgate Harbour and the North Foreland. A mile or two more brought them round the Elbow, into the great expanse starred with beacons, the Prince's Channel and the Girdler, with Shoebury far beyond. The night came cold and quiet, with a clear sky, into which the moon rose triumphing.

All through the night they towed, from the Channels to the Deeps and from the Deeps into the Reaches. The hard work of the voyage was over, but all hands stayed on deck ready for a call. Perrot made them suppers at odd times; some of them slept and others sang. Edgeworth stretched canvas over the ends of a cask and made a drum.

Before morning came, as Cruiser walked with the Pilot watching sleeping England and the unsleeping life of the river, a Kentish cock crowed for morning in some unseen roost. The faint magical noise reached the *Bird of Dawning,* and instantly her cock flapped on his perch in the coop and crowed in answer. Far away ashore on both sides of the river the cry passed from roost to roost. Cockcrow surely will rouse the dead at the dawn of judgment.

Soon light came into the sky: factory whistles blew to work, chimneys smoked; bells rang and the life of the port became busy about them. At eight o'clock, as they drew near to dock, a big steamer, coming down, beat her bells to them; her crowd of passengers, stewards and deck-hands clustered at the rail and cheered them: she blew her siren, and passed them, dipping colours. Now down the river towards them came a flotilla of tugs, river-craft, skiffs, wherries and launches, all crowded, all gay with flags. The pierhead loomed up, black with people. The dock-side railwaymen began to let off detonators. All those multitudes cheered and cheered, waved flags and streamers, flung their hats aloft and cried for the *Bird of Dawning*.

"You're for it, Captain," the Pilot said. "If you'll cast an eye down the Reach you'll see your rival."

Far down the river, too far down perhaps to be a serious rival, a big ship without topgallant masts was towing up in a cloud of black smoke.

"She's the *Fu-Kien*," Cruiser said.

"She's got three tugs to her," the Pilot said. "She'll run you close still. The worst of these races is that they're never decided till the ship's docked. And we're far from docked yet."

"Yes, there's many a slip," Cruiser said. "And she's coming up fast."

"If we can see the gates closed behind us, before she's ready to enter, we'll beat her," the Pilot said. "But in this river anything may delay us, a barge or one of your admirers in a skiff here."

The crew of the *Bird of Dawning* had done their best to fit her for her coming in. Ever since dawn they had been at her, getting harbour stows on her sails, squaring her yards, washing down, coiling up, and brightening her brass. All her flags were aloft between trucks, and her colours and number at the peak. Now, as she loitered down and checked and took position to enter dock, the boats closed in upon her and the world of the shore came crowding on board, press-men first, to get the story, ship-owners and their friends, men who had betted on the race, ship-designers, ships' builders and ships' captains, with the runners and the sharks who live on sailors. They were pressing everywhere, bearing a hand at the gear, questioning, cheering and cutting bits of rope as souvenirs.

Now, slowly, the ship moved up to the dock-gate, with both tugs ahead. Kemble steered her; old Fairford stood on her fo'c's'le; Cruiser eyed her aft. As the figurehead drew past the gate, the tense crowd on the wharves seemed to grow white. A man, stepping forward, put fire to the breech of a signal canon. At the crash of the gun the Father of the Port, an old white-headed sea-captain, took off his white top-hat and cried, "Three cheers for the *Bird of Dawning,* winner of the China Tea Race." Then all the crowds broke into a roaring of cheering: all ships in the port beat bells, fired guns, hooted with sirens and cheered with throats.

Old Fairford lifted his hat and cried, "Three cheers for Old Pierhead." The little crowd of neversinks cheered and cheered as they passed into the dock.

Then Old Fairford cried, "Three cheers, boys, for Captain Trewsbury." As they finished the cheers Edgeworth leaped to his drum and beat upon it, others beat marline-spikes together, and all sang the words and tune of *See, the Conquering Hero Comes.*

More yet remained to be done. As the ship took sheer to sidle in, Coates and Chedglow went aloft to the main truck and secured to the spindle of the wind-vane the gilt cock made by Clutterbucke some days before. He steadied to the wind there and swung proudly as a *Bird of Dawning* should. The two lads came slithering down the backstays to the deck.

As they slid down, they saw the dock-gates slowly draw together and lock themselves close. They were shut. Three hundred yards downstream, the *Fu-Kien* checked her way: she was beaten. Now the *Bird of Dawning's* bow-and-stern-fasts were pitched over the bollards ashore. All hands, crews and visitors, took them to the capstan, and old Edgeworth began his song:

> *"I thought I heard the Captain say,*
> *Leave her, Johnny, leave her.*
> *I thought I heard the Captain say,*
> *It's time for us to leave her."*

They walked her up "for a full due" to the dock-side, till her fenders touched the coping. "That'll do, men," old Fairford said.

~~~~~~

Duty Steam Boat

The Midshipman of the Second Picket Boat—that is to say, the boat with the bell-mouthed funnel of burnished brass and vermilion paint inside her cowls—was standing under the electric light at the battery door reading the Commander's night order-book.

"Second Picket Boat to have steam by 5 a.m., and will perform duties of Duty Steam Boat for the Second Division." He closed the book and stood meditatively looking out into the darkness beyond the quarter-deck rails. It was blowing fitfully, gusts of wind shaking the awning in a manner that threatened dirty weather on the morrow. "Why the deuce couldn't the other Picket Boat . . . ? But she hadn't got a brass funnel—only a skimpy painted affair. Decidedly it was the fatal beauty of his boat that had influenced the Commander's decision. Still . . ." He yawned drearily, and opening the deck log, ran his finger down the barometer readings. "Glass low—beastly low—and steady. Wind 4–5, overcast, squally, raining. H'm'm." The cryptic quotations did not appear to add joy to the outlook. Ten o'clock had struck, and forward in the waist the boatswain's mate was "piping down", the shrill cadence of his pipe floating aft on the wind. Sorrowfully the Midshipman descended to the steerage flat, and crouching beneath the hammocks that hung from the overhead beams, reached his chest and noiselessly un-dressed,—noiselessly, because the sleeping occupant of the adjacent hammock had the morning watch, and was prone to be unreasonable when accidentally awakened.

In rather less than a minute he had undressed and donned his pyjamas; then delving amid the mysterious contents of his sea-chest, produced a pair of sea-boots, an oilskin and sou'wester and a sweater. He made his preparations mechanically, propping the sea-boots where they would be handiest when he turned out. Lastly, he hung his cap over a police-light, because he knew from experience that the light caught his eyes when he was in his hammock, locked his chest, and, choosing a spot where two mess-mates (who were scuffling for the possession of a hammock-stretcher) would not fall over his feet, he unconcernedly knelt down and said his prayers. The corporal of the watch passed on his rounds: the sentry clicked to attention an instant, and resumed his beat: above his head the ward-room door opened to admit a new-comer, and the jangle of a piano drifted down the hatchway; then the door closed again, shutting out the sound, and the kneeling figure, in rather dilapidated pyjamas, rose to his feet. Steadying himself by a ringbolt overhead, he swung lightly into his hammock and wriggled down between the blankets. From the other side of the flat came a voice:

"Freckles, you're Duty Steam Boat to-morrow."

The Midshipman of the Second Picket Boat grunted in reply and pulled the blanket close under his chin. Presently the voice sounded again:

"Freckles, dear, aren't you glad you sold your little farm and came to sea?"

But he who had sold a farm only snuggled his face against the pillow, sighed once and was asleep.

Had you seen the sleeper in waking hours, nursing a cutter close-reefed through a squall, or handling a launch-load of up-roarious liberty-men, you might, passing by at this moment, have found food for meditation. For the vibration of the dynamo a deck below presently caused the cap to fall from the police-light it had shielded, and the glare shone full in a face which (for all the valiant razor locked away in its owner's chest) was that of a very tired child.

.   .   .   .   .   .

"Orders for the Picket Boat, sir?"

The Officer of the Morning Watch, who was staring through his binoculars into the darkness, turned and glanced at the small figure muffled in oilskins at his side. Many people would have smiled in something between amusement and compassion at the earnest tone of inquiry. But this is a trade in which men get out of the way of smiling at 5 a.m.—besides, he'd been through it all himself.

"Flagship's signalled some empty coal-lighters broken adrift up to windward—cruisin' independently. Go an' round 'em up before they drift down on the Fleet. Better man your boat from the boom and shove straight off. Smack it about!"

The small figure in oilskins—who, as a matter of fact, was none other than the Midshipman of the Second Picket Boat, brass funnel, vermilion-painted cowls and all—turned and scampered forward. It was pitch dark, and the wind that swept in rainy gusts along the battery caught the flaps of his oilskins and buffeted the sleep out of him. Overside the lights of the Fleet blinked in an indeterminate confusion through the rain, and for an instant a feeling of utter schoolboy woe, of longing for the security of his snug hammock, filled his being. Then the short years of his training told. Somewhere ahead, in that welter of rain and darkness, there was work to be done—to be accomplished, moreover, swiftly and well. It was an order.

Stumbling on to the forecastle, he slipped a life-belt over his shoulders, climbed the rail, and descended the ship's side by a steel ladder, until he reached the lower boom. It jutted out into the darkness, a round, dimly-discerned spar, and secured to it by a boat-rope at the farthest point of his vision, he saw his boat. The circular funnel-mouth ringed a smoky glow, and in the green glare of a side-light one of the bowmen was reaching for the ladder that hung from the boom. Very cautiously he felt his way out along it, steadied by a man-rope, breast high. Looking downward, he saw the steam boat fretting like a dog in leash; the next instant she was lurching forward on the crest of a wave, and as suddenly dropped away again in a shower of spray. Releasing his grip with one hand he slipped astride of the boom, wriggled on his stomach till his feet touched the rungs of a Jacob's ladder, and so hung swaying a few feet above the tumbling water.

"'Arf a mo', sir," said a deep voice behind him. The boat's bows were plunging just below . . . the ladder tautened with a jerk.

"Now, sir!" said the voice. He relaxed his hold and dropped nimbly on to the triangular space in the bows. As he landed, the Jacob's ladder shot upwards into the darkness, as though snatched by an unseen hand.

Steadying himself by the rail along the engine-room casing he hurried to the wheel. A bearded petty-officer moved aside as he came aft. This was his Coxswain, a morose man about the age of his father, who obeyed orders like an automaton, and had once (mellowed by strong waters) been known to smile.

"Cast off forward!" The engine-room bell rang twice, and the Midshipman gave a quick turn to the wheel. For an instant the boat plunged as if in uncertainty, then swung round on the slope of a slate-grey wave and slid off on her quest. Forward in the bows the bowmen were crouched through the rain. Presently one of them hailed hoarsely.

"Port a bit, sir," supplemented the Coxswain. "That's them, there!" He pointed ahead to where indistinct shapes showed ahead black against the troubled waters. The bell rang again in the tiny engine-room, and the Leading Stoker, scenting adventures, threw up the hatch and thrust a head and hairy chest into the cold air. His interest in the proceedings apparently soon waned, however, for he shut the hatch down again and busied himself mysteriously—always within reach of the throttle and reversing-lever—with an oil-can.

Going very slow, the boat crept alongside the foremost lighter, a huge derelict that, when loaded, carried fifty tons of coal. They had been moored alongside one another to the wharf, but, rocking in the swell, had chafed through their moorings and broken adrift.

Now to take in tow an unwieldy lighter in the dark with a heavy swell running, and to moor it safely in the spot whence it came, is a piece of work that requires no small judgment. However, one by one, the three truants were captured and secured, and then, with the grey dawn of a winter morning breaking overhead, the picket boat swung round on her return journey. On the way she passed another boat racing shoreward for the mails. The Midshipman at the wheel raised his hand with a little gesture of salutation, and she went by in a shower of spray.

Half an hour later the Midshipman of the Second Picket Boat, garbed in the "rig of the day", was ladling sugar over his porridge with the abandon of one who is seventeen and master of his fate. A messenger appeared at the gunroom door:

"Duty Steam Boat's called away, sir."

Her Midshipman locked away his pet marmalade-pot (for there are limits even to the communism of a gunroom) and reached for his cap and dirk. "We ain't got much money," he observed grimly, "but we *do* see life!"

LEO WALMSLEY

~~~~~~

Three Fevers

It was dawn of a day in December, the weather deceptively calm and mild, with a moderately heavy ground swell running into the shore.

We had helped the Fosdycks launch their coble. With Tindal and Avery Fosdyck at the oars and old Luke in the stern standing by the lines, she was already abreast of the two posts which marked the hidden ends of the east and scars and the mouth of the Landing. She rose and dipped steeply to the swell which broke on the scars not more than a coble's length on either side.

The Lunns' coble was now afloat at the shoreward end of the tranquil landing. John, the elder son, was priming the engine. Marney was bending the buoy and anchor of the first line. Henry, with one hand on the tiller, was watching the Fosdycks' coble.

"They're going to shoot straight out from the landing posts into deep water," he remarked. "They're not going to risk the weather."

Marney gave a contemptuous grunt.

"Quick off and quick in," he mocked. "That's their motto. Cod run close in to the scar ends when there's a swell like this. The closer we go in the better . . . Come on, John, get that damned engine started. You're like an old woman. Here, I'll give her a swing."

"You leave the engine alone. Then we'll know who's fault it is if owt goes wrong."

"If I had charge of it it never would go wrong! Hurry up. We've seven lines to shoot, and we're not going to shoot in deep water. We're going to put them where there's some fish."

"That's for father to say," John remarked. "There's only one boss in this boat remember."

"And that's me," was Marney's ready answer: with the smiling qualification, "Isn't it, father?"

Henry, who had never relaxed his observation of the Fosdycks, suddenly turned to me and winked. But he did not speak. John gave the engine a couple of powerful turns. It started, and he looked up beaming:

"How's that?" he said triumphantly. "Second swing. That's because I had the magneto ashore last night and gave it a proper fettling."

At half tide the Landing measured a rough two hundred yards from its shallow shore end to the marking posts. Soon we had passed the bared ends of the scars. The crash of the breakers now made almost inaudible the steady tug-tug of the engine. Marney was standing up with the buoy in his hand. We drew abreast of the posts. The coble climbed a big roller and dipped with an easy crash into its trough. At the same time the roller split on the sunken scar ends close to each side of us and went shorewards leaving a mass of seething foam in its wake.

Henry waved his disengaged hand to the foam.

"It's a nasty spot, this," he said quietly. "It's all right when you can see where you're going. But in mucky weather it's hard to see the posts until you're right on them, and of course in a really heavy sea the waves may be breaking right across. Once you've started running in it's too late to turn back and make for deep water. If it wasn't for this we could fish in almost any weather," he added regretfully.

"And it's a damned good thing we can't," put in John, and to his brother, "You needn't think we're going to start shooting in here with the swell like it is."

"You hold your jaw," Marney said. "You're the engineer not

the navigation officer. What about it, father? You know there's most fish close in."

Again father winked, but he said nothing. He kept the coble on a course straight out of the Landing and then slightly north-west until we were about a hundred yards from the posts and the nearest broken water. Then he swung round until we were pointing for Low Batts cliff, and signed to Marney to heave the buoy overboard.

"We're near enough in and far enough out to suit both of you here," he said, smiling. "If it blows up we'll just be able to pick our end up here. The Fosdycks have only just started shooting. Throttle your engine, John. Now, Marney, soon as your buoy is clear."

One never had any real doubt as to who was boss of that boat. The buoy was trailing out astern. Marney had the first line along-side him. He gave the buoy line a last clearing tug, heaved over the small anchor, and, as soon as its line was paid out, started to shoot. For a while there was no more talking.

It was tricky work. Each line measured four hundred fathoms: and there was a yard-long "snood" and hook, at each second fathom. They were coiled on the wicker "skeps" so that the baited hooks lay together in a neat heap clear of the line. Even so there was a chance of a hook fouling, either the line, or the boat's gunwale, or even the "shooter's" hands, which meant that the hook would have to bear the entire strain of the heavy and fairly fast-moving boat.

Henry, when I knew him first, had the reputation of being the smartest hand at shooting on the coast. Now, he admitted, he was not so good as Marney. His fingers had become too stiff. It needed a marvellously quick eye, a dainty touch, unerring judgment. John's ambitions had never lain this way. He was the mechanic, and when occasion arose, the second strong man of the trio. He had a prodigious strength.

There was an immense fascination in seeing these three men at their job; Marney deftly lifting the coils of line, flinging them, with their vicious hooks, clear of the boat; John watching him, with his hand on the throttle, ready to ease down or stop if anything fouled; Henry standing with one sea-booted foot on the stern thwart, the long tiller boom under his left arm, alert, watchful, quietly and supremely in command. He looked like a Viking chief with his bristly, straw-coloured moustache projecting above his tightly closed lips, his bright audacious eyes roving restlessly from the boat, across that heaving, windless, enigmatic sea.

Our course continued towards Low Batts, parallel to the rocky shore, and just clear of the breaking surf. But soon the shore began to sweep out north-east in conformity with the strike of the headland cliff, and we turned north-east, riding the swell head-on. The first line was nearly shot.

"Stand by!" Marney shouted to me. "Don't make a mess of it!"

I lifted the "skep" of the second line alongside that of the first, took off its lashings, bent its beginning to the loose end of the first, and as the last coil of the latter went overboard, moved the empty "skep" out of the way, an effort which afforded me considerable satisfaction, but which produced from Marney only a sarcastic grunt.

"Slow," he said, flinging a coil of line into the air as though it were a living snake. "Slow. You're nearly as slow as our John, and there never was anything slower. . . . Keep closer in, father. We're getting off the rock edge here."

The coble rose almost on its end as he spoke, mounting a huge roller. A petrol can came crashing down from a thwart. Marney swayed, but the net coil, with its baited hook, shot out as clear as the first.

"Sea's growing like hell," John complained. "We'll be lucky if it's not breaking here when we come back. Why can't you have a bit of sense, the pair of you? You know the Fosdycks will be only too pleased to have the lifeboat out after us, and make fools of us."

"Stop your damned croaking," put in Marney.

Being "made fools of" was the one thing the Lunns really feared, and nothing came so completely within their conception of the term as an active challenge on the part of the Fosdycks to their sea judgment, of their ability to get back to shore unassisted.

But Henry, taking a glance at the Fosdycks' boat, now about a mile to the south-east of us, smiled complacently.

"They'll be back before us," he said. "But they'll know better than try that game on. If they do they'll only have it to launch back. . . . They're queer chaps, the Fosdycks," he added, turning to me. "You'd think that in a place like this, with only two boats working, it would pay you both to pull together. But it seems they can't forget father and them coming here and showing 'em how to fish. And they've not liked us starting with a motor-coble. Yet they've got enough brass to buy an engine if they wanted. If they worked the same way we do they'd catch just as much fish. But they'll go on sticking to their old-fashioned ways until they die, I reckon. They're queer. That's all I can say about them."

"But I could say more," put in Marney darkly, leaning almost horizontal with the boat as she rode another great roller.

"And so could I," added John.

"Then you can both hold your jaws," said father with a surprising severity. "Least said, soonest mended."

Both Marney and John grinned, but they did not speak again for a while. We were now running parallel with Low Batts cliff, still head-on to the rollers which broke, not against, but along the cliff foot; chasing each other for half a mile before they finally crashed on the shores of the bay itself. They were typical deep-sea waves, very long and regular in their incidence. It seemed incredible that we should ride over them in safety and tolerable comfort, while not more than eighty yards away they could have smashed our coble to pieces in a matter of minutes.

Would the wind that had transmitted this awful energy to the sea follow on? The sun had risen, but the sky remained completely overcast. Round the distant headland of High Batts a steamer had appeared; but its smoke trailed languidly astern, denoting a complete absence of wind. Yet the swell obviously was growing. The noise of it, reverberating from the precipitous walls of the adjacent cliff, was like that of an immense cataract. Over the entire shore of the bay the breakers were throwing up a fine white mist, which almost obscured the land, and the village itself. The unnatural closeness of the air helped to increase one's apprehension about the weather. Yet the business of shooting went steadily on with only that gloomy look in John's eyes to suggest that my apprehension might be shared; and that look I knew was more or less habitual, and signified a resistance to his brother's recklessness, rather than a fear of the sea itself.

Each line took roughly a quarter of an hour to shoot. The second was now nearly gone. I bent on the third, earning from Marney this time a curt, "That's better."

"Where have the Fosdycks got to now, father?" he asked, almost in the same breath.

Henry glanced over his shoulder.

"Still shooting straight out. They must be on their second line."

"Look out!"

A sudden shout from Marney caused John instinctively to throw the engine out of gear. A hook had fouled. Quickly Marney's hand shot out and seized the receding line, and he held on to it against the way of the boat while with the other hand he deftly caught the offending hook from a bunch of theirs it had caught.

"That's one of your lines," he shouted at John when the line was clear, and the boat, in gear again, took an almost vertical plunge down the back of a roller. "You must have been thinking of that lass you were going to meet in Burnharbour on Saturday night while you were baiting it. My lines never foul. Nor father's. You ought to have been a grocer."

"And I might have to be one yet," John answered, "when you two have gone and drowned yourselves!"

There was another battle of wits between the two brothers, which went on until Henry, glancing south-east, remarked suddenly:

"Damned if the Fosdycks haven't started to haul. They're hauling before they've started their third line. Summat must have scared them."

"So they are," John muttered slowly. "I wonder what's up?" And then suddenly he shouted, "I know why. Look at the coast-guard station. North cone's up." He turned to Marney. "Now will you say I'm croaking?"

The coastguard station was built on high ground at the back of the village, and its flag-staff rose clear above the white mist shrouding the village itself. A small, black, conical bag was just discernible, hanging from the signal yard. Its point was upwards, denoting the conventional warning of an approaching gale from the north.

"Now will you say I'm croaking?" John repeated. "There's evidence for you. We'd best get this line shot, and then start hauling straight away."

"Don't talk so daft!" was Marney's comment. "We've come out to fish, not to play at launching boats up and down."

Quite unperturbed, he went on with his occupation, while Henry, looking again towards the Fosdycks, said complacently:

"Aye. That's what's turned them about. They've seen the cone, only they could have told it was going to blow without that. I don't blame them for hurrying in with a coble like theirs. So long as they don't expect us to join them. It just beats me why they don't get an engine. Look at us, and where we've got to already. They couldn't have worked this end of the bay this morning if they'd had six men to pull for them."

John shook his head despairingly, and bent gloomily over his engine.

The third line was shot. We started on the fourth, and not by a yard did Henry deviate from that course which was steadily bringing us nearer to the extremity of Low Batts. Yet despite their outward complacence, I knew that both Henry and Marney were aware that we were running into danger; that every fathom of line shot was a fathom between ourselves and the safe water behind that perilous landing mouth.

Not a word was spoken while the fourth and fifth lines were shot. We were practically opposite Low Batts point when I stood by to bend on the sixth. But before Marney was ready we cleared the point, and a line of rough, breaker-fringed coast came in view beyond it. And with that line of coast, terminating at the high bluff called Kettlenab, which bears a light of the same name and hides the port of Burnharbour from the south, came in view the open sea, the northern skyline, the wind itself.

For two miles to the north, the surface of the slowly heaving sea was dully polished under the low-lying pall of pewter-grey cloud that obscured the sky. Beyond, divided by a line as clear cut as the contour of that forbidding coast, reaching from the coast to the north-east skyline, the sea was almost black; the cloud above it was almost black, save for one small gap of startling blue sky, across which a wisp of white cloud moved like a ragged sail torn from a ship.

The wind! One saw it in that wisp of scurrying cloud; in that expanse of dark furrowed sea, whose clear-cut margin was travelling south-west, as fast almost as the wind itself. And suddenly one felt it in the air; not a movement, but a peculiar coldness, as though one had plunged into an icy bath.

I thought John would be the first one to break the silence with which we surveyed that disquieting prospect, but I was wrong. He merely glanced from the sea to his father, whose expression remained completely unperturbed; and it was Marney, swaying to the wild movement of the boat, who spoke, with a rather uncertain defiance:

"Stand by with that other line."

"You needn't trouble. Throttle your engine, John. Hold on your line, Marney. Start hauling soon as she comes about."

There was no alarm in Henry's voice. He had made the

decision of a cool gambler who knows the precise limit of his stake. We turned. For a moment we were broadside on to the swell, and the coble rolled violently. But before the next roller came we were facing the land, John had opened his throttle to half-speed again, Marney had started hauling.

For a time we were silent. Despite that we were all conscious of the approaching wind and its significance, we watched the line coming on board with undivided interest. The fascination of a fisherman's life is that he reaps his harvest from an unseen world through whose insecure and perilous crust he throws down his sacrificial gifts for a reward that may be small, or may be great, but is always uncertain. All that he knows of that obscure region beneath him is that it is inexhaustibly rich.

True that we expected nothing of that first line. In normal weather we should have waited an hour at least before hauling. The last few fathoms had not even touched the bottom. Marney's face took on an expression of profound disgust, as hook after hook came up with its bait intact.

"If there's one thing I hate," he grumbled, "it's hauling a line that hasn't had a chance. We might just as well have waited twenty minutes before we hauled."

"You have a look nor'ard, and you'll not talk so daft," said John. "You'll be glad enough of that twenty minutes when we come to the far end of the line. If it's not breaking across the Landing by then it'll be a wonder to me."

"What if it is?" shouted Marney with a sudden cheerfulness. "You can swim ashore and then start that grocery business of yours. . . . Gaff—father. Here's the first, and a good fish, too."

We had drawn under Low Batts again. The coast beyond had disappeared, and with it that threatening expanse of furrowed sea: and the wind itself was temporarily forgotten in the excitement of bringing on board a twenty-pound cod.

"Now will you stop your croaking!" Marney shouted, continuing to haul while father deftly unhooked it. "Here's another. Damned if it isn't its mate!"

A second fish of about the same weight was gaffed and brought aboard, followed shortly by a third, only a pound or two smaller.

Marney was beaming now. Even John looked less gloomy. Henry's face still wore that expression of absolute imperturbability as his eyes roved without rest from the boat to the crashing breakers between ourselves and the cliff; to the seaward horizon, and to the mist-hung shore.

About fifty fathoms came in blank. Then came a codling which did not need the gaff. The end of the first line was reached without another fish. I unbent the line and stowed it out of the way. Marney had stopped beaming. He hauled half of the next line before swinging another codling on board.

"They're not so plentiful as I thought," he muttered then. "The Fosdycks will have the laugh on us if we don't do better than this. Where have they got to?"

We looked shorewards. The other coble had nearly reached the Landing posts.

"They're just about in," said Henry laconically.

"And I shouldn't mind if we were too," said John. "Look nor'ard now. It's coming, and no mistake."

Within a space of less than ten minutes the entire aspect of the seaward horizon had changed. From the extremity of Low Batts, as far as eye could reach to the south-east, it was as though that inert mass of low-lying cloud was being rolled up from the line of the sea in dark, horizontal, moving folds, from which drooped folds of paler colour, trailing like an immense opaque curtain over a sea that was dark furrowed and flecked white by the advancing wind.

"It's coming," John repeated. "It's a squall, too. That's either hail or snow behind the wind. . . . Now where should we have been if we'd waited? It's going to be a devil. I tell you we're not going to get in a minute too soon."

Whether Marney glanced seawards or not, I did not know. He created a diversion at that moment with a shout of, "Eh! What's this damned thing coming up? Look out—father. Quick!"

Henry, gaff in hand, leaned smartly over the gunwale; but instead of the gaff he reached his bare hand into the sea, and lifted a big lobster out of it clean into the boat.

Again it seemed that the weather was forgotten. Both Henry and John stared at that utterly unexpected crustacean, flapping on its back on the boat's bottom as though it was a bar of gold from a sunken galleon.

"Well, I'm damned!" said Henry.

"If that doesn't beat the band!" said John.

"First I've heard of a lobster being hauled close-in in December," was Marney's contribution, as he continued to haul. "And it looks as surprised as we are. I should think it's gone and eaten something that hasn't agreed with it, and put its compass wrong."

"I don't know," said John, with a new seriousness. "They're making lobster-pots already at Burnharbour. I was talking to a chap on Saturday night, and he said they were all starting for lobsters in February. He'd got a proper lobster fever on him. Couldn't talk about anything else but the brass Burnharbour chaps made out of lobsters last year. If we had a couple of score of fine ones like that it would pay us better than cod. I reckon we ought to start making pots now, so we can start fishing when prices are good."

Marney swung another codling into the boat. He grinned, but he was taking John quite seriously.

"So you went and caught lobster fever on Saturday night," he said. "Well," he added, "those chaps did make some brass by all accounts. There was one boat that made nearly a hundred quid in a week."

"There was one made over a hundred," put in Henry quietly. "Lobsters were bringing three shillings each all week."

I was aware that Henry's eyes had an unusual sparkle in them as he took another glance at the lobster; but I had still to become really acquainted with those peculiar and highly infectious fevers, which, as one season declines, spread among the fishermen of the coast, firing them with a wild enthusiasm for the next.

Nothing more was said about lobsters then. The end of the second line came with a single fourteen-pound cod. The third line was hauled without a fish. There were two lines left. We were more than halfway home; and still there was no wind. Yet despite that the swell was less noticeable now that we were moving with it, the margin between the boat and the edge of the broken water was steadily decreasing as we moved into the bay. Without exchanging a word, I knew that each of the Lunns was thinking of the buoy, the Landing mouth, and the squall behind us.

Were the seas breaking across the Landing? The Fosdycks' coble long ago had disappeared between the posts. Presumably they had safely navigated the passage. Since we had lost sight of them, however, the swell had measurably grown. Ten minutes of a squall on top of it might make the difference between a safe entry and an impossible one.

With the fourth line our luck began to change again. Two more good cod came in quick succession. There was a blank, then a run of about a dozen—not big, but respectable fish. Their appearance was greeted in silence, however. Every fathom was bringing us nearer to where the rollers were breaking. As the end of the fourth line drew near with another small batch of fish we were obliged to wait while a breaking roller charged past us, before dodging into its churning wake, and out again before the next one came.

And as the end of that line, and the beginning of the last one came on board, came the first warning puff of wind. No one remarked upon it. No one troubled to look round. We felt its chilly blast, we saw it, like the shadow of a menacing hand, move across the grey water ahead. There was a moment's lull; then came a stronger gust of icy air that whipped the crest of a near-by breaker into smoke. There was a sharp patter of hailstones. The gust passed over and ahead. Another quickly followed; and in the short succeeding lull I saw Marney take a quick glance shorewards to where, close by the west Landing post, the buoy had become visible as it rode the crest of what appeared to be an unbroken sea.

But he said nothing. He went on steadily hauling. For several minutes the whole view shorewards was obscured by the driving hail, which pattered on the thwarts and bottom of the heaving coble. The squall was on us. All round, the sea was whipped white by the wind, which was now continuous, and rapidly growing in force.

There was no fish during that period. Then they began to come in again: a batch of codling, a stray pollack, a conger which required all of Henry's strength and dexterity to bring on board. The hail continued. Only by that steadily growing pile of line by Marney's side was it possible to measure the distance which separated us from the buoy. Yet still Henry's face, reddened by the bite of the freezing wind and the sting of hail, was unperturbed as he helped with the fish, steered the boat and kept up a keen watch ahead. More than two-thirds of the last line was hauled when the hail stopped. The land cleared again. We saw the Landing posts, and then the wind-whipped pennant of the buoy, poised for a moment on the crest of a wave that was beginning to break not more than a coble's breadth to the west of it.

John, hanging on to the wood casing of the engine as the boat pitched wildly, gave a shout.

"It's breaking! Right on the buoy. That means across the Landing too! We'd best cut away now, and make a dash for it. Cut the line!"

"Garn!" Marney shouted back. "We're not going to cut before there's need to, and very likely not at all. We're not going to throw away twenty fathoms of good line and maybe a dozen fish just to keep your shirt dry. You look after your engine. We can look after the boat. Can't we, father? We've got in when it's been twice as bad as this."

My sympathies at that moment were entirely with John. But Henry answered neither of them. He was staring hard towards the shore. Suddenly he said:

"There's a lot of folks on the slipway. I believe there's somebody waving summat. Can any of you make it out?"

The wind, which had now reached gale force, had flattened the mist from the near-in breakers. The hail shower had swept over the village top, leaving the front and the slipway clear. One could vaguely distinguish, near to a group of figures standing on the slipway, a tall man in yellow oilskins, energetically waving a long pole with a black cloth on its end.

"It's Luke Fosdyck!" John shouted. "He's waving us to stop. It must be breaking across the Landing. He's——"

Before John had finished, there came from the shore the muffled report of a gun. As we looked, against the dark scurrying smoke from the shot came down three scintillating red stars. And as the stars died there came the muffled report of that second explosion.

I had lived my whole boyhood in Bramblewick and that signal was too familiar for me not to understand it. It was the call-signal for the lifeboat crew. The figure we believed to be Luke Fosdyck was now moving up the slipway. The group had dispersed in the same direction. In a minute or two, the double doors of the lifeboat-house would be opened wide. Men would be rushing down, hurriedly strapping on their life-belts. . . .

"There you are! Didn't I say they'd do it?"

I looked at John. But it was anger, not fear, that made his shout hoarse. And for the first time in my life I saw Henry really angry too. He was standing up, with the tiller boom under his arm, his oilskin cracking in the wind: and I heard him mutter between his teeth:

"The damned fools! Do they think we're kids?"

Then he suddenly looked towards the buoy, now not more than thirty yards away, and said quietly to Marney:

"Have your knife ready, and cut when I say. Never mind the buoy. It'll wash ashore"; and to John, "When I say 'go', let her have it!"

The buoy had disappeared in the trough between two great rollers over which we had already ridden. It appeared again on the crest of the second one, which broke clean on top of it, hiding its flapping pennant in a torrent of spray. We drew down upon it, Marney still calmly hauling. He swung another big cod on board without waiting for the gaff: another pollack, and two more codling. Then, as another roller lifted the coble up not a dozen yards from the buoy, Henry's curt order came:

"Cut!"

And as Marney slashed at the line, with one steady glance towards that gap between the marking posts a hundred yards diagonally to our left, Henry put the helm hard over. We swung round on the very crest of that breaking sea. We sank sideways into its trough. Its successor rose above us—began to break.

"Look out!" Henry shouted.

It caught the low gunwale of the boat before we had time to rise, and sent a torrent of water smashing over us. But we were not aware then that we were wet. The coble rode that wave broadside on, and sank sideways down its back. And as a third and bigger wave still began to rise to charge straight between the Landing posts, Henry put the tiller over again, and shouted violently:

"Let her go!"

I did not know then if John obeyed that order. From that moment we were not aware of any other power than the sea. We swung round as the wave lifted us. For a time it seemed we were poised on its absolutely rigid crest, that the two posts on either side of us were themselves moving towards us, out to sea. Then our stern began to sink. The wave appeared to become mobile, it passed on, reared its crest higher, split, and abandoned us in its boiling wake, with the posts appearing to move land-wards again as the undertow took us back into the path of the following wave.

I did not look at that wave. I expected it to swamp us; and I was struggling to kick off my sea-boots when, like an immense hand, it gripped us from behind. We rose. Again there was that illusion of immobility as the boat balanced on its crest and travelled with it shorewards. Again the posts appeared to move while we were still. But this time the posts passed us. The shallow ends of the scars passed us. We saw the bare rock, east and west. Then again we began to sink down the back of the carrying wave. The illusion of immobility went. The wave advanced, passed on. But it did not break, except on the scars alongside us. We sank easily into its trough. We were consciously moving under our own power on the undulating, gale-swept, but unbroken surface of the Landing.

For a while none of us spoke. John throttled the engine. Henry steered in towards the shore end of the east scar, where the Fosdycks' coble was beached. There was no sign of the lifeboat. The beach between the Landing and the village was deserted, but for a small boy running our way. But as we looked, the Fosdyck brothers with their lifebelts on appeared on the slipway. The engine stopped. We moved gently into shallow water. Our bow touched the bottom. The coble became still.

And then Marney emitted a triumphant grunt.

"How was that for a bit of surf-riding? Well done, father. You couldn't have done it better if you'd trained at Honolulu. Now what about the lifeboat and making fools of us? I bet old Luke there is wishing he'd saved his fireworks for next Gunpowder Plot night. Who's got a fag?"

"Here, I have," said John. "If that damned sea we shipped hasn't spoiled the whole damned packet." He produced from his trousers a packet of Woodbines. "Did you notice how that damned engine picked up when father said go? I tell you there isn't a finer engine on the whole damned coast. Hello. Here's our Steve."

The boy, easily recognizable as another member of the Lunn family, had halted, panting, on the scar close by.

"Eh!" he hailed. "They were just going to put the lifeboat off for you. Crew were getting their belts on. Mother says if you've got a nice cod you're to keep it for dinner. . . . Eh! Marney!" he hailed again.

"What's up?" Marney demanded.

Steve grinned.

"Your Amy's on the slipway. She's been watching you come into the Landing. She says she's going to murder you. She says you've got to come straight up and change your clothes."

"You can tell her he'll do nowt of the sort," put in John indignantly. "There's the fish to clean and get away by the one o'clock train, and the cobles to haul up yet. She ought to have more sense."

"You tell her I'll be up in a few minutes," said Marney quietly. "Aye, and you can tell her summut else." He suddenly held up the lobster. "Tell her to get this boiled for our tea. . . . Come on, father," he added briskly, as he got out of the boat. "Let's get the fish ashore. The Fosdycks are coming to haul up. We didn't do so bad after all. But we'd have done better if we'd waited a bit before we hauled."

Henry, unfastening his oilskin, turned his eyes to the gale-swept roaring sea.

"Aye," he said quietly, "that landing mouth's a nuisance. . . . How many fish did the Fosdycks get, Steve?" he added, turning to the shore.

Steve grinned again.

"Five codling," he answered.

C. S. FORESTER

Hornblower and McCool

The Channel fleet was taking shelter at last. The roaring
westerly gales had worked up to such a pitch that timber and
canvas and cordage could withstand them no longer, and nineteen
ships of the line and seven frigates, with Admiral Lord Bridport
flying his flag in H.M.S. *Royal George,* had momentarily abandoned that watch over Brest which they had maintained for six
years. Now they were rounding Berry Head and dropping anchor
in the shelter of Tor Bay.

A landsman, with that wind shrieking round him, might be
pardoned for wondering how much shelter was to be found there,
but to the weary and weatherbeaten crews who had spent so long
tossing in the Biscay waves and clawing away from the rocky
coast of Brittany, that foam-whitened anchorage was like paradise.
Boats could even be sent in to Brixham and Torquay to return
with letters and fresh water; in most of the ships, officers and men
had gone for three months without either. Even on that winter
day there was intense physical pleasure in opening the throat and
pouring down it a draught of fresh clear water, so different from
the stinking green liquid doled out under guard yesterday.

The junior lieutenant in H.M.S. *Renown* was walking the deck
muffled in his heavy pea-jacket while his ship wallowed at her
anchor. The piercing wind set his eyes watering, but he continually gazed through his telescope nevertheless; for, as signal lieutenant, he was responsible for the rapid reading and transmission
of messages, and this was a likely moment for orders to be given

regarding sick and stores, and for captains and admirals to start chattering together, for invitations to dinner to be passed back and forth, and even for news to be disseminated.

He watched a small boat claw its way towards the ship from the French prize the fleet had snapped up yesterday on its way up-channel. Hart, master's mate, had been sent on board from the *Renown,* as prizemaster, miraculously making the perilous journey. Now here was Hart, with the prize safely anchored amid the fleet, returning on board to make some sort of report. That hardly seemed likely to be of interest to a signal lieutenant, but Hart appeared excited as he came on board, and hurried below with his news after reporting himself in the briefest terms to the officer of the watch. But only a very few minutes passed before the signal lieutenant found himself called upon to be most active.

It was Captain Sawyer himself who came on deck, Hart following him, to supervise the transmission of the messages. "Mr. Hornblower!"

"Sir!"

"Kindly send this signal."

It was for the admiral himself, from the captain; that part was easy; only two hoists were necessary to say *"Renown* to Flag". And there were other technical terms which could be quickly expressed—"prize" and "French" and "brig"—but there were names which would have to be spelled out letter for letter. "Prize is French national brig *Espérance II* having on board Barry McCool."

"Mr. James!" bellowed Hornblower. The signal midshipman was waiting at his elbow, but midshipmen should always be bellowed at, especially by a lieutenant with a very new commission.

Hornblower reeled off the numbers, and the signal went soaring up to the yardarm; the signal halyards vibrated wildly as the gale tore at the flags. Captain Sawyer waited on deck for the reply; this business must be important. Hornblower read the message again, for until that moment he had only studied it as something to be transmitted. But even on re-reading it he did not know why the message should be important. Until three months before, he had been a prisoner in Spanish hands for two weary years, and there were gaps in his knowledge of recent history. The name of Barry McCool meant nothing to him.

On the other hand, it seemed to mean a great deal to the admiral, for hardly had sufficient time elapsed for the message to be carried below to him than a question soared up to the *Royal George's* yardarm.

"Flag to *Renown*," Hornblower read those flags as they broke and was instantly ready for the rest of the message. "Is McCool alive?"

"Reply affirmative," said Captain Sawyer.

And the affirmative had hardly been hoisted before the next signal was fluttering in the *Royal George*.

"Have him on board at once. Court martial will assemble."

A court martial! Who on earth was this man McCool? A deserter? The capture of a mere deserter would not be a matter for the commander in chief. A traitor? Strange that a traitor should be court-martialled in the fleet. But there it was.

A word from the captain sent Hart scurrying overside to bring this mysterious prisoner on board, while signal after signal went up from the *Royal George* convening the court martial in the *Renown*.

Hornblower was kept busy enough reading the messages; he had only a glance to spare when Hart had his prisoner and his sea chest hoisted up over the port side. A youngish man, tall and slender, his hands were tied behind him—which was why he had to be hoisted in—and he was hatless, so that his long red hair streamed in the wind. He wore a blue uniform with red facings— a French infantry uniform, apparently. The name, the uniform and the red hair combined to give Hornblower his first insight into the situation. McCool must be an Irishman.

While Hornblower had been a prisoner in Ferrol, there had been, he knew, a bloody rebellion in Ireland. Irishmen who had escaped had taken service with France in large numbers. This must be one of them, but it hardly explained why the admiral should take it upon himself to try him instead of handing him over to the civil authorities.

Hornblower had to wait an hour for the explanation, until, at two bells in the next watch, dinner was served in the gun room.

"There'll be a pretty little ceremony tomorrow morning," said Clive, the surgeon. He put his hand to his neck in a gesture which Hornblower thought hideous.

"I hope the effect will be salutary," said Roberts, the second lieutenant. The foot of the table, where he sat, was for the moment the head, because Buckland, the first lieutenant, was absent attending to the preparations for the court martial.

"But why should we hang him?" asked Hornblower.

Roberts rolled an eye on him.

"Deserter," he said, and then went on. "Of course, you're a newcomer. I entered him myself, into this very ship, in '98. Hart spotted him at once."

"But I thought he was a rebel?"

"A rebel as well," said Roberts. "The quickest way out of Ireland—the only way, in fact—in '98 was to join the armed forces."

"I see," said Hornblower.

"We got a hundred hands that autumn," said Smith, another lieutenant.

And no questions would be asked, thought Hornblower. His country, fighting for her life, needed seamen as a drowning man needs air, and was prepared to make them out of any raw material that presented itself.

"McCool deserted one dark night when we were becalmed off the Pointe de Penmarch in Brittany," explained Roberts. "Got through a lower gunport with a grating to float him. We thought he was drowned until news came through from Paris that he was there, up to his old games. He boasted of what he'd done—that's how we knew him to be O'Shaughnessy, as he called himself when we had him."

"Wolfe Tone had a French uniform," said Smith. "And they'd have strung him up if he hadn't cut his own throat first."

"Uniform only aggravates the offence when he's a deserter," said Roberts.

Hornblower had much to think about. First there was the nauseating thought that there would be an execution in the morning. Then there was this eternal Irish problem, about which the more he thought the more muddled he became. If just the bare facts were considered, there could be no problem. In the world at the moment, Ireland could choose only between the domination of England and the domination of France; no other possibility existed in a world at war. And it seemed unbelievable that anyone would wish to escape from English overlordship—absentee landlords and Catholic disabilities notwithstanding—in order to submit to the rapacity and cruelty and venality of the French republic. To risk one's life to effect such an exchange would be a most illogical thing to do, but logic, Hornblower concluded sadly, had no bearing upon patriotism, and the bare facts were the least considerable factors.

And in the same way the English methods were subject to criticism as well. There could be no doubt that the Irish people looked upon Wolfe Tone and Fitzgerald as martyrs, and would look upon McCool in the same light. There was nothing so effective as a few martyrdoms to ennoble and invigorate a cause.

The hanging of McCool would merely be adding fuel to the fire that England sought to extinguish. Two peoples actuated by the most urgent of motives—self-preservation and patriotism—were at grips in a struggle which could have no satisfactory ending for a long time to come.

Buckland, the first lieutenant, came into the gun room with the preoccupied look commonly worn by first lieutenants with a weight of responsibility on their shoulders. He ran his glance over the assembled company, and all the junior officers, sensing that unpleasant duties were about to be allocated, did their unobtrusive best not to meet his eye. Inevitably it was the name of the most junior lieutenant which rose to Buckland's lips.

"Mr. Hornblower," he said.

"Sir!" replied Hornblower, doing his best now to keep resignation out of his voice.

"I am going to make you responsible for the prisoner."

"Sir?" said Hornblower, with a different intonation.

"Hart will be giving evidence at the court martial," explained Buckland—it was a vast condescension that he should deign to explain at all. "The master-at-arms is a fool, as you know. I want McCool brought up for trial safe and sound, and I want him kept safe and sound afterwards. I'm repeating the captain's own words, Mr. Hornblower."

"Aye, aye, sir," said Hornblower, for there was nothing else to be said.

"No Wolfe Tone tricks with McCool," said Smith.

Wolfe Tone had cut his own throat the night before he was due to be hanged, and had died in agony a week later.

"Ask me for anything you may need, Mr. Hornblower," said Buckland.

"Aye, aye, sir."

"Side boys!" suddenly roared a voice on deck overhead, and Buckland hurried out; the approach of an officer of rank meant that the court martial was beginning to assemble.

Hornblower's chin was on his breast. It was a hard, unrelenting world, and he was an officer in the hardest and most unrelenting service in that world—a service in which a man could no more say "I cannot" than he could say "I dare not".

"Bad luck, Horny," said Smith, with surprising gentleness, and there were other murmurs of sympathy from round the table.

"Obey orders, young man," said Roberts quietly.

Hornblower rose from his chair. He could not trust himself to speak, so that it was with a hurried bow that he quitted the company at the table.

"'E's 'ere, safe an' sound, Mr. 'Ornblower," said the master-at-arms, halting in the darkness of the lower 'tween decks.

A marine sentry at the door moved out of the way, and the master-at-arms shone the light of his candle lantern on a keyhole in a door and inserted the key.

"I put 'im in this empty storeroom, sir," went on the master-at-arms. "'E's got two of my corporals along with 'im."

The door opened, revealing the light of another candle lantern. The air inside the room was foul; McCool was sitting on a chest, while two of the ship's corporals sat on the deck with their backs to the bulkhead. The corporals rose at an officer's entrance, but even so, there was almost no room for the two newcomers.

Hornblower cast a vigilant eye round the arrangements. There appeared to be no chance of escape or suicide. In the end, he steeled himself to meet McCool's eyes.

"I have been put in charge of you," he said.

"That is most gratifying to me, Mr.—Mr.——" said McCool, rising from the chest.

"Hornblower."

"I am delighted to make your acquaintance, Mr. Hornblower."

McCool spoke in a cultured voice, with only enough of Ireland in it to betray his origin. He had tied back the red locks into a neat queue, and even in the faint candlelight his blue eyes gave strange reflections.

"Is there anything you need?" asked Hornblower.

"I could eat and I could drink," replied McCool. "Seeing that nothing whatsoever has passed my lips since *Espérance II* was captured."

That was yesterday. The man had had neither food nor water for more than twenty-four hours.

"I will see to it," said Hornblower. "Anything more?"

"A mattress or a cushion—something on which I can sit," said McCool. He waved a hand towards his sea chest. "I bear an honoured name, but I have no desire to bear it imprinted on my person."

The sea chest was of a rich mahogany. The lid was a thick slab of wood whose surface had been chiselled down to leave his name, B. I. McCool, standing out in high relief.

"I'll send you in a mattress, too," said Hornblower.

A lieutenant in uniform appeared at the door.

"I'm Payne, on the admiral's staff," he explained to Hornblower. "I have orders to search this man."

"Certainly," said Hornblower.

"You have my permission," said McCool.

The master-at-arms and his assistants had to quit the crowded little room to enable Payne to do his work, while Hornblower stood in the corner and watched.

Payne was quick and efficient. He made McCool strip to the skin and examined his clothes with care—seams, linings and buttons. He crumpled each portion carefully, with his ear to the material, apparently to hear if there were papers concealed inside. Then he knelt down to the chest; the key was already in the lock, and he swung it open. Uniforms, shirts, underclothing, gloves; each article was taken out, examined and laid aside. There were two small portraits of children, to which Payne gave special attention without discovering anything.

"The things you are looking for," said McCool, "were all dropped overside before the prize crew could reach *Espérance II*. You'll find nothing to betray my fellow countrymen, and you may as well save yourself that trouble."

"You can put your clothes on again," said Payne curtly to McCool. He nodded to Hornblower and hurried out again.

"A man whose politeness is quite overwhelming," said McCool, buttoning his breeches.

"I'll attend to your requests," said Hornblower.

He paused only long enough to enjoin the strictest vigilance on the master-at-arms and the ship's corporals before hastening away to give orders for McCool to be given food and water, and he returned quickly.

McCool drank his quart of water eagerly, and made an effort to eat the ship's biscuit and meat.

"No knife. No fork," he commented.

"No," replied Hornblower in a tone devoid of expression.

"I understand."

It was strange to stand there gazing down at this man who was going to die tomorrow, biting not very efficiently at the lump of tough meat which he held to his teeth.

The bulkhead against which Hornblower leaned vibrated slightly, and the sound of a gun came faintly down to them. It was the signal that the court martial was about to open.

"Do we go?" asked McCool.

"Yes."

"Then I can leave this delicious food without any breach of good manners."

They climbed the ladders to the main deck, two marines leading, McCool following them, Hornblower following him, and two ship's corporals bringing up the rear.

"I have frequently traversed these decks," said McCool, looking round him, "with less ceremonial."

Hornblower was watching carefully lest he should break away and throw himself into the sea.

The court martial had begun. There was much gold lace and curt efficient routine, as the *Renown* swung to her anchors and the timbers of the ship transmitted the sound of the rigging vibrating in the gale. Evidence of identification came first, followed by a series of curt questions.

"Nothing I could say would be listened to amid the emblems of tyranny," said McCool in reply to the president of the court.

It needed no more than fifteen minutes to condemn a man to death: "The sentence of this court is that you, Barry Ignatius McCool, be hanged by the neck——"

The storeroom to which Hornblower escorted McCool back

was now a condemned cell. A hurrying midshipman asked for Hornblower almost as soon as they arrived there.

"Captain's compliments, sir, and he'd like to speak to you."

"Very good," said Hornblower.

"The Admiral's with him, sir," added the midshipman in a burst of confidence.

Admiral the Honourable Sir William Cornwallis was indeed in the captain's cabin, along with Payne and Captain Sawyer. He went straight to the point the moment Hornblower had been presented to him.

"You're the officer charged with carrying out the execution?" he asked.

"Yes, sir."

"Now look'ee here, young sir——"

Cornwallis was a popular admiral, strict but kindly, and of unflinching courage and towering professional ability. Under his nickname of "Billy Blue" he was the hero of uncounted anecdotes and ballads. But having got so far in what he was intending to say, he betrayed a hesitation alien to his character. Hornblower waited for him to continue.

"Look'ee here," said Cornwallis again. "There's to be no speechifying when he's strung up."

"No, sir?" said Hornblower.

"A quarter of the hands in this ship are Irish," went on Cornwallis. "I'd as lief have a light taken into the magazine as have McCool make a speech to 'em."

"I understand, sir," said Hornblower.

But there was a ghastly routine about executions. From time immemorial the condemned man had been allowed to address his last words to the onlookers.

"String him up," said Cornwallis, "and that'll show 'em what to expect if they run off. But once let him open his mouth—— That fellow has the gift of the gab, and we'll have this crew unsettled for the next six months."

"Yes, sir."

"So see to it, young sir. Fill him full o' rum, perhaps. But let him speak at your peril."

"Aye, aye, sir."

Payne followed Hornblower out of the cabin when he was dismissed.

"You might stuff his mouth with oakum," he suggested. "With his hands tied he could not get it out."

"I've found a priest for him," went on Payne, "but he's Irish too. We can't rely on him to tell McCool to keep his mouth shut."

"Yes," said Hornblower.

"McCool's devilish cunning. No doubt he'd throw everything overboard before they captured him."

"What was he intending to do?" asked Hornblower.

"Land in Ireland and stir up fresh trouble. Lucky we caught him. Lucky, for that matter, we could charge him with desertion and make a quick business of it."

"Yes," said Hornblower.

"Don't rely on making him drunk," said Payne, "although that was Billy Blue's advice. Drunk or sober, these Irishmen can always talk. I've given you the best hint."

"Yes," said Hornblower, concealing a shudder.

He went back into the condemned cell like a man condemned himself. McCool was sitting on the straw mattress Hornblower had had sent in, the two ship's corporals still had him under their observation.

"Here comes Jack Ketch," said McCool with a smile that almost escaped appearing forced.

Hornblower plunged into the matter in hand; he could see no tactful way of approach.

"Tomorrow——" he said.

"Yes, tomorrow?"

"Tomorrow you are to make no speeches," he said.

"None? No farewell to my countrymen?"

"No."

"You are robbing a condemned man of his last privilege."

"I have my orders," said Hornblower.

"And you propose to enforce them?"

"Yes."

"May I ask how?"

"I can stop your mouth with tow," said Hornblower brutally.

McCool looked at the pale, strained face. "You do not appear to me to be the ideal executioner," said McCool, and then a new idea seemed to strike him. "Supposing I were to save you that trouble?"

"How?"

"I could give you my parole to say nothing."

Hornblower tried to conceal his doubts as to whether he could trust a fanatic about to die.

"Oh, you wouldn't have to trust my bare word," said McCool bitterly. "We can strike a bargain, if you will. You need not carry out your half unless I have already carried out mine."

"A bargain?"

"Yes. Allow me to write to my widow. Promise me to send her the letter and my sea chest here—you can see it is of sentimental value—and I, on my side, promise to say no word from the time of leaving this place here until—until——" Even McCool faltered at that point. "Is that explicit enough?"

"Well——" said Hornblower.

"You can read the letter," added McCool. "You saw that other gentleman search my chest. Even though you send these things to Dublin, you can be sure that they contain nothing of what you would call treason."

"I'll read the letter before I agree," said Hornblower.

It seemed a way out of a horrible situation. There would be small trouble about finding a coaster destined for Dublin; for a few shillings he could send letter and chest there.

"I'll send you in pen and ink and paper," said Hornblower.

It was time to make the other hideous preparations: to have a whip rove at the portside fore yardarm, and to see that the line ran easily through the block; to weight the line and mark a ring with chalk on the gangway where the end rested; to see that the noose ran smooth; to arrange with Buckland for ten men to be detailed to pull when the time came. Hornblower went through it all like a man in a nightmare.

Back in the condemned cell, McCool was pale and wakeful, but he could still force a smile.

"You can see that I had trouble wooing the muse," he said.

At his feet lay a couple of sheets of paper, and Hornblower, glancing at them, could see that they were covered with what looked like attempts at writing poetry. The erasures and alterations were numerous.

"But here is my fair copy," said McCool, handing over another sheet.

My darling wife, the letter began. *It is hard to find words to say farewell to my dearest . . .*

It was not easy for Hornblower to force himself to read that letter. It was as if he had to peer through a mist to make out the words. But they were only the words of a man writing to his beloved, whom he would never see again. That at least was plain. He compelled himself to read through the affectionate sentences. At the end it said:

I append a poor poem by which in the years to come you may remember me, my dearest love. And now goodbye, until we shall be together in Heaven.

Your husband, faithful unto death,

Barry Ignatius McCool.

Then came the poem—
> *Ye heavenly powers! Stand by me when I die!*
> *The bee ascends before my rolling eye.*
> *Life still goes on within the heartless town.*
> *Dark forces claim my soul. So strike 'em down.*
> *The sea will rise, the sea will fall. So turn*
> *Full circle. Turn again. And then will burn*
> *The lambent flames while hell will lift its head.*
> *So pray for me while I am numbered with the dead.*

Hornblower read through the turgid lines and puzzled over their obscure imagery. But he wondered if he would be able to write a single line that would make sense if he knew he was going to die in a few hours.

"The superscription is on the other side," said McCool, and Hornblower turned the sheet over. The letter was addressed to the Widow McCool, in some street in Dublin.

"Will you accept my word now?" asked McCool.

"Yes," said Hornblower.

The horrible thing was done in the grey hours of the morning.

"Hands to witness punishment."

The pipes twittered and the hands assembled in the waist, facing forward. The marines stood in lines across the deck. There were masses and masses of white faces, which Hornblower saw when he brought McCool up from below. There was a murmur when McCool appeared.

Around the ship lay boats from all the rest of the fleet, filled with men—men sent to witness the punishment, but ready also to storm the ship should the crew stir. McCool stood in the chalk ring on the gangway. Then came the signal gun, and the rush of feet as the ten hands heaved away on the line. And McCool died, as he had promised, without saying a word.

The body hung at the yardarm, and as the ship rolled in the swell that came round Berry Head, so the body swung and dangled, doomed to hang there until nightfall, while Hornblower, sick and pale, began to seek out a coaster which planned to call at Dublin from Brixham, so that he could fulfil his half of the bargain. But he could not fulfil it immediately; nor did the dead body hang there for its allotted time.

The wind was backing northerly and was showing signs of moderating. A westerly gale would keep the French fleet shut up in Brest; a northerly one might well bring them out, and the Channel fleet must hurry to its post again. Signals flew from the flagships.

"Hands to the capstan!" bellowed the bosuns' mates in twenty-four ships. "Hands make sail!"

With double-reefed topsails set, the ships of the Channel fleet formed up and began their long slant down-Channel. In the *Renown* it had been "Mr. Hornblower, see that *that* is disposed of". While the hands laboured at the capstan the corpse was lowered from the yardarm and sewn into a weighted bit of sail-cloth. Clear of Berry Head it was cast overside without ceremony or prayer. McCool had died a felon's death and must be given a felon's burial. And, close-hauled, the big ships clawed their way back to their posts amid the rocks and currents of the Brittany coast. And on board the *Renown* there was one unhappy lieu-tenant, at least, plagued by dreadful memories.

In the tiny cabin which he shared with Smith there was some-thing that kept Hornblower continually reminded of that morn-ing: the mahogany chest with the name "B. I. McCoOL" in high relief on the lid. And in Hornblower's letter-case lay that last letter and the rambling, delirious poem. Hornblower could send neither on to the widow until the *Renown* should return again to an English harbour, and he was irked that he had not yet ful-filled his half of the bargain. The sight of the chest under his cot jarred on his nerves; its presence in their little cabin irritated Smith.

Hornblower could not rid his memory of McCool; nor, beating about in a ship of the line on the dreary work of blockade, was there anything to distract him from his obsession. Spring was approaching and the weather was moderating.

When he opened his leather case and found that letter staring at him again, he felt undiminished that revulsion of spirit. He turned the sheet over; in the half dark of that little cabin he could hardly read the gentle words of farewell. He knew that strange poem almost by heart, and he peered at it again, sacrilege though it seemed to try to analyse the thoughts of the brave and frightened man who had written it during his final agony of spirit. *"The bee ascends before my rolling eye."* What could possibly be the feeling that inspired that strange imagery? *"Turn full circle. Turn again."* Why should the heavenly powers do that?

A startling thought began to wake to life in Hornblower's mind. The letter, with its tender phrasing, had been written without correction or erasure. But this poem; Hornblower remembered the discarded sheets covered with scribbling. It had been written with care and attention. A madman, a man distraught with trouble, might produce a meaningless poem with such prolonged effort, but then he would not have written that letter. Perhaps—perhaps——

Hornblower sat up straight instead of lounging back on his cot. *"So strike 'em down."* There was no apparent reason why McCool should have written *"'em"* instead of *"them"*. Hornblower mouthed the words. To say "them" did not mar either euphony or rhythm. There might be a code. But then why the chest? Why had McCool asked for the chest to be forwarded with its uninteresting contents of clothing? There were two portraits of children; they could easily have been made into a package. The chest with its solid slabs of mahogany and its raised name was a handsome piece of furniture, but it was all very puzzling.

With the letter still in his hand, he got down from the cot and dragged out the chest. B. I. McCOOL. Barry Ingatius McCool. Payne had gone carefully through the contents of the chest. Hornblower unlocked it and glanced inside again; he could see nothing meriting particular attention, and he closed the lid again and turned the key. B. I. McCOOL. A secret compartment! In a fever, Hornblower opened the chest again, flung out the contents and examined sides and bottom. It called for only the briefest examination to assure him that there was no room there for anything other than a microscopic secret compartment. The lid was thick and heavy, but he could see nothing suspicious about it. He closed it again and fiddled with the raised letters, without result.

He had actually decided to replace the contents when a fresh thought occurred to him. *"The bee ascends!"* Feverishly Hornblower took hold of the "B" on the lid. He pushed it, tried to turn it. *"The bee ascends!"*

He put thumb and finger into the two hollows in the loops of the "B", took a firm grip and pulled upward. He was about to give up when the letter yielded a little, rising up out of the lid half an inch. Hornblower opened the box again, and could see nothing different. Fool that he was! *"Before my rolling eye."* Thumb and forefinger on the "I". First this way, then that way—and it turned!

Still no apparent further result. Hornblower looked at the poem again. *"Life still goes on within the heartless town."* He could make nothing of that. *"Dark forces claim my soul."* No. Of course! *"Strike 'em down."* That "'em". Hornblower put his hand on the "M" of "McCool" and pressed vigorously. It sank down into the lid. *"The sea will rise, the sea will fall."* Under firm pressure the first "C" slid upward, the second "C" slid downward. *"Turn full circle. Turn again."* Round went one "O", and then round went the other in the opposite direction. There was only the "L" now. Hornblower glanced at the poem. *"Hell will lift its head."* He guessed it at once; he took hold of the top of the "L" and pulled; the letter rose out of the lid as though hinged along the bottom, and at the same moment there was a loud decisive click inside the lid.

Nothing else was apparent, and Hornblower gingerly took hold of the lid and lifted it. Only half of it came up; the lower half stayed where it was, and in the oblong hollow between there lay a mass of papers, neatly packaged.

The first package was a surprise. Hornblower, peeping into it, saw that it was a great wad of five-pound notes—a very large sum of money. A second package also contained notes. There was ample money here to finance the opening moves of a new rebellion. The first thing he saw inside the next package was a list of names, with brief explanations written beside each. Hornblower did not have to read very far before he knew that this package contained the information necessary to start the rebellion. In the last package was a draft proclamation ready for printing. *"Irishmen!"* it began.

Hornblower took his seat on the cot again and tried to think, swaying with the motion of the ship. There was money that would make him rich for life. There was information which, if given to the government, would clutter every gallows in Ireland. Struck by a sudden thought, he put everything back into the chest and closed the lid.

For the moment it was a pleasant distraction, saving him from serious thought, to study the ingenious mechanism of the secret lock. Unless each operation was gone through in turn, nothing happened. The "I" would not turn unless the "B" was first pulled out, and it was most improbable that a casual investigator would pull at that "B" with the necessary force. It was most unlikely that anyone without a clue would ever discover how to open the lid, and the joint in the wood was marvellously well concealed. It occurred to Hornblower that when he should announce his discovery, matters would go badly with Payne, who had been charged with searching McCool's effects. Payne would be the laughing-stock of the fleet, a man both damned and condemned by everyone.

Hornblower thrust the chest back under the cot and, secure now against any unexpected entrance by Smith, went on to try to think about his discovery. That letter of McCool's had told the truth. *"Faithful unto death."* McCool's last thought had been for the cause in which he died. If the wind in Tor Bay had stayed westerly another few hours, that chest might have made its way to Dublin.

On the other hand, now there would be commendation for him, praise, official notice—all very necessary to a junior lieutenant with no interests behind him to gain him his promotion to captain. And the hangman would have more work to do in Ireland. Hornblower remembered how McCool had died, and felt fresh nausea at the thought. Ireland was quiet now. And the victories of St. Vincent and the Nile and Camperdown had put an end to the imminent danger which England had gone through. England could afford to be merciful. He could afford to be merciful. And the money?

Later on, when Hornblower thought about this incident in his past life, he cynically decided that he resisted temptation because bank notes are tricky things, numbered and easy to trace, and the ones in the chest might even have been forgeries manufactured by the French government. But Hornblower misinterpreted his own motives, possibly in self-defence, because they were so vague and so muddled that he was ashamed of them. He wanted to forget about McCool. He wanted to think of the whole incident as closed.

There were many hours to come of pacing the deck before he reached his decision, and there were several sleepless nights. But Hornblower made up his mind in the end, and made his preparations thoughtfully, and when the time came he acted with decision.

It was a quiet evening when he had the first watch; darkness had closed in on the Bay of Biscay, and the *Renown*, under easy sail, was loitering along over the black water with her consorts just in sight. Smith was at cards with the purser and the surgeon in the gun room. A word from Hornblower sent the two stupidest men of the watch down below to his cabin to carry up the sea chest, which he had laboriously covered with canvas in preparation for this night. It was heavy, for buried among the clothing inside were two twenty-four-pound shot. They left it in the scuppers at Hornblower's order. And then, when at four bells it was time for the *Renown* to tack, he was able, with one tremendous heave, to throw the thing overboard. The splash went unnoticed as the *Renown* tacked.

There was still that letter. It lay in Hornblower's writing case to trouble him when he saw it. Those tender sentences, that affectionate farewell; it seemed a shame that McCool's widow should not have the privilege of seeing them and treasuring them. But—but——

When the *Renown* lay in the Hamoaze, completing for the West Indies, Hornblower found himself sitting at dinner next to Payne. It took a little while to work the conversation around in the right direction.

"By the way," said Hornblower with elaborate casualness, "did McCool leave a widow?"

"A widow? No. Before he left Paris he was involved in a notorious scandal with La Gitanita, the dancer. But no widow."

"Oh," said Hornblower.

That letter, then, was as good a literary exercise as the poem had been. Hornblower realized that the arrival of a chest and a letter addressed to the Widow McCool at that particular house in Dublin would have received the attention it deserved from the people who lived there. It was a little irritating that he had given so much thought to the widow, but now the letter could follow the chest overside. And Payne would not be made the laughing-stock of the fleet.

RICHARD HUGHES

~~~~~~

In Hazard

I

Dick Watchett could hardly believe his senses when he found that the wind had dropped, and the risen barometer proved that this was no "centre" again, but at last the storm's periphery. He hurried to the bridge—to get the good news confirmed. He found the captain and Mr. Buxton in the chart-room, both holding on to the built-in chart-roller.

"Is it true, sir?" he burst out. "Are we really out of the storm?"

Captain Edwardes nodded. And then, looking at the captain's face, Dick saw an astonishing thing. Captain Edwardes was, for the first time in that storm, afraid.

Dick looked back at the ship beneath him: and saw why. He saw the poop disappear in a shifting tumble of foam that raced forward right to the very centre-castle. She winced under it; her bows, even viewed from the height of the bridge, mounting almost to the horizon. It passed; but her stern did not very greatly rise. Without doubt she was now down by the stern.

Just at that moment Sparks appeared on the bridge, to report his emergency set was once more working.

"Send a call to all ships," said Captain Edwardes. "*'Estimated position so-and-so, require immediate assistance!'* And keep on sending."

Sparks, with blanched face, departed on his ominous duty.

But it is not much use sending out a call for urgent help unless you know your actual position pretty certainly. There are methods by which other vessels can get a rough idea of your direction: but even then they may have a long search before they find you.

The estimated position Captain Edwardes sent out was plainly very wrong, by the messages that presently came pouring in—from vessels near that position, who found no *Archimedes*; not even weather like hers.

If they had to make a prolonged search, help would arrive too late. For if the *Archimedes* was going down, she would do it quickly.

But if she did not sink in the next hour or so, with the wind gone the sea must presently moderate. Then she would be comparatively safe.

But still the sky was obscured: no chance of a sight of the sun, to tell him where he was.

One message that came was relayed from Boston—it was from its owners, in Bristol:

"Master Archimedes Salvage vessel Patricia been searching you three days stop Are you sinking condition query Endeavour utmost to ascertain your true position stop Sage."

Captain Edwardes, his brown eyes staring brightly and his lower lip drawn over his teeth, seemed suddenly moved by determination and a kind of anger. He fished out a sodden wireless pad from his pocket, dented it laboriously with a stubby black-lead:

"Sage. Bristol. Hurricane moderating. Am confident of safety of ship will proceed Kingston. Edwardes."

He pushed the original and his reply under Mr. Buxton's nose. The latter whistled faintly through a hollow tooth.

"Will proceed?" he said.

"Will proceed," answered the captain.

Captain Edwardes blew a double blast on his whistle, and a little quartermaster came padding along.

"Ask Mr. MacDonald to step on the bridge."

Presently the chief engineer appeared: his eyes wild and bleary, his false teeth in his hand.

"Mr. Macdonald, what is to prevent you getting steam on the donkey?"

"Nae funnel."

"Well, the wind has moderated now. What's to prevent you rigging a jury-funnel? I want enough steam for the pumps in two hours. Can you do it?"

"A canna," said Macdonald. "Bu' A can try."

So the engineers broke off one of the few tall, hooded ventilators that had remained unsmashed: and with the help of some cement stopped it on the stump of the old donkey-funnel: they guyed it very firmly with wire guys (which was very clever in that motion): then went below again to try to light the donkey-furnace.

Four hours, not two, had passed when they had reluctantly to admit it was still no go. Even with a jury-funnel, the hot oil still ran out of the furnace-door.

Captain Edwardes set his teeth, his bright eyes seeming concentrated on the problem of the present: but in reality his mind was travelling back into the past. His own past, before he joined the Sage Line: when he was still in Sail. For, like every other senior officer in the Fleet, his training had been in Sail, not steam. It is only lately, when the supply of sail-trained officers had begun to run short, that most of the first-class steamship lines have begun to accept officers trained in steam alone: have begun to train such officers themselves.

This seems an anomaly, to landsmen: that steamship companies should actually require their officers to have been trained in Sail: landsmen are inclined to smile, as at a piece of foolish conservatism—as if London bus-drivers were required to serve for seven years as stable-boys and grooms before they were allowed to handle motor-buses. With so much technical knowledge to acquire anyhow, why waste the man's time in learning a useless and outmoded technique as well?

The answer is a matter of Virtue, really. For an inclination towards virtue (such as sent Mr. Buxton to sea) is not enough in itself: it must be trained, like any other aptitude. Now there is a fundamental difference in kind between the everyday work of a sailing-vessel and the everyday work of a steamer. The latter does not essentially differ from a shore job: it is only occasionally, rarely, that emergencies arise in steam. But every common action in the working of a sailing-vessel, all the time, partakes of something of the nature of an emergency. Everything must be done with your whole heart, and a little more than your whole strength. Thus is natural aptitude for virtue increased by everyday practice. For changing a jib in a stiff breeze is a microcosm, as it were, of saving the ship in a storm.

So the officer in Sail acquires a training in virtue that may later, in Steam, mean the saving of some hundred lives, and a million or so of property.

If this had been a sailing-ship, Captain Edwardes reflected, now something could have been done. Jury-masts rigged, jury-sails bent, so she could escape out of the seething of this hell-broth. But what can you do in a steamer?

He remembered one of his early voyages, in a little Portmadoc schooner of a hundred and fifty tons. They were dismasted in a North Sea gale, fastened themselves below and rolled helplessly as the *Archimedes* now rolled. They were bringing home a cargo of timber: the holds were packed tight with it, and their decks had been piled high with it too till the storm washed those decks as clean as a brass door-plate. Presently she had rolled clean over and up the other side. I know it sounds incredible, but that is what happened. For proof, there were the burns on the cabin ceiling, where hot cinders from the cabin stove had fallen on it! (But if the *Archimedes* rolled over like that, she would not come up again before the Day of Judgment.)

Once the storm relaxed, captain and crew of the schooner had reappeared—like head and legs of a reassured tortoise. Her masts were gone: but they had plenty of timber below-decks, with which they built up small masts, and stepped them in the pumps. She would not come to windward under this improvised rig; but she made a port to leeward without too much difficulty. No salvage-ship was sent combing the seas for *her*.

And then Captain Edwardes recalled his first voyage as a steamship officer. On watch on the bridge, he had seen a squall coming. In a sailing-vessel, there would have been plenty for the officer of the watch to do. But what do you do on a steamer, when you see a squall coming? Nothing, except stroll into the wheelhouse to shelter from the rain.

It cuts both ways. The knight in armour could laugh at the slings and stones of the footboys. But once he fell off his horse, there he stayed—he could not even stand up again on his feet without help. The steamship officer can laugh at squalls, and contrary winds. But once he is in a real hole, there he stops.

And yet, surely something could be done. For a moment Edwardes had a mad idea of putting the *Archimedes* also under jury-rig; sailing her to safety. Bend awnings to her few remaining derricks. But all the awnings were cut up, for hatch-covers. And again, without steam how could he shift the bloody rudder? It is no good sailing if you cannot steer.

Well, they could rig tackles on the rudder-head: and perhaps all heaving together they could shift the rudder, in time. But that is not steering: why, it might take ten minutes to shift the rudder a few degrees.

Still, perhaps it might be done . . . and at least the sails might stop her rolling like this . . .

Again he remembered that his awnings were all cut up, now, for hatch-covers: there was nothing to make sails out of.

If they were ever to move again, it must be by steam. And the oil would not burn.

After all, she was a *steamer*: everything in her depended on steam. You could not carry her back into the days of sail, not effectively. If you improvised anything, it must be a way to raise steam you improvised.

In short, if the oil would not burn they must burn something else.

Captain Edwardes sought out Mr. MacDonald, and found him staring at the still dribbling donkey.

"Mr. MacDonald," he said, "what about solid fuel?"

"Aye, gin we had coal, an' fire-bars. But we ha's nae coal, let be fire-bars."

"Wood?"

Mr. Macdonald looked at the captain for a moment as if the latter had gone insane: then he gave his thigh a great slap.

At first sight it would appear as difficult to burn solid fuel in an oil-furnace as to stoke up your gas-ring with lumps of charcoal. But it is not so bad, really. The chief thing you need is fire-bars, for the fuel to rest on. Some ships (though not many nowadays) actually have convertible furnaces, and carry fire-bars so that they can change over from oil to coal fuel if necessary or convenient. The *Archimedes* did not: but all the same, fire-bars could surely be improvised.

So Mr. MacDonald set the engineers to work on a new task: they collected a number of superheat elements (these are fasces of thin tubes, four or five together), and with hack-saws cut them off to the length of the furnaces, supporting them on fire-bricks. The short ends they laid over them crosswise. Then the furnaces were stuffed with dunnage and broken furniture, and they were fired.

By the time they came to fix the bars her motion must have been noticeably easier: or they would never have succeeded in doing it.

II

Indeed, it was certainly easier, that afternoon: and Captain Edwardes began to believe that the confidence which he had expressed but not felt had been after all justified. The pooping was rarer; until at last it was possible to cover Number 6 hatch properly. After that, no more water went below. But she must have eleven hundred tons in her at least, by now: she was listed at 35° and down by the stern: head up and only one ear cocked, as it were. The position was still critical.

Now that the danger seemed somewhat relaxed, and the incessant buffeting was over, the famishment of everyone became very serious. Dick took to walking about in a slightly bent position so as to ease his emptiness. Then the first officer suggested that it might be possible, now her motion was eased, to get something at last out of the flooded store-room. The store-room was right forward, under the fo'c'sle. No one could possibly have entered it while her motion was still fierce, even during a lull.

The ladder down into the store-room had broken loose, broken a hole in the floor, broken itself, and disappeared. Beneath the floor were bags of rice: and swelling in all that sea-water they had burst the whole floor up, and then began to ferment horribly. If they had had time, they would have made it impossible to enter the store-room without a gas mask; but they had only just begun fermenting now. So Dick was lowered down, sitting in the bight of a rope, with an iron hook in his hand. It was a dizzy business: he swung on the rope one way, while the water beneath him sloshed the other way. So he, and the cans and cases he was trying to grapple, rushed about, with great violence in many directions, but (like two relatives who have arranged to meet in a huge crowd) never seemed able to collide.

At last, however, he managed to grapple two cases, and they were pulled up. One was a case of Bass, the other of tinned peaches. Then he was hauled up himself—half-unconscious, what with the swinging and the gases from the rice.

The chief steward, of course, was at hand to receive the stores: and at once he issued the canned peaches. But he would not allow one single bottle of the Bass to be opened till he had found his book of chits. He did not like irregularity of any kind.

When the cans of peaches were first opened, the glands in their jaws hurt excruciatingly at the sight. For this was Sunday; and they had only had one other snack since Thursday morning: no proper meal for nearly a week.

III

By now the engineers were beginning to cry out for more wood. There was no dry wood to be had, of course: but apparently once the centre donkey-furnace was going they could dry wood sufficiently by it to light the other two. The thing was now that they must have quantities of wood: for the furnaces had to be kept roaring if they were to raise any steam, and wood burnt away in no time. So everyone was kept running hither and thither for more. It was like trying to get a kettle to boil at a picnic, with only bits of paper to burn. There was plenty of spoilt stuff of all kinds in the *Archimedes,* from packing-cases in the holds to the saloon furniture: the only job was to break it up and to bring it up to the donkey-room fast enough. So all the officers hacked with axes, breaking and splitting and busting, and all the Chinamen ran with bundles of faggots—earning their blessed "cumshaws".

It is wonderful how the free busting of anything, especially valuable stuff, goes to your head. Dick grinned with pleasure as he cleft bunks into faggots. Even Mr. Buxton grinned as he chopped at the broken, mahogany turned legs of the saloon table. The Chinamen, carrying the stuff, wore broad grins. Mr. Rabb, now working as hard as anyone, was the only one who did not grin: but his axe fell with the unerring skill, and the force, of personal enmity.

Soon the donkey-room, and all spaces near it, were piled high with wood like a junk-yard. And the engineers everlastingly stoked like devils. They would have to keep it up all night, though, if they were to raise the steam to any usable pressure.

IV

Dick was on watch, that night, from twelve till four. As he climbed the bridge he noticed a change in the air: a softness.

Rain still fell in showers: but they pattered on your face delicately, refreshingly, instead of lashing your skin like dog-whips. Being (like them all) very deaf, the quiet seemed to him unnatural. The sea now had settled down to a steady, very long swell.

All was dark, except where a glow showed from the donkey-room: occasionally broken by a dark figure passing in or out. The stoking, the carrying of wood, still went on.

Visibility was not very good: the night seemed very dark, the clouds low and close, so that you could not tell the level of the horizon at all: a warm, moist, woolly night.

Suddenly the heavens opened, and a patch of brilliant starlit sky appeared. At the same time the horizon showed, stark and clear. After so long in the dark, the stars seemed to shine with an almost blinding, icy fire. Dick caught his breath in wonder: then made a dash to the chart-room to get out his sextant.

V

After a long period without sleep, a healthy young man likes to make it up by sleeping for fourteen hours or so at a stretch. But the routine of watch-keeping makes this impossible on a ship.

The older man, after five days and nights without sleep, found it very difficult to sleep at all. Captain Edwardes still did not feel himself justified in going to bed, but picked an occasional nap on his cabin sofa. Mr. MacDonald, on the other hand, made no attempt to sleep—he knew it would be hopeless. He walked about ceaselessly, talking chiefly about Chinamen and water (though not saying anything very sensible about either). The younger men, on the other hand (such as Gaston and Dick Watchett), once they were asleep, found waking after a few hours an agony: they were dragged back to consciousness as miserably as a partially drowned man is restored—wishing they had never slept at all, rather than that they should have been dragged back like that.

When a man is in that state, it is hard to say exactly when he does wake. Certainly not when he first answers you, in his bunk, in crisp tones but with his eyes closed, and not moving. Is it when he jumps out on to the floor, and, his eyes still shut, feels about for his boots? Or perhaps after he has been going about his duties for a quarter of an hour?

Dick certainly had no memory of getting out of his bunk that morning. The first thing he could remember was when he was on deck. It was a limpid and lovely morning. The sea was smooth, except for a slight, very long, very rapid swell, that passed almost faster than the eye could follow it, and gave the ship no time to rise and fall. The sky was the blue of a field of gentians: the air clear as glass, but warm: the very sea seemed washed, it sparkled so blue, so diamond-bright. The blue wood-smoke from the improvised donkey funnel floated up into the still air, and hung there, the only cloud there was, scenting all the horrible litter of the decks with its sweet smell. It was such a morning that you could hardly believe no larks would presently rise, ascending on their clear voices into the clear sky.

The voices of the woodmen in the donkey-room rose sharp but still faint; and the occasional blow of an axe.

Dick heard an order given, in a confident voice. There was a hiss, as steam-cocks were turned on: then the sudden clanging of the pumps: loud at first till the water began to rise; then steady, and slow. They were pumping out Number 6 hold. A brown and filthy stream, creamy with air-bubbles, began to cascade into the clean sea.

The pool of brown in the clear blue spread. Presently Dick noticed a queer thing: fish rising to the surface of it floating dead, their white bellies up. It was so impregnated with tobacco juice, it poisoned any fish who came near it. Imagine all that nicotine, flowing through delicate gills!

The pumps could not work for long at a time: the highest pressure of steam the wood-furnace could raise was forty pounds (roughly, the pressure in a motor-tyre); and they could not hold it long. A brief spell of work: and then a rest, while they stoked the furnace once more. Meanwhile, the brown stain in the sea faded to a yellow opaqueness. But the poisoned fish remained, floating round the *Archimedes* in hundreds, with staring eyes and fixed, gaping mouths.

Presently the pumps began their painful and poisonous vomiting once more.

It may have killed the fish, but it put wonderful new heart into the crew of the *Archimedes*: and as the level of water in the after-holds fell they sang, and worked like blazes. In their zeal they smashed for firewood even objects that were not really seriously damaged. For there were a few of these, after all, saved in a miraculous way. The bookcase in the smoking-room for instance: a flimsy affair with a glass front. It had fallen on its face on the floor, and in some unaccountable way not even the glass was broken. Yet a saloon table, I told you, had been snapped off its clamped legs. It was not as if the bookcase contained a Bible—you could not even find a superstitious reason for its being saved. It only contained ordinary literature.

Another pretty miraculous thing, when you come to think of it, was that nobody had been killed. Things had been happening all round them as lethal as an air-raid: yet there were no casualties. Not even a broken bone. Everyone, nearly, was cut and bruised, but that was all. The worst sufferer was Mr. Soutar: at one moment the heaviest midshipman had been flung on to a particularly bad bunion he had; and he had yelled with agony. He limped from it still.

VI

By sight of a star at dawn, and a solar sight later, Captain Edwardes was at last able to fix his position. Being so far from his estimated position, the calculation took him some time. And when he plotted the result in the chart, he rubbed his eyes. He was a hundred miles north of Cape Gracias: all banks passed. The storm had carried him nearly four hundred miles from the point at which it had struck him: in five days. Moreover, it had probably not taken him direct there: curving, they had probably drifted at least a hundred miles a day. An average speed of four knots—travelled, for the most part, broadside on. Of course, a speed through the water of four knots, broadside on, was hardly possible. The storm must have carried the sea along with it too. And indeed, when he examined the chart, he saw that his earlier surmise must have been true: that the sea was raised up, near the centre of the storm, in a flattish cone, with a circular motion (only slower) like that of the wind: and so they had passed safely over banks they could never have crossed if the sea had been at its normal level!

The first thing he did, of course, when he found his position, was to announce it to the *Patricia*: and when he got her reply, he was thankful. For this steam raised on wood—it was, after all, only make-believe. It enabled them to do a bit of pumping: or when in tow, perhaps it would work the steering-gear. It could work the fans: but he knew very well the fans could never get the main furnaces going, from cold, without a main funnel. It could never really enable them to raise main steam again.

Nevertheless, it had served two useful purposes. Most of them knew that yesterday, the day the storm had abandoned them, had been the most dangerous day of all. For six hours at least the ship might have sunk any minute. Without hard and hopeful work could these worn men have borne the strain? That was one thing: and there was another. They would presently have to be taken in tow by the salvage vessel: and the salvage the Owners would have to pay would in any case be very heavy. But salvage is proportional to the helplessness of the vessel salved. Captain Edwardes might save a lot off the award if the *Archimedes* had at least auxiliary steam on her.

Meanwhile the engineers continued pumping: and the Deck set about a new task. They borrowed a little steam for a winch, to haul some hawsers up on deck. They were preparing a tow-rope. For by now they were in constant communication with the *Patricia*: already acting largely under her orders. And to all other offers of assistance a general reply was sent: thanks, but it was not needed.

It was at one that midday that the *Patricia* was sighted. First her smoke above the horizon. Thereupon (since the *Archimedes'* little whiff would hardly be visible to her) Edwardes wirelessed his bearing to her: and she was soon close.

She looked like a small black steamer, rather than a tug.

She steamed right round the *Archimedes,* taking a good look at her. Well she might! I doubt if she had ever seen a vessel like the *Archimedes* floating the sea. You see vessels like the *Archimedes* lying up on a reef somewhere, sometimes: but you do not see them floating on the sea.

Then she stopped, and lowered a boat. Sixteen men climbed into it, and rowed across. It was a romantic sight, these sixteen men coming to the rescue of the stricken vessel. Captain Edwardes on the bridge counted them—sixteen. And Dick also counted them, as he stood at the rail, waiting to lower a pilot-ladder to them (for both gangways were gone). *Sixteen.*

Sixteen men! Captain Edwardes was almost too shaken to speak.

"Mr. Buxton," he said, "stand by that pilot-ladder and allow no man on board but the master only."

Buxton picked up a thick piece of wood: gave another to Dick:

"If anyone but the master tries to board us, club him back into the sea!"

Other officers joined them.

Captain Abraham was standing in the boat's sternsheets: his bowman had laid hold on the ladder.

"Keep your men in the boat, Captain," roared Edwardes from the bridge. "I allow no man on board but yourself!"

"What the hell, Captain?" Captain Abraham began. "I insist. . . ."

Then he looked up at the line of faces at the ship's rail. They were faces as ravaged as the ship herself: maniac faces. Mr. Soutar, a length of iron pipe in his hand, was even foaming at the mouth: a fleck blew from his lips and slanted into the sea, where it floated. Dick felt the rage of his companions fill him: he too was trembling with rage. All these men, to board *their* ship!

". . . Stay where you are," Captain Abraham said quietly to his men, and climbed the ladder alone.

He passed through the silent guard: who took no notice of him, their eyes never leaving for a moment the boat below: only Mr. Buxton followed him, and he climbed to the lower bridge.

There the two captains met: and shook hands.

"I congratulate you, Captain," said the stranger.

"Thank you," said Edwardes. "Come to my cabin."

So the three of them entered the captain's cabin. Captain Edwardes produced a bottle of gin from a cupboard, doing the honours as host. Each took a ceremonial sip.

After that, they talked business: signed Lloyd's contract. The destination was to be Belize, in British Honduras.

Captain Edwardes now looked sane enough: so Abraham ventured to ask him:

"Why won't you allow my men on board?"

Edwardes turned red as a colonel, his neck swelling over his collar.

"I allow no man to board without my permission."

"Why?" said Abraham bluntly. "Have you got an infectious disease on board?"

"If I refuse permission, no man on earth has a right to ask my reason!" cried Edwardes, thumping the table.

"Well, I'm in charge of salvaging this vessel, and I insist on having my men!"

"Your men can work for you on your own ship, they won't work on mine!" said Captain Edwardes.

Abraham rose to his feet. "Then I shall tear up this contract," he said.

"You can tear up your own copy if you like," said Edwardes. "But I don't tear up my copy, and you have signed it."

Captain Abraham was bewildered: simply did not know what to do. After all, *he* was responsible that the towing-line was properly fixed. His own men were experts at the job, it was their business. These lunatic scarecrows? How could he rely on them to do it? And besides, his human heart told him that what these men needed was rest, not more work.

"Captain Edwardes," he said, "do you imagine that if I use my own men it's going to affect the salvage claim?"

A flicker of Edwardes's eyes betrayed that one nail at least was hit on the head. But he answered in a strangled voice:

"I'll have you know, Captain, that anything needful on this ship my own men can do. We don't need any help from strangers to work our own ship, *thank you*—what do you think my men are? Passengers?"

This was no ordinary situation, to be dealt with by cold logic. Such high-pitched emotion could only be answered in the same key. Captain Abraham rose from his seat, moved into the centre of the cabin, and there fell on both his knees. He lifted his right hand above his head, fixed his worldly, hatchet-face in as other-worldly an expression as he could manage.

"Captain!" he said. "I swear by Almighty God, that if I have my own men on board to fix the tow it shall not affect the salvage question, not by one jot nor one tittle! Nor it don't derogate any from your crew! I swear by Almighty God that it's just the usual procedure!"

"Very well," said Captain Edwardes, a tear in his eye. "Mr. Buxton, let them come up."

It is an uncommon sight nowadays, that: to see one captain, in his uniform, kneeling in another captain's cabin.

NICHOLAS MONSARRAT

~~~~~~

The Cruel Sea

It was more than a full gale at sea; it was nearer to a great roaring battlefield, with ships blowing across it like scraps of newspaper. The convoy no longer had the shape of a convoy, and, indeed, a ship was scarcely a ship, trapped and hounded in this howling wilderness. The tumult of that southerly gale, increasing in fury from day to day, had a staggering malice from which there was no escape: it was as if each ship were some desperate fugitive, sentenced to be lynched by a mob whose movements had progressed from clumsy ill-humour to sightless rage.

Huge waves, a mile from crest to crest, roared down upon the pigmies that were to be their prey; sometimes the entire surface of the water would be blown bodily away, and any ship that stood in the path of the onslaught shook and staggered as tons of green sea smote her upper deck and raced in a torrent down her whole length. Boats were smashed, funnels were buckled, bridges and deck-houses were crushed out of shape: men disappeared overboard without trace and without a cry, sponged out of life like figures wiped from a blackboard at a single imperious stroke. Even when the green seas withheld their blows for a moment, the wind, screaming and clawing at the rigging, struck fear into every heart; for if deck-gear and canvas screens could vanish, perhaps even men could be whipped away by its furious strength. . . . For the crew of *Saltash* there was no convoy and no other ships, save their own; and she and they were caught in a mesh of fearful days and nights, which might defeat them by their sheer brutal force. Normally a good sea boat, *Saltash* had ridden out many storms and had often had strength to spare for other ships that might be in difficulties; now, entirely on her own, she laboured to stay afloat, wearily performing for hour after hour and day after day the ugly antics of a ship which refused, under the most desperate compulsion, to stand on her head.

Throughout it all the ship's relay-loudspeaker system, monotonously fed by a satirical hand, boomed out a tune called *"Someone's Rocking My Dream-Boat"*.

Each of them in the wardroom had problems of a special sort to cope with, over and above the ones they shared with the rest of the crew—the problem of eating without having food flung in their faces, of sleeping without being thrown out of their bunks, of getting warm and dry again after the misery of a four-hour watch: above all, the problem of staying unhurt.

Scott-Brown, the doctor, was kept busy with this human wreckage of the storm, treating from hour to hour the cuts, the cracked ribs, the seasickness that could exhaust a man beyond the wish to live. His worst casualty, the one which would have needed all his skill and patience, even if he had been able to deal with it in a quiet, fully-equipped operating-theatre ashore, was a man who, thrown bodily from one side of the mess-deck to the other, had landed on his knee-cap and smashed it into a dozen bloody fragments.

Johnson, the engineer officer, had a problem calling for endless watchfulness—the drunken movements of the ship, which brought her stern high out of the water with every second wave, and could set the screws racing and tearing the shaft to bits, unless the throttle were clamped down straight away.

Raikes, in charge of navigation, was confronted by a truly hopeless job. For days on end there had been no sun to shoot, no stars to be seen, no set speed to give him even a rough position: where *Saltash* had got to after five days and nights of chaos was a matter of pure guesswork, which any second-class stoker, pin in hand, could have done just as well as he. Ill-balanced on the Arctic Circle, sixty-something North by nothing West—that was the nearest he could get to it: *Saltash* lay somewhere inside these ragged limits, drifting slowly backwards within the wild triangle of Iceland, Jan Mayen Island and Norway.

The ship's organization was, as usual, Lockhart's responsibility; and the ship's organization had become a wicked sort of joke. Between decks *Saltash* was in chaos—the wardroom uninhabitable, the mess-decks a shambles: there could be no hot food, no way of drying clothes, no comfort for anyone under the ceaseless battering of the storm. Deck-gear worked loose, boats jumped their chocks and battered themselves to bits, water fell in solid tons on every part of the ship: after facing with hope a thousand dawns, Lockhart now dreaded what might meet his eye at the end of his watch, when daylight pierced the wild and lowering sky and showed him the ship again. An upper deck swept clean, a whole watch of thirty seamen vanished overboard—these were the outlines of a waking nightmare which might with a single turn of fortune come hideously true.

As *Saltash* laboured, as *Saltash* faltered and groaned, as *Saltash* found each tortured dawn no better than the last, he, along with the rest, could only endure and curse the cruel sea.

No one cursed it with more cause and with less public demonstration than Ericson, who, self-locked into one corner of the bridge, was fulfilling once more his traditional rôle of holding the whole thing together. After five days and nights of storm he was so exhausted that the feeling of exhaustion had virtually disappeared: anchored to the deck by lead-like legs and soaked seaboots, clamped to the bridge rail by weary, half-frozen arms, he seemed to have become a part of the ship herself—a fixed pair of eyes, a watchful brain welded into the fabric of *Saltash*. All the way north to Murmansk he had had to perform the mental acrobatics necessary to the control of twenty escorts and the repelling of three or four different kinds of attack: now the physical harassing of this monstrous gale was battering at his body in turn, sapping at a lifetime's endurance which had never had so testing a call made upon it, had never had to cope with an ordeal on this scale.

Assaulted by noise, bruised and punished by violent movement, thrown about endlessly, he had to watch and feel the same things happening to his ship.

The scene from the bridge of *Saltash* never lost an outline of senseless violence. By day it showed a square mile of tormented water, with huge waves flooding in like mountains sliding down the surface of the earth: with a haze of spray and spume scudding across it continually: with gulfs opening before the ship as if the whole ocean were avid to swallow her. Outlined against a livid sky, the mast plunged and rocked through a wild arc of space, flinging the aerials and the signal-halyards about as if to whip the sea for its wickedness. Night added the terrible unknown; night was pitch-black, unpierceable to the eye, inhabited by fearful noises and sudden treacherous surprises: by waves that crashed down from nowhere, by stinging spray that tore into a man's face and eyes before he could duck for shelter. Isolated in the blackness, *Saltash* suffered every violence: she pitched, she rolled, she laboured; she met the shock of a breaking wave with a jar that shook her from end to end, she dived shuddering into a deep trough, shipping tons of water with a noise like a collapsing house, and then rose with infinite slowness, infinite pain, to shoulder the mass of water aside, and shake herself free, and prepare herself for the next blow.

Ericson watched and suffered with her, and felt it all in his own body: felt especially the agony of that slow rise under the crushing weight of the sea, felt often the enormous doubt as to whether she would rise at all. Ships had foundered without trace in this sort of weather: ships could give up and lie down under punishment, just as could human beings: here, in this high corner of the world where the weather had started to scream insanely, and the sea to boil, here could be murder: here, where some of *Compass Rose's* corpses might still be wandering, here

187

he might join them, with yet another ship's company in his train. He stayed where he was on the bridge and waited for it to happen, or not to happen. He was a pair of red eyes, inflamed by wind and salt water: he was a brain, tired, fluttering, but forced into a channel of watchfulness: he was sometimes a voice, shouting to the helmsman below to prepare for another threatening blow from the sea. He was a core of fear and of control, clipped small and tight into a body he had first ill-treated, and then begun perforce to disregard.

No gale of this force could last for ever, or the very fabric of the globe would long ago have been torn to bits, and presently, as a grudging act of grace, the weather took a turn for the better. The sea was still jumbled and violent, but it was no longer on the attack: the wind still sang on a high note, but it had lost its venom: the ship still rolled and staggered, but she could at least now steer a single fixed course. There came a day when the upper deck began to dry off and a start could be made with cleaning up the shambles below: when a hot meal could be cooked and eaten in comfort: when a man could climb from the fo'c'sle to the bridge without running a gauntlet of green seas that might toss him into the scuppers or straight overboard: when the Captain could leave the bridge for more than half a watch, and sleep for more than an hour at a stretch. . . . The sun pierced the clouds for the first time for many days and set the grey water gleaming: it warmed the shoulders of their duffelcoats and sent up a small haze of steam from the drying decks. It also showed them exactly three ships in sight, over a space of a hundred square miles of ocean, which should have held fifty-four vessels in orderly convoy formation.

But perhaps that was too much to expect. . . . The process of rounding up the convoy took *Saltash* nearly forty-eight hours, steaming all the time at an average of twenty knots on a dozen different schemes of search: it was not eased by the fact that each individual escort was doing the same thing simultaneously, trying to marshal whatever merchantmen were in their immediate area, and that there were at one time six of these small convoys of half a dozen ships each all trying to attract fresh customers to the only true fold, and all steering different courses. On one occasion *Saltash,* coming across the frigate *Streamer* with five ships in company, signalled to her: "The convoy is 200 degrees, fourteen miles from you," only to receive the answer: "The convoy is here." It was, for a tired Senior Officer on the edge of irritation, a pregnant moment which Ericson longed to exploit.

But for him there could be no such delaying luxury: the crisp orders which went to *Streamer* were neither brutal nor sarcastic, simply explicit and not to be argued. They formed a pattern with all the other crisp orders of the last two days, and presently, as a result, things were under control again; presently *Saltash* could station herself at the van of what really looked something like a convoy—straggling, woefully battered, but still a body of ships which could be honestly reported to Their Lordships as Convoy R.C. 17. Ericson made this report and disposed of his escorts in their night positions and handed over to Allingham, who was officer-of-the-watch; and then, with a drugged thankfulness, he took his aching body down the ladder, in search of the shelter of his cabin, and of longed-for rest.

The weather was still wild; but with the convoy intact and the main chaos retrieved, the hours ahead seemed bearable and hopeful, and, above all, suitable for oblivion.

Then, not a mile astern of *Saltash,* a ship was torpedoed.

Ericson had just passed the first sweet margin of sleep when the alarm-bells clanged: for a moment he could not really believe that they were ringing, and then, as he felt the loathed sound drilling deep into his brain, he had such a violent upsurge of rage and disappointment that he came near to childish tears. It was too much altogether, it wasn't fair. . . . He heaved himself out of his bunk and followed the many other running feet up the ladder again, conscious only of an enormous weariness and a brain suddenly and brutally robbed of the sleep it craved. How could a man or a ship cope with this? How could they be expected to fight anything except the weather?

It seemed that they would have to: it seemed that as soon as the weather gave a foot of ground the other enemy, ready in the wings, stepped in with fresh violence, fresh treachery. The scene that greeted Ericson had a pattern made familiar by a hundred convoys: it showed the ships in station, the dusk gathering around them, the heaving sea, and then the ugly deformity which meant disaster—the single winged ship sagging away out of line, already listing mortally, already doomed. She was a small ship: she must, as a prelude to her defeat, have had to endure a special form of hell during the last week of storm. . . . Ericson looked at Allingham.

"What happened, Guns?"

"She just went, sir." The Australian accent, as usual in moments of excitement, was thick and somehow reassuring. "Fired a distress rocket about a minute ago. But how the hell could they hit her in this sort of weather?"

"M'm." Ericson grunted. The astonishing question had already occurred to him, but it was useless to speculate. Probably there was yet another new weapon: probably U-boats could now fire a torpedo vertically from the bed of the ocean and hit a ship plumb in its guts. One could think of a nice expressive name for it. But it was no use being surprised at anything in this bloody, this immensely long war. . . . "Who's the wing escort?"

"*Pergola,* sir. She's making a sweep to starboard."

Ericson grunted again. That was all that could be done at the moment: *Pergola* could sweep the suspect area, the stern escort could pick up the bits. *Saltash* could plod along at the head of the convoy, he himself could think it all out, with cutting logic, using an ice-cold brain. . . . He saw Allingham looking at him with a rough sort of compassion in his glance, taking in his inflamed eyes, half sunk in sleep, his swollen face, the twitching on his cheek-bone—all the marks of exhaustion which Ericson was aware of himself and which could not be disguised. He smiled ruefully.

"I'd just got my head down."

"Bad luck, sir." Allingham paused. "Shall I go along to the fo'c'sle, sir? Or stay up here?"

Ericson smiled again, acknowledging the line of thought. "You go down, Guns. I've got the ship."

When he had gone there was silence among the men now gathered at Action Stations on the bridge. Ericson watched the convoy, Lockhart watched the sinking ship, Holt and the signalmen watched *Pergola,* the look-outs watched their appointed arcs, the bridge-messenger watched Ericson. It was a closed circle, of men in danger doing nothing at a moment when active movement would have been a relief, carried in a ship which might herself be doing the wrong thing for want of a single clue. When Ericson said, suddenly and aloud: "We'll wait," it was as much to bridge the dubious pause in his own mind as to inform the men round him.

But the pause was not long. There was an exclamation from Holt, the midshipman, and then he said excitedly:

"*Pergola's* got a signal hoisted!" He stared through his glasses at the corvette, rooting away to starboard like a questing terrier. "Large flag, sir."

The yeoman of signals called out: "*Pergola* in contact, sir."

I wonder, thought Ericson; but he did not say it aloud. *Pergola,* young and enthusiastic, was always ready to depth-charge anything, from a clump of sea-weed to a shoal of sardines, but he did not want to discourage her. Depth-charges were cheap, ships and men were not. . . . Now all of them, save the stolid lookouts dedicated to their arc of vision, turned to watch *Pergola.* Three miles to starboard, she was steering obliquely away from the convoy: she was rolling and pitching drunkenly, and her increased speed sent the spray in great clouds over her bridge. Steaming full ahead, thought Ericson appraisingly: she must be going to drop some for luck. And as he thought it, and wished that *Saltash* might have an excuse for doing the same, another flag fluttered up to *Pergola's* cross-trees, and the yeoman of signals called out:

"*Pergola* attacking, sir."

Now they all watched with increased attention, wondering how good the asdic contact was, knowing with professional insight just how difficult it must be for *Pergola* to get her depth-charges cleared away and ready for dropping while steaming full ahead in this immensely troubled sea. *Compass Rose* used to do this sort of thing, thought Lockhart, as *Pergola* gave an especially vicious lurch and shipped a green sea on her quarter: *Compass Rose* used to sweep into action balanced inelegantly on one ear and one leg, while poor old Ferraby danced a jig round the depth-charge rails as he tried to get his charges ready, with a bunch of ham-handed stokers to help him and plenty of caustic comment from the bridge. It was nice to have graduated from corvettes. . . . Lockhart watched *Pergola* reminiscently: Holt and the signal-men watched her with a professional eye to her signals: below on the plotting-table Raikes, the navigator, watched her with the searching beam of the radar set, and Ericson watched her with a proprietary interest. For him she was simply an extension of his own armament, a probing steel finger sent out from *Saltash* to find and hit the enemy. The torpedoed ship had been his, and *Pergola* was his, too: if the one balanced the account of the other it would not be so bad, it would justify the escort-screen, it would appease the sense of failure that nagged his tired brain. It would let him sleep once more.

Pergola went in like an express train somehow diverted on to a switch-back railway. They saw her charges go down, they saw her sweep round to port as soon as they were dropped: then after a few moments the huge columns of grey-green water were tossed into the air by the explosion. When the spray settled they waited again, their glasses trained on the place of execution; but the surface of the sea was innocent, the expected black shape did not appear. *Pergola,* now at half-speed, headed back towards the explosion area uncertainly, like a small boy who has made far too much noise in his mother's drawing-room and wishes he were safely and anonymously back in the nursery. There was a pause and then a third flag went up from her bridge.

"From *Pergola,* sir," said the yeoman of signals promptly. "'Lost contact.'"

"Call her up," said Ericson. "Make: 'Continue to search your area. Report nature of original contact.'"

The lamps flickered between the two ships.

"Contact was firm, moving left, classified as U-boat," came *Pergola's* answer.

"What is your estimate now?" was Ericson's next signal.

"I still think it was a U-boat," said *Pergola* manfully. Then she added, as if with an ingenuous smile: "It was where a U-boat ought to have been."

Now there, thought Ericson, there I agree with you. The attack had certainly come from that side, the U-boat would naturally have tried to move away to starboard, she would have been steering the course that *Pergola* indicated; she might well have been just about where *Pergola* had dropped her depth-charges. That being so, it was worth while *Pergola* staying where she was and continuing the hunt: in fact, he thought, with sudden vehemence, it was worth while staying there himself and organizing the hunt on a two-ship basis. He would be taking a chance if he detached two escorts from the screen; but it was very unlikely that the U-boat was one of a pack: in this weather the convoy could only have been sighted by chance from close to, and there would have been no time to assemble other craft for a concerted attack. She was, therefore, a lone wolf, sinking her fangs once, swiftly, and then slinking off into the forest again. Lone wolves of this sort deserved special attention, special treatment. The chance was worth taking.

The pattern of action emerged new-minted from his brain, as if, however tired he were, he had only to press a button marked "Detach two escorts for independent search" in order to produce a typed schedule of operational orders. The necessary directions were dictated in a smooth series which kept all three signalmen busy at the same time. Signals went to the Admiralty and the commodore of the convoy, to tell them what was happening: to *Harmer,* to take over as Senior Officer: to *Pergola,* to continue her search until *Saltash* joined her: to *Rose Arbour,* to take *Pergola's* place on the screen: to *Streamer,* to dispatch the sinking merchantman by gun-fire, and then rejoin: and to the other escorts, to station themselves according to the new diagram. Then Ericson summoned Lockhart and Johnson, the engineer-officer, to the bridge to explain what he proposed to do: he conferred, lengthily and technically, with Raikes at the plotting-table; and then he took *Saltash* round in a wide sweep to starboard, and, coming up on *Pergola's* quarter, started sending a final long signal, beginning: "We will organize our search in accordance with two alternative possibilities."

Lockhart had never admired the Captain more than during the twelve hours that followed. In the end, he thought, for all these new machines and scientific stuff, war depends on men. . . . He knew that Ericson must have been desperately tired even before the new crisis arrived: if the exacting trip north-bound to Murmansk and the last five days of battering weather did not suggest it, then his grey, lined face and humped shoulders supplied a reliable clue. And yet there was in all his actions, both now and during the subsequent long, intricate and determined hunt for the submarine, no trace of tiredness or of readiness to compromise: he rose to the moment and kept at the required pitch of alertness, as if he had come to the task fresh from a six weeks' holiday; and the result, in addition to being a remarkable physical effort, was, in the realm of submarine detection, a tactical masterpiece as well.

Ericson must have been very sure, thought Lockhart, that the submarine was there and that *Pergola*—the happy-go-lucky *Pergola*—had for once been on the right track and might well have damaged her: he must have conquered his tiredness with this knowledge that the quarry was immediately to hand. For it was not enough to keep in mind that a ship had been sunk and men killed in the process: that was a commonplace of the Atlantic and the revengeful energy it bred soon petered out. It was the professional sense which was now the mainspring of every sustained effort of will: the feeling, present all the time, that senior officers of escorts were specifically hired to sink U-boats and that for this reason U-boats must never be allowed to go to waste.

Certainly Ericson clung on to his quarry, or the hope of it, as if he would have been personally ashamed to forfeit the chance of a kill. . . . It was six o'clock in the evening when *Saltash* and *Pergola* separated to start their different schemes of search: it was midnight before any results rewarded either of them. Earlier, down in *Saltash's* plotting-room, Ericson and Raikes had made a detailed appreciation of the prospects, involving three different suppositions. Firstly, the U-boat might have been slightly damaged by *Pergola's* attack, in which case she would dive deep and stay there, in the hope of fooling the pursuit and patching herself up in the meantime. Alternatively, she might have been badly damaged and would need to start creeping for the shelter of the nearest home-port as soon as she could. Lastly, she might have escaped damage altogether—or have been outside the area of attack in the first place: she would then probably decide, after the initial scare, to follow the convoy at a distance and come in for a second helping later that night. There were variations latent in all these possibilities, but thus the broad outlines had confronted Ericson as he started his reasoned, highly technical guesswork on the plotting-table.

The last possibility—that the U-boat would continue to follow the convoy—was something which *Saltash* must now disregard if the U-boat were going to try again, *Harmer* and the rest of the escort-screen must cope with it themselves. That left the other two alternatives: the lurking in the deep or the immediate creep for home. Lurking meant for the hunting escort a long and patient period of waiting up above: it might involve circling the area slowly for as long as twenty-four hours, all the time on the alert for any sign of a break-out. If, on the other hand, the U-boat had already started for home, the journey might be eastwards towards Norway, or south-east to the German coast, or due south to one of the Biscay ports: it meant, in any case, a rapidly extending range of search, becoming more like a needle-in-the-haystack proposition with every hour that passed.

Of the two, Ericson finally chose for himself the patient, stalking wait above the spot where the U-boat ought to be: it was the one he thought most likely, and *Saltash's* superior asdic and radar would give her a decided advantage if the U-boat tried to run for it. The other—the cast for home, in an ever-widening arc—was a somewhat forlorn venture: in assigning it to *Pergola*, he tried not to feel that he was giving the junior ship a dubious chance of distinguishing herself. . . . Something of the sort must have occurred to the irrepressible *Pergola*, who, on taking her leave, signalled:

"Don't forget it was originally my bird."

Ericson, hovering between the alternative answers, "We'll go fifty-fifty on the medals" and "Confine your signals to essential traffic," finally sent none at all. All that he really wanted to say to *Pergola*, as she drew away and the darkness thickened between them, was that she carried his blessings with her. But there was really no official version of this.

The next six hours had not the smallest excitement for anyone aboard *Saltash*: they had, in fact, a deadly sameness, an unrewarding monotony, the hardest thing of all for tired men to support. Ericson remained on the bridge the whole time, hunched in his chair, wide awake, while *Saltash* quartered the suspect area at half-speed; for hour after hour her asdic recorded nothing at all and her radar simply the diminishing speck of light which was *Pergola* sweeping deeper and deeper to the south-east. Ericson ate a scratch meal at eight o'clock: relays of cocoa reached him at hourly intervals: the moon came up and then left them again: the sea flattened as the wind died. It was cold: the cold attacked not only the body, it chilled the mind as well, so that to keep alert, to believe that what one was doing was right, became more and more difficult.

At times Ericson's thoughts wandered so far that the effort to bring them back was like a physical ordeal, a cruel tug on some stretched sinew of the brain. I am very tired, he thought: I have this pain of tiredness in my legs and across my shoulders and under my heart: that thing inside my head is starting to flutter again. This search may go on for hours, this search may go on for ever: we are probably doing the wrong thing, we have probably guessed wrong in every respect from the very beginning: there was probably a pack of six or eight U-boats in this area all the time, and they are preparing to fall upon the convoy at this moment, while we fool about fifty miles astern of it. I have weakened the escort-screen at this crucial time, I have taken away two ships out of eight, I have been, by one quarter, unforgivably stupid and rash, I am ripe for a court-martial. . . . The asdic pinged away like a nagging insect: the tick-tick of the motor on the plotting-table reached Ericson continually up the voice-pipe, like some infernal metronome, reminding him that everything he did was out of joint. The hours crept past and the change of course, which came every fifteen minutes, seemed a futile break in a pattern already futile.

Now and again he spoke to Raikes, the navigator, who had the first watch; and Raikes answered him quietly, unhurriedly, without turning from his place at the front of the bridge. But these exchanges never contained what Ericson really wanted to say, and never what he wanted to hear either: they simply featured a comment on the weather, a query about the distance run, a neutral remark on any neutral subject that occurred to him. For his own comfort, his own hunger, he wanted to say: do you think we are right, do you think we are wasting our time: is the U-boat here at all or have I, in diluting the escort-screen by a quarter, made what may turn out to be a murderous mistake? But none of these were captain's questions and so they remained unasked, prisoners in the brain; while *Saltash* covered the same square of ocean once every hour and *Pergola* gradually faded out of range, and the black and empty sea, deserted even by the moon, offered to *Saltash* only a cold, derisive hissing as she passed.

But the change of watch at midnight marked a change of fortune as well; Allingham and Vincent had hardly taken over from Raikes—indeed, Raikes was still writing up his meagre entry in the deck-log—when the pattern of the night quickly flowered in the only way that could bring any pleasure to the senses. The asdic repeater, which could be heard all over the bridge and which had been sounding an identical, damnable note for six hours on end, suddenly produced an astonishing variation—a solid echo, an iron contact in a featureless ocean. . . . Ericson jumped when he heard it, as did everyone else within earshot: the bridge sprang to life as if the darkness had become charged with an electric fervour that reached them all instantly.

"Sir!" began Allingham.

"Bridge!" called the asdic rating.

"Captain, sir!" said the yeoman of signals.

"All right," said Ericson, slipping down off his chair. "I heard it. . . . What a nice noise. . . . Hold on to it. . . . Sound Action Stations. . . . Yeoman!"

"Sir?" said the yeoman of signals.

"Make to *Pergola*: 'Return to me with all dispatch.'"

That's a guess, he thought as he said it—but the echo, loud and clear, confirmed him in the belief that this, the blank stretch of ocean which had suddenly blossomed, was now the place for all available hunting escorts to be. Only U-boats sounded like that, only U-boats could produce that beautiful metallic ring; and this U-boat, which had struck once and then lain in hiding for so long, must now be finally cornered. It would take *Pergola* over two hours to get back from her search, even "with all dispatch"—the Navy's most urgent order; but she deserved to be in at the kill, and she could play a useful supporting rôle if the U-boat were elusive. . . . The asdic echo sharpened: Lockhart, now

stationed on the set, called out: "Target moving slowly right":
Vincent, from aft, reported his depth-charges ready: *Saltash*
began to tremble as the revolutions mounted and the range
shortened down to striking distance.

But this was to be no swift kill: perhaps, indeed, it was to be
no kill at all. During the next hour *Saltash* dropped a total of
sixty-eight depth-charges without apparently the slightest effect:
the echo remained constant, the U-boat still twisted and turned
and doubled back with limitless cunning. It seemed as if no
attack, however carefully calculated, was sufficiently accurate
to bring her up short; they might have been launching snowballs
into the fire, they might have been dropping cotton-wool bombs
on the nursery floor, for all the difference their efforts made.
Time and again *Saltash* swept in for the assault: the depth-
charges went down, the surface of the sea leapt and boiled astern
of her; but when she came round again in a tight circle she found
that her searchlight still shone on a blank sea, and presently she
would pick up the contact again—always there, always solid, but
never to be grasped, and seemingly unaffected by the fury of the
attack. Sixty-eight depth-charges, thought Ericson wearily: most
of them had been pretty close: the men down there in the U-
boat must be going through hell: why doesn't something happen,
why doesn't it *work* . . . ? He shaped up for yet another attack,
on a contact which was as firm as ever, and then he suddenly
lifted his head and sniffed.

"Number One!" he called out.

"Sir?" said Lockhart.

"Smell anything?"

After a pause: "Yes—oil," said Lockhart.

Oil. The hateful smell, which to them had always meant a
sinking ship, could now mean a sinking U-boat instead . . .
Ericson, walking to the wing of the bridge, sniffed violently again
and the smell of oil came thick and strong to his nostrils: taken
at its face-value, it meant damage, it meant, at least, a crushed
and leaking bulkhead inside the U-boat, and it could mean total

success. He ordered the searchlight to be trained right ahead, and there, where they had dropped their last charges, they presently saw the patch of oil—glistening, sluggish, reflecting the light most prettily, and spreading outwards in a heartening circle. They dropped another pattern of depth-charges as they rode over the area, and then, as they turned in again, the asdic failed, and Lockhart reported: "Lost contact."

The silence that fell on the bridge seemed to be a self-congratulatory one, but it was not so for Ericson. He would have liked to believe in that patch of oil and that fading contact, which everyone else took to be the U-boat slowly sinking beneath the beam of the asdic; but he suddenly found that he could not believe it. Oil, for his private satisfaction, was not nearly enough: he wanted wreckage, woodwork, an underwater explosion, bits of men weaving gently to the surface. Oil could come from a minor leak, oil could even be a subterfuge; the U-boat might have released some on purpose and then crept away, leaving the feeble English sailors to celebrate their skill in feeble English beer. Oil, like wine, could be a mocker. . . . She has gone deep again, he thought, with sudden, illogical conviction: maybe she is damaged, but she is not yet done to death: she will wait and then come up again. We will wait, too, he told himself grimly, with a new access of determination which must have come from the very core of his brain; and then, aloud to Lockhart, he called out:

"Carry out lost-contact procedure. I'm going to go on with the attack."

To his tautened nerves it seemed as if the bridge-personnel, and indeed the whole tired ship, had sighed as he said the words. I do not care how sick of it you are, he said, almost aloud, instantly angry: if I am the last man to keep awake in this ship, if I am the last man left alive, I will still drive her, and you, and myself for just as long as I want to. But no one had sighed, and no one had spoken, save Lockhart, who repeated: "Lost-contact procedure" to his asdic operator; and *Saltash,* settling down to her steady half-speed progress, began again her interminable search, as if the past six hours now counted for nothing and they were starting again from the beginning.

The trouble was that, ludicrously, there was nothing to start on. For the second time the U-boat, with her leak or her oil-decoy, with her shaken or exultant crew, with her dubious amount of damage, had vanished.

Surveying the fact dispassionately, Ericson found it hard to believe: continuing to survey it, his dispassion gave way to the beginnings of a blind rage. When Lockhart had reported "Lost contact", he imagined that it was because of the disturbed state of the water, and that they would pick the U-boat up again in a matter of minutes, as had happened before; but when those minutes went by, and added up to five, and then ten, and then twenty, without a single trace of an echo on the asdic, he found himself face to face with the fact that they might have lost her. After seven hours of trying, after nearly eighty depth-charges, after this enormous and sustained effort which was eating into the last reserves of his endurance. . . . He stood over the two operators at the asdic set, and looked down at the backs of their stupid, doltish heads, and wanted above all else to take a revolver from the rack and put a bullet through the pair of them. *This could not happen to him*—the U-boat was *there*—they had had her almost in their hands, and now Lockhart and his two bloody fools of operators and his rotten set had let her slip away again. . . . When Lockhart reported, for the tenth time: "No contact," and added: "She could have been sunk, don't you think, sir?" Ericson, with a spurt of anger, answered: "I wish to Christ you'd mind your own business and get on with your job!" and strode out of the asdic-compartment as if he could bear the infected air no longer.

But: I should not have said that, he thought immediately, leaning against the front of the bridge: it comes of being tired, it comes of losing the U-boat when we were so close. . . . He turned round.

"Number One!"

Lockhart came out of the asdic-hut and walked towards him in the darkness. "Sir?" he said, with extreme formality.

"Sorry I said that," grunted Ericson. "Forget it."

"That's all right, sir," said Lockhart, who could rarely resist an apology and certainly not one so promptly offered.

"I don't think she was sunk," went on Ericson. "Not enough evidence for it."

"No, sir," answered Lockhart. He did not agree, but this was not the moment to say so.

"I'm going back to that square search again. We'll keep at Action Stations."

"Aye, aye, sir."

Not Action Stations, but sleep, thought Lockhart, returning to the set: that's what I want, that's what he wants, that's what we all want: and we're none of us going to get it, because the obstinate old bastard won't listen to reason. . . . He was quite sure, as was his leading asdic-rating, that the U-boat had been destroyed, crushed or battered to bits by the cumulative effect of seventy or eighty near-misses: she had probably collapsed and was going down slowly, leaving that trail of oil which had so cheered him when he caught sight of it. But, since it seemed that the slightest hint to this effect was enough to start a riot, it was better to carry on without comment. . . . He shut the door of the asdic-compartment and said in a non-committal voice:

"Normal sweep. We're doing a box search again."

The senior rating on the set repeated: "Normal sweep, sir," and then sucked his teeth in unmistakable reproach.

"Don't make that filthy noise!" snapped Lockhart. "Without comment" covered that sort of thing as well.

"Hollow tooth, sir," said the man rebelliously.

"Get on with your work."

The rating, now breathing heavily, bent over the set and made an adjustment to it, as noisily as he could. They were all of them a bit short-tempered, thought Lockhart: it's catching, it's an inevitable product of tiredness. He smiled to himself as he looked at the asdic-rating, who was normally one of his favourites: he could have quoted with reasonable accuracy most of the thoughts and phrases that were going through the man's head. (*All you get is threats and abuse. . . . The skipper gives him a rocket and he passes it on to me. . . . Bloody officers. . . . Roll on my twelve. . . .*) With just enough friendliness in his voice to bring things back to normal without surrendering his point, Lockhart said:

"We'd better have another brew of cocoa. This is going to take a long time."

It took a very long time indeed; and as the hours went by, without change, without significance, it began to seem as if the futile hunt might well continue to the end of time itself—or until, for some reason unrelated to their private effort, the war came to a finish, one side was declared the winner and the other not, and *Saltash,* receiving a postcard about the result, would be able to set course for home in reasonable time to claim her old-age pension. . . . *Pergola* joined them at three o'clock, coming up from the south-east at a speed which seemed to spurn the wasted hours of her diversion: her arrival enabled Ericson to extend the scope of the search, to guard the back door as well as the front, but she was no more successful than *Saltash* in picking up the scent again. The watch changed at four, the sky began to lighten from the eastwards, illuminating a sea as grey and flat and worthless as a washed-out water-colour: it showed also the two ships, five miles apart, seemingly intent but scarcely convincing—in fact, plodding to and fro like a couple of myopic old women making the rounds of the dust-bins, not knowing that these had been emptied hours before.

To Ericson the dawn, and the outlines of his ship, and the grey faces of the men on the bridge brought a sudden bleak doubt. He could be wrong, he could be wasting his time, for two reasons which now began to appeal irresistibly: the U-boat might be many miles away or she might have been sunk by their original attack. At this, the lowest hour dividing night and day, when *Saltash* had been hunting for eleven hours on end, and he himself had been on the bridge the entire time, he was assailed by the most wretched sense of futility he had ever known; the temptation to call the thing off, to take the oil patch at its face value and claim a victory which no one would seriously deny them—this nagged at him like a cat mewing endlessly outside a door, his own door, which, sooner or later, he would have to open. It would stop the noise; it would please the neighbours. And it would bring, for his own relief, the prospect of sleep. . . .

He was aware that all round him were men who had long ago made up their minds on these very lines: that Lockhart thought the U-boat had been sunk, that the hard-driven asdic operators were sulky and sullen for the same reason; that *Pergola*, reading the report he had given her, to bring her up to date when she arrived, must have wondered why on earth they had not packed up and joined the convoy hours before, signalling a definite kill to the Admiralty as they did so.

The doubt and uncertainty increased his weariness: slumping in his chair, with nothing to break the monotony and no glimmer of success to sustain him, he found himself in mortal fear of falling asleep. He felt his whole brain and body being lulled into a delicious weary doze by the sounds round him—the noise of the asdic, the slice-slice of *Saltash's* bow wave, the men washing down the upper deck: even the movement each half hour, as the look-outs changed and the helmsman was relieved, could be strung together as part of the same sleep-inducing chain. To resist it was agony, not to resist it gave him a feeling of sick foreboding: if he stayed awake he would begin to weep, if he slept he would fall off his chair, and then they would all think he was cracking up, and it would be true. . . .

Lockhart, who now had the watch, came out of the asdic-hut for the twentieth time and said:

"Nothing on the recorder, sir."

Involuntarily Ericson's nerves began to jump. "What about it?"

Lockhart stared. "Nothing, sir. Routine report. It's the end of another sweep."

"What do you mean, *another* sweep?"

Lockhart swallowed, as he had had to do many times during the past twelve hours. "I thought you said, sir——"

"Jesus Christ, Number One——" began Ericson, and then stopped. His heart was thudding, his brain felt like a box with a little bird fluttering about inside it. He thought: this won't do at all—I really will crack up, I'll be shooting somebody in a minute. . . . He stood up and flexed his shoulders, sharpening and then easing the pain that lay across them. His head swam with the effort. But he knew now what he had to do next.

Two minutes later, down in his cabin, he confronted Scott-Brown, the doctor. The latter, routed out of his sleep as a matter of urgency by a startled bridge-messenger, was dressed in a pair of pyjama trousers and an inflated life-belt; he still maintained, unimpaired, his Harley Street air of complete dependability. He took one look at the Captain and said, in a tone of reproof which Ericson did not mind:

"Time you turned in, sir."

"I know, doc. But I can't."

"How long have you been up on the bridge?"

"Since that ship went down."

"It's too long."

"I know," repeated Ericson. "But I've got to stay there. Can you fix me up with something?"

Scott-Brown frowned at him. "Is it necessary? What's this all about?"

Ericson flared: "Christ, don't *you* start——" And then, his heart thudding again, he sat down suddenly. "There's a U-boat here," he said quietly, trying to conserve every effort, every urge of feeling. "I know damned well there is, and I'm going to get her. I want something to keep me awake while I'm doing it."

"How long for?"

"Another night, maybe. . . . Can you do it?"

"Oh, I can do it all right. It's just a question of——"

Ericson's nerves were starting to jump again. "Well, do it then," he interrupted roughly. "What does it involve? An injection?"

Scott-Brown smiled, recognizing the point where medical prudence succumbed to the lash of discipline. "Just a pill or two. Benzedrine. You'll feel like a spring lamb."

"How long will it last?"

"We'll start with twenty-four hours." The doctor smiled again, turning for the door. "After that you'll go out like a light and wake up with the hell of a hangover."

"Is that all?"

"Probably. How old are you, sir?"

"Forty-eight."

Scott-Brown wrinkled his nose. "Benzedrine isn't a thing to play with, you know."

"I wasn't intending to make a habit of it," said Ericson sourly. "This is a special occasion."

Another two minutes and Scott-Brown was back again with two grey pills and a glass of water. Ericson had disposed of the first one and had the second poised on his tongue, when the bell at the head of his bunk began to ring.

He bent to the voice-pipe, swallowing as he did so, and called out:

"Captain."

"Bridge, sir!" came Lockhart's voice, off-key with excitement. "*Pergola's* got a contact."

He felt like saying, "I told you so," he felt like shouting, "Nuts to all of you. . . ." He caught Scott-Brown's eye, expectant, slightly amused. He said, "Thanks, doc.," and started for the door. Behind him the doctor said: "In theory you ought to lie down for ten minutes, and then——" and then the measured voice was lost as he turned the corner of the passage-way and began to race up the bridge-ladder.

Whether it was the benzedrine or the feeling of eleventh-hour reprieve, or *Pergola's* activity, or the heartening effect of full daylight, he felt like a king when he stood on the bridge again and looked round him. Now it was a different sort of scene. . . . Five miles away across the flat sea *Pergola* was turning under full helm and at full speed: the water creamed at her bow as, coming obliquely towards *Saltash,* she roared in for her attack. She flew the two flags, which meant: "I have an under-water contact" and "I am attacking": she looked everything that a corvette, viewed at dawn, after a long and exhausting night, should look. . . . Ericson called to Lockhart in the asdic-hut: "Have you got anything?" and then there was a pause, and Lockhart answered suddenly: "In contact—starboard bow—bearing one-nine-oh!" and the asdic-repeater began to produce a loud, clear, singing echo on a cross-bearing, which could only be the U-boat which *Pergola* was attacking.

Pergola's charges exploded half a mile ahead of them: *Saltash,* weaving in at right angles to complete a lethal tapestry, dropped her own not more than twenty yards from the discoloured, still-frothing patch of water. Then the two ships turned together, heading back towards the fatal area, ready to do it all again, but this time there was no need. There came a sudden dull, under-water explosion, clearly audible all over the ship: a great gout of oily water burst upwards from the heart of the sea and it was followed by other things—bits of wood, bits of clothing, bits of things which might later need a very close analysis. . . . Ericson called for "Stop engines" and *Saltash* came to a standstill, surrounded now by a bloody chaplet of wreckage; the crew crowded to the rails, the curious debris thickened and spread, a working party aft got busy with buckets and grappling hooks. This was a victory which called for trophies. . . . It took us twelve hours, thought Ericson, leaning against the front of the bridge, hugely exultant, but we did it; she *was* there all the time. I was right. . . . He turned and caught Lockhart's eye—Lockhart, whose last attack must have been accurate to within five yards—and Lockhart smiled ruefully and said: "Sorry, sir!" to cover the past night of disbelief and the bad judgment which had prompted it. But it did not matter now, and Ericson sat down in his chair, himself sorry for only one thing—the benzedrine which he need not have taken, which he should have saved for a really exhausting occasion. . . .

The bell rang from the quarter-deck aft and Vincent said, in the voice of a man facing grisly reality rather too early in the morning:

"We've got lots of woodwork, sir, and some clothes, and some other things as well. Two buckets full."

"What other things, Sub?"

After a pause: "The doctor says, sir, they're clearly in his department."

WILLIAM GOLDING

~~~~~~

Pincher Martin

He was struggling in every direction, he was the centre of the writhing and kicking knot of his own body. There was no up or down, no light and no air. He felt his mouth open of itself and the shrieked word burst out.

"Help!"

When the air had gone with the shriek, water came in to fill its place—burning water, hard in the throat and mouth as stones that hurt. He hutched his body towards the place where air had been but now it was gone and there was nothing but black, choking welter. His body let loose its panic and his mouth strained open till the hinges of his jaw hurt. Water thrust in, down, without mercy. Air came with it for a moment so that he fought in what might have been the right direction. But water reclaimed him and spun so that knowledge of where the air might be was erased completely. Turbines were screaming in his ears and green sparks flew out from the centre like tracer. There was a piston engine too, racing out of gear and making the whole universe shake. Then for a moment there was air like a cold mask against his face and he bit into it. Air and water mixed, dragged down into his body like gravel. Muscles, nerves and blood, struggling lungs, a machine in the head, they worked for one moment in an ancient pattern. The lumps of hard water jerked in the gullet, the lips came together and parted, the tongue arched, the brain lit a neon track.

"Moth——"

But the man lay suspended behind the whole commotion, detached from his jerking body. The luminous pictures that were shuffled before him were drenched in light but he paid no attention to them. Could he have controlled the nerves of his face, or could a face have been fashioned to fit the attitude of his consciousness where it lay suspended between life and death, that face would have worn a snarl. But the real jaw was contorted down and distant, the mouth was slopped full. The green tracer that flew from the centre began to spin into a disc. The throat at such a distance from the snarling man vomited water and drew in again. The hard lumps of water no longer hurt. There was a kind of truce, observation of the body. There was no face but there was a snarl.

A picture steadied and the man regarded it. He had not seen such a thing for so many years that the snarl became curious and lost a little intensity. It examined the picture.

The jam jar was standing on a table, brightly lit from O.P. It might have been a huge jar in the centre of a stage or a small one almost touching the face, but it was interesting because one could see into a little world there which was quite separate but which one could control. The jar was nearly full of clear water and a tiny glass figure floated upright in it. The top of the jar was covered with a thin membrane—white rubber. He watched the jar without moving or thinking while his distant body stilled itself and relaxed. The pleasure of the jar lay in the fact that the little glass figure was so delicately balanced between opposing forces. Lay a finger on the membrane and you would compress the air below it which in turn would press more strongly on the water. Then the water would force itself farther up the little tube in the figure, and it would begin to sink. By varying the pressure on the membrane you could do anything you liked with the glass figure which was wholly in your power. You could mutter,—sink now! And down it would go, down, down; you could steady it and relent. You could let it struggle towards the surface, give it almost a bit of air then send it steadily, slowly, remorselessly down and down.

The delicate balance of the glass figure related itself to his body. In a moment of wordless realization he saw himself touching the surface of the sea with just such a dangerous stability, poised between floating and going down. The snarl thought words to itself. They were not articulate, but they were there in a luminous way as a realization.

Of course. My lifebelt.

It was bound by the tapes under that arm and that. The tapes went over the shoulders—and now he could even feel them—went round the chest and were fastened in front under the oilskin and duffel. It was almost deflated as recommended by the authorities because a tightly blown-up belt might burst when you hit the water. Swim away from the ship then blow up your belt.

With the realization of the lifebelt a flood of connected images came back—the varnished board on which the instructions were displayed, pictures of the lifebelt itself with the tube and metal tit threaded through the tapes. Suddenly he knew who he was and where he was. He was lying suspended in the water like the glass figure; he was not struggling but limp. A swell was washing regularly over his head.

His mouth slopped full and he choked. Flashes of tracer cut the darkness. He felt a weight pulling him down. The snarl came back with a picture of heavy seaboots and he began to move his legs. He got one toe over the other and shoved but the boot would not come off. He gathered himself and there were his hands far off but serviceable. He shut his mouth and performed a grim acrobatic in the water while the tracer flashed. He felt his heart thumping and for a while it was the only point of reference in the formless darkness. He got his right leg across his left thigh and heaved with sodden hands. The seaboot slipped down his calf and he kicked it free. Once the rubber top had left his toes he felt it touch him once and then it was gone utterly. He forced his left leg up, wrestled with the second boot and got it free. Both boots had left him. He let his body uncoil and lie limply.

His mouth was clever. It opened and shut for the air and against the water. His body understood too. Every now and then it would clench its stomach into a hard knot and sea water would burst out over his tongue. He began to be frightened again—not with animal panic but with deep fear of death in isolation and long drawn out. The snarl came back but now it had a face to use and air for the throat. There was something meaningful behind the snarl which would not waste the air on noises. There was a purpose which had not yet had time and experience to discover how relentless it was. It could not use the mechanism for regular breathing but it took air in gulps between the moments of burial.

He began to think in gulps as he swallowed the air. He remembered his hands again and there they were in the darkness, far away. He brought them in and began to fumble at the hard stuff of his oilskin. The button hurt and would hardly be persuaded to go through the hole. He slipped the loop off the toggle of his duffel. Lying with little movement of his body he found that the sea ignored him, treated him as a glass figure of a sailor or as a log that was almost ready to sink but would last a few moments yet. The air was regularly in attendance between the passage of the swells.

He got the rubber tube and drew it through the tapes. He could feel the slack and uninflated rubber that was so nearly not holding him up. He got the tit of the tube between his teeth and unscrewed with two fingers while the others sealed the tube. He won a little air from between swells and puffed it through the rubber tube. For uncounted numbers of swell and hollow he taxed the air that might have gone into his lungs until his heart was staggering in his body like a wounded man and the green tracer was flickering and spinning. The lifebelt began to firm up against his chest but so slowly that he could not tell when the change came. Then abruptly the swells were washing over his shoulders and the repeated burial beneath them had become a wet and splashing slap in the face. He found he had no need to play catch-as-catch-can for air. He blew deeply and regularly into the tube until the lifebelt rose and strained at his clothing. Yet he did not stop blowing at once. He played with the air, letting a little out and then blowing again as if frightened of stopping the one positive action he could take to help himself. His head and neck and shoulders were out of the water now for long intervals. They were colder than the rest of his body. The air stiffened them. They began to shake.

He took his mouth from the tube.

"Help! Help!"

The air escaped from the tube and he struggled with it. He twisted the tit until the air was safe. He stopped shouting and strained his eyes to see through the darkness but it lay right against his eyeballs. He put his hand before his eyes and saw nothing. Immediately the terror of blindness added itself to the terror of isolation and drowning. He began to make vague climbing motions in the water.

"Help! Is there anybody there? Help! Survivor!"

He lay shaking for a while and listened for an answer but the only sound was the hissing and puddling of the water as it washed round him. His head fell forward.

He licked salt water off his lips.

"Exercise."

He began to tread water gently. His mouth mumbled.

"Why did I take my sea boots off? I'm no better off than I was." His head nodded forward again.

"Cold. Mustn't get too cold. If I had those boots I could put them on and then take them off and then put them on——"

He thought suddenly of the boots sinking through water towards a bottom that was still perhaps a mile remote from them. With that, the whole wet immensity seemed to squeeze his body as though he were sunk to a great depth. His chattering teeth came together and the flesh of his face twisted. He arched in the water, drawing his feet up away from the depth, the slopping, glutinous welter.

"Help! Help——"

He began to thresh with his hands and force his body round. He stared at the darkness as he turned but there was nothing to tell him when he had completed the circle and everywhere the darkness was grainless and alike. There was no wreckage, no sinking hull, no struggling survivors but himself, there was only darkness lying close against the balls of the eyes. There was the movement of water.

He began to cry out for the others, for anyone.

"Nat! Nathaniel! For Christ's sake! Nathaniel! Help!"

His voice died and his face untwisted. He lay slackly in his lifebelt, allowing the swell to do what it would. His teeth were chattering again and sometimes this vibration would spread till it included his whole body. His legs below him were not cold so much as pressed, squeezed mercilessly by the sea so that the feeling in them was not a response to temperature but to weight that would crush and burst them. He searched for a place to put his hands but there was nowhere that kept the ache out of them. The back of his neck began to hurt and that not gradually but with a sudden stab of pain so that holding his chin away from his chest was impossible. But this put his face into the sea so that he sucked it into his nose with a snoring noise and a choke. He spat and endured the pain in his neck for a while. He wedged his hands between his lifebelt and his chin and for a swell or two this was some relief but then the pain returned. He let his hands fall away and his face dipped in the water. He lay back, forcing his head against the pain so that his eyes if they had been open would have been looking at the sky. The pressure on his legs was bearable now. They were no longer flesh, but had been transformed to some other substance, petrified and comfortable. The part of his body that had not been invaded and wholly subdued by the sea was jerking intermittently. Eternity, inseparable from pain, was there to be examined and experienced. The snarl endured. He thought. The thoughts were laborious, disconnected but vital.

Presently it will be daylight.

I must move from one point to another.

Enough to see one move ahead.

Presently it will be daylight.

I shall see wreckage.

I won't die.

Not me——

Precious.

He roused himself with a sudden surge of feeling that had nothing to do with the touch of the sea. Salt water was coming fast out of his eyes. He snivelled and gulped.

"Help, somebody—help!"

His body lifted and fell gently.

If I'd been below I might have got to a boat even. Or a raft. But it had to be my bloody watch. Blown off the bloody bridge. She must have gone on perhaps to starboard if he got the order in time, sinking or turning over. They'll be there in the darkness somewhere where she sank asking each other if they're downhearted, knots and stipples of heads in the water and oil and drifting stuff. When it's light I must find them, Christ I must find them. Or they'll be picked up and I'll be left to swell like a hammock. Christ!

"Help! Nathaniel! Help——!"

And I gave the right orders too. If I'd done it ten seconds earlier I'd be a bloody hero—Hard a-starboard for Christ's sake!

Must have hit us bang under the bridge. And I gave the right order. And I get blown to buggery.

The snarl fixed itself, worked on the wooden face till the upper lip was lifted and the chattering teeth bared. The little warmth of anger flushed blood back into the tops of the cheeks and behind the eyes. They opened.

Then he was jerking and splashing and looking up. There was a difference in the texture of the darkness; there were smears and patches that were not in the eye itself. For a moment and before he remembered how to use his sight the patches lay on the eyeballs as close as the darkness had been. Then he firmed the use of his eyes and he was inside his head, looking out through the arches of his skull at random formations of dim light and mist. However he blinked and squinted they remained there outside him. He bent his head forward and saw, fainter than an after-image, the scalloped and changing shape of a swell as his body was lifted in it. For a moment he caught the inconstant outline against the sky, then he was floating up and seeing dimly the back top of the next swell as it swept towards him. He began to make swimming motions. His hands were glimmering patches in the water and his movements broke up the stony weight of his legs. His thoughts continued to flicker.

We were travelling north-east. I gave the order. If he began to turn she might be anywhere over there to the east. The wind was westerly. That's the east over there where the swells are running away down hill.

His movements and his breathing became fierce. He swam a sort of clumsy breast-stroke, buoyed up on the inflated belt. He stopped and lay wallowing. He set his teeth, took the tit of the lifebelt and let out air till he was lying lower in the water. He began to swim again. His breathing laboured. He stared out of his arches intently and painfully at the back of each swell as it slunk away from him. His legs slowed and stopped; his arms fell. His mind inside the dark skull made swimming movements long after the body lay motionless in the water.

The grain of the sky was more distinct. There were vaporous changes of tone from dark green to gloom, to grey. Near at hand the individual hillocks of the surface were visible. His mind made swimming movements.

Pictures invaded his mind and tried to get between him and the urgency of his motion towards the east. The jam jar came

back but robbed of significance. There was a man, a brief inter-
view, a desk-top so polished that the smile of teeth was being
reflected in it. There was a row of huge masks hung up to dry
and a voice from behind the teeth that had been reflected in the
desk spoke softly.

"Which one do you think would suit Christopher?"

There was a binnacle-top with the compass light just visible,
there was an order shouted, hung up there for all heaven and
earth to see in neon lighting.

"Hard a-starboard, for Christ's sake!"

Water washed into his mouth and he jerked into consciousness
with a sound that was half a snore and half a choke. The day was
inexorably present in green and grey. The seas were intimate
and enormous. They smoked. When he swung up a broad, hilly
crest he could see two other smoking crests, then nothing but a
vague circle that might be mist or fine spray or rain. He peered
into the circle, turning himself, judging direction by the run of
the water until he had inspected every part. The slow fire of his
belly, banked up to endure, was invaded. It lay defenceless in
the middle of his clothing and sodden body.

"I won't die! I won't!"

The circle of mist was everywhere alike. Crests swung into
view on that side, loomed, seized him, elevated him for a
moment, let him down and slunk off, but there was another crest
to take him, lift him so that he could see the last one just dim-
ming out of the circle. Then he would go down again and another crest would loom weltering towards him.

He began to curse and beat the water with the flat of his white
hands. He struggled up the swells. But even the sounds of his
working mouth and body were merged unnoticed in the in-
numerable sounds of travelling water. He hung still in his belt,
feeling the cold search his belly with its fingers. His head fell on
his chest and the stuff slopped weakly, persistently over his face.
Think. My last chance. Think of what can be done.

She sank out in the Atlantic. Hundreds of miles from land.

She was alone, sent north-east from the convoy to break WT silence. The U-boat may be hanging round to pick up a survivor or two for questioning. Or to pick off any ship that comes to rescue survivors. She may surface at any moment, breaking the swell with her heavy body like a half-tide rock. Her periscope may sear the water close by, eye of a land-creature that has defeated the rhythm and necessity of the sea. She may be passing under me now, shadowy and shark-like, she may be lying down there below my wooden feet on a bed of salty water as on a cushion while her crew sleeps. Survivors, a raft, the whaler, the dinghy, wreckage may be jilling about only a swell or two away hidden in the mist and waiting for rescue with at least bully and perhaps a tot.

He began to rotate in the water again, peering blearily at mist; he squinted at the sky that was not much higher than a roof; he searched the circle for wreckage or a head. There was nothing. She had gone as if a hand had reached up that vertical mile and snatched her down in one motion. When he thought of the mile he arched in the water, face twisted, and began to cry out.

"Help, curse you, sod you, bugger you—— Help!"

Then he was blubbering and shuddering and the cold was squeezing him like the hand that had snatched down the ship. He hiccuped slowly into silence and started to rotate once more in the smoke and green welter.

One side of the circle was lighter than the other. The swell was shouldering itself on towards the left of this vague brightness; and where the brightness spread, the mist was even more impenetrable than behind him. He remained facing the brightness not because it was of any use to him but because it was a difference that broke the uniformity of the circle and because it looked a little warmer than anywhere else. He made swimming movements again without thought and as if to follow in the wake of that brightness was an inevitable thing to do. The light made the sea-smoke seem solid. It penetrated the water so that between him and the very tops of the restless hillocks it was bottle green. For a moment or two after a wave had passed he could see right into it but the waves were nothing but water—there was no weed in them, no speck of solid, nothing drifting, nothing moving but green water, cold persistent idiot water. There were hands to be sure and two forearms of black oilskin and there was the noise of breathing, gasping. There was also the noise of the idiot stuff, whispering, folding on itself, tripped ripples running tinkling by the ear like miniatures of surf on a flat beach; there were sudden hisses and spats, roars and incompleted syllables and the soft friction of wind. The hands were important under the bright side of the circle but they had nothing to seize on. There was an infinite drop of the soft cold stuff below them and under the labouring, dying body.

The sense of depth caught him and he drew his dead feet up to his belly as if to detach them from the whole ocean. He arched and gaped, he rose over the chasm of deep sea on a swell and his mouth opened to scream against the brightness.

It stayed open. Then it shut with a snap of teeth and his arms began to heave water out of the way. He fought his way forward.

"Ahoy—for Christ's sake! Survivor! Survivor! Fine on your starboard bow!"

He threshed with his arms and legs into a clumsy crawl. A crest overtook him and he jerked himself to the chest out of water.

"Help! Help! Survivor! For God's sake!"

The force of his return sent him under but he struggled up and shook the wave from his head. The fire of his belly had spread and his heart was thrusting the sluggish blood painfully round his body. There was a ship in the mist to port of the bright patch. He was on her starboard bow—or—and the thought drove him to foam in the water—he was on her port quarter and she was moving away. But even in his fury of movement he saw how impossible this was since then she would have passed by him only a few minutes ago. So she was coming towards, to cut across the circle of visibility only a few yards from him.

Or stopped.

At that, he stopped too, and lay in the water. She was so dull a shape, little more than a looming darkness that he could not tell both her distance and her size. She was more nearly bows on than when he had first seen her and now she was visible even when he was in a trough. He began to swim again but every time he rose on a crest he screamed.

"Help! Survivor!"

But what ship was ever so lop-sided? A carrier? A derelict carrier, deserted and waiting to sink? But she would have been knocked down by a salvo of torpedoes. A derelict liner? Then she must be one of the Queens by her bulk—and why lop-sided? The sun and the mist were balanced against each other. The sun could illumine the mist but not pierce it. Then darkly in the sun-mist loomed the shape of a not-ship where nothing but a ship could be.

He began to swim again, feeling suddenly the desperate exhaustion of his body. The first, fierce excitement of sighting had burned up the fuel and the fire was low again. He swam grimly, forcing his arms through the water, reaching forward under his arches with sight as though he could pull himself into safety with it. The shape moved. It grew larger and not clearer. Every now and then there was something like a bow-wave at the forefoot. He ceased to look at her but swam and screamed alternately with the last strength of his body. There was green force round him, growing in strength to rob, there was mist and glitter over him; there was a redness pulsing in front of his eyes—his body gave up and he lay slack in the waves and the shape rose over him. He heard through the rasp and thump of his works the sound of waves breaking. He lifted his head and there was rock stuck up in the sky with a sea-gull poised before it. He heaved over in the sea and saw how each swell dipped for a moment, flung up a white hand of foam then disappeared as if the rock had swallowed it. He began to think swimming motions but knew now that his body was no longer obedient. The top of the next swell between him and the rock was blunted, smoothed curiously, then jerked up spray. He sank down, saw without comprehension that the green water was no longer empty. There was yellow and brown. He heard not the formless mad talking of uncontrolled water but a sudden roar. Then he went under into a singing world and there were hairy shapes that flitted and twisted past his face, there were sudden notable details close to of intricate rock and weed. Brown tendrils slashed across his face, then with a destroying shock he hit solidity. It was utter difference, it was under his body, against his knees and face, he could close fingers on it, for an instance he could even hold on. His mouth was needlessly open and his eyes so that he had a moment of close and intent communion with three limpets, two small and one large that were only an inch or two from his face. Yet this solidity was terrible and apocalyptic after the world of inconstant wetness. It was not vibrant as a ship's hull might be but merciless and mother of panic. It had no business to interrupt the thousands of miles of water going about their purposeless affairs and therefore the world sprang here into sudden war. He felt himself picked up and away from the limpets, reversed, tugged, thrust down into weed and darkness. Ropes held him, slipped and let him go. He saw light, got a mouthful of air and foam. He glimpsed a riven rock face with trees of spray growing up it and the sight of this rock floating in mid-Atlantic was so dreadful that he wasted his air by screaming as if he had been a wild beast. He went under into a green calm, then up and was thrust sideways. The sea no longer played with him. It stayed its wild movement and held him gently, carried him with delicate and careful motion like a retriever with a bird. Hard things touched him about the feet and knees. The sea laid him down gently and retreated. There were hard things touching his face and chest, the side of his forehead. The sea came back and fawned round his face, licked him. He thought movements that did not happen. The sea came back and he thought the movements again and this time they happened because the sea took most of his weight. They moved him forward over the hard things. Each wave and each movement moved him forward. He felt the sea run down to smell at his feet then come back and nuzzle under his arm. It no longer licked his face. There was a pattern in front of him that occupied all the space under the arches. It meant nothing. The sea nuzzled under his arm again.

He lay still.

Acknowledgments

Although the choice of items is the editor's responsibility, it would be unpardonable on his part not to acknowledge the help he has had from others well qualified as judges. He would like to particularise Professor Bonamy Dobrée, and Messrs Charles Causley, T. O. Beachcroft, John Munday and Richard Goffin. Those who have charge in matters of copyright have invariably been courteous, and the formal acknowledgments and references are as follows: thanks are due to Messrs Macmillan and the Trustees of the Estate for leave to reproduce the passage from Chapter 34 of *The Trumpet Major* by Thomas Hardy; to Messrs J. M. Dent and Sons Ltd as Agents for the Trustees of the Author's Estate for the extract from Joseph Conrad's *Typhoon*; to Mrs George Bambridge, Messrs Macmillan & Co. and the Macmillan Company of Canada for "The Ship that Found Herself" by Rudyard Kipling; to Dr John Masefield, O.M., the Society of Authors and the Macmillan Company, New York, for the passage from *The Bird of Dawning* published by Messrs Heinemann; to Mr Leo Walmsley and Messrs Collins for the passage from *Three Fevers*; to Mr C. S. Forester and Messrs A. D. Peters for "Hornblower and McCool"; to Mr Richard Hughes, Messrs Chatto and Windus and Messrs Harper and Row for the passage from *In Hazard*; to Mr Nicholas Monsarrat and Messrs D. C. Benson and Campbell Thompson Ltd for the passage from Part Five of *The Cruel Sea,* published by Messrs Cassell & Co. Ltd, and to Mr William Golding and Messrs Faber and Faber for the opening of *Pincher Martin*.